The Theocrat

The Theocrat

Bensalem Himmich

Translated by Roger Allen

The American University in Cairo Press
Cairo — New York

English translation copyright © 2005 by
The American University in Cairo Press
113 Sharia Kasr el Aini, Cairo, Egypt
420 Fifth Avenue, New York, NY 10018
www.aucpress.com

Copyright © 1989 by Bensalem Himmich
First published in Arabic in 1989 as *Majnun al-hukm*
Protected under the Berne Convention

First paperback edition 2009

Dar el Kutub No. 16762/08
ISBN 978 977 416 251 0

Dar el Kutub Cataloging-in-Publication Data

Aslan, Ibrahim
        The Theocrat / Bensalem Himmich; translated by Roger Allen.—Cairo: The
American University in Cairo Press, 2008
        p.   cm.
        ISBN 977 416 251 X
        1. Arabic fiction   I. Allen, Roger (Trans.) II. Title
        892.73

1 2 3 4 5 6 7 8   14 13 12 11 10 09

Designed by Andrea El-Akshar/AUC Press Design Center
Printed in Egypt

contents

Translator's introduction

I begin this translator's note to *The Theocrat*, the English translation of Bensalem Himmich's novel, *Majnun al-hukm* (1989), with what may be a somewhat unusual admission: my reasons for selecting this particular work for translation are, firstly, that my reading of the original Arabic text suggested to me almost immediately that it would pose unusually difficult challenges for the translator, and secondly (as a consequence of those challenges), that the resulting English version would almost certainly confront its readers with a narrative that illustrates some of the particularities of contemporary Arabic novel writing.

In the context of Western reactions to the award of the Nobel Prize for literature to the Egyptian novelist, Naguib Mahfouz in 1988 and to the published translations of Arabic novels that have followed that event, I have been concerned, in selecting novels for translation, to identify works that tend to distance themselves from the expectations (whether implicit or explicit) of Western readers regarding the nature, techniques, and purposes of fiction. In other words, I have hoped to find examples of Arabic novels that, through the process of transfer, of "translation," across the cultural divide between Arabic-speaking and English-speaking countries, will manage to convey to readers of English aspects of the more intrinsically Arab and Arabic contributions to contemporary Arabic fiction rather than those which, in one way or another, can be seen as replications of the Western tradition of fiction, albeit transplanted to a different (and even, exotic) cultural environment. This perception does not, needless to say, reflect an either/or situation. After all, the novel has been and remains a world-wide phenomenon of breath-taking variety. However, as students who investigate the pleasing varieties of this maximally adaptive genre search for elements of innovation and change in other world cultural traditions as well as their own, it is to be hoped that the enormous variety of the contemporary Arabic novelistic tradition may also become a participant in and a focus of such investigations.

In making the above statement about confrontation, I am not merely alluding to the fact that *The Theocrat* is a translation in English of an Arabic novel written by a Moroccan. One of the more fortunate consequences of the Nobel award to Naguib Mahfouz has been an increase in the selection of Arabic novels that are available in English translation, although admittedly there are more from some countries (particularly Egypt) than others. Even so, Moroccan fiction is represented in current (2001) listings by works of Muhammad Shukri, Muhammad Barrada, and Leila Abouzeid. Nor am I referring to the fact that *The Theocrat* advertises itself as a "novel of historical fiction." For, quite apart from the long-established European tradition of historical novels, for which a short list would include writers such as Walter Scott, Alexandre Dumas, Leo Tolstoy, and Umberto Eco, the modern tradition of the Arabic novel also provides some notable examples of this subgenre of novel-writing. Among those available in English translation are the Egyptian novelist, Gamal al-Ghitani's, *Zayni Barakat* and 'Abd al-Rahman Munif's *Variations on Night and Day* (that being the third volume of a quintet of novels, under the general title of *Cities of Salt [Mudun al-milh]*). In talking above about a text that confronts, what I do have in mind is that, with *The Theocrat*, Bensalem Himmich writes a novel that challenges its readers with not only the organizational logic of the narrative but also the sheer virtuosity of his varied application of language in order to revive and imitate samples from the great narrative traditions of the Arabic heritage. In the context of this English version, it probably does not need to be emphasized that, as part of the translation process, the very challenge that Himmich's novel presents to readers of the Arabic original is not merely transferred but amplified.

To begin with, the topic of Himmich's novel—as the Arabic title, *Majnun al-hukm* (literally, he who is crazy in rule) makes clear—is one of Arab and Islamic history's most perplexing figures, al-Hakim bi-Amr Illah ('the one who rules by order of God'), the Fatimid caliph and ruler of Egypt during the tenth century of our era (r. 996–1020). Al-Hakim's reign was marked by considerable chaos on the economic, political, and social levels, as he subjected the Egyptian people to a series of extraordinary decrees regarding their beliefs and public behavior (some of which are briefly discussed below) and implemented them through a campaign of terror that reached astonishing proportions. His death or disappearance has always been a matter of intense speculation in historical accounts, not least because groups of his devotees believed him to have gone into a state of occultation. After his death, those devotees fled to the "mountains of Syria" where they took the name "Druze" after one of their leaders, Muhammad al-Druzi (who, as this narrative informs us, was himself murdered).

The chapters of Himmich's narrative treat different aspects of al-Hakim's extraordinary regime. Each one begins with often extensive quotations from the writings of historians from the pre-modern period of Arab-Islamic history: many of the most famous names are cited—al-Maqrizi, 'Izz al-Din ibn al-Athir, Ibn Iyas, Ibn Taghribirdi, and al-Qalqashandi, for example. In addition, the text itself often contains quotations from these same sources, each of which is duly footnoted at the end of the book. After these historical references to time, place, and events, Himmich then proceeds to replicate the particular discourse of the textual genre that is being invoked.

Following a "prelude" in which readers are introduced to a predominant image in the narrative—al-Hakim's adoption of a Qur'anic verse to reflect his own complexities—"the clear smoke," the first two chapters of the narrative provide ample evidence of the problematic nature of al-Hakim's personality. As we read the sections of these chapters devoted to al-Hakim's mental illness and the behavior which seems to have been its consequence, we come to admire, among other things, the state of medical knowledge within Arab-Islamic dominions in the tenth century. We are provided with detailed historical and medical records (and their elaboration in Himmich's own narrative), pointing out in some detail that al-Hakim suffered from a chemical imbalance in the brain. The evidence is not clear enough for us to determine whether this condition constituted what would now be termed schizophrenia or some kind of bipolar condition. However, what becomes abundantly clear (and from both the historical and fictional-historical narratives) is that the consequences of al-Hakim's mental state for Egypt, its people, and everyone who had to deal with him, were dire indeed.

What is truly remarkable about Himmich's blending of actual historical sources and modern fictional narrative is that certain sections of the novel are written as replications of the language of al-Hakim's ecstatic visions. There are a number of "sessions" in which groups of his devotees gather together, whether with his knowledge or not, and record his utterances, with all their multiple symbolic resonances and unusual metaphoric linkages. These visions and utterances, whether recorded while he is sitting in a bath of violet oil or observing stars in the Muqattam Hills above Cairo, are gathered into collections and eagerly studied by groups of al-Hakim's devotees eager to unravel their concealed significances.

In the lengthy third chapter, occupying fully one third of the entire narrative, a vivid account is provided of the rebellion which Abu Rakwa, descendant of the former Umayyad house of caliphs, mounted against the Fatimid (in other words, Shi'ite) caliph, al-Hakim. While providing readers with a gripping chronological record of the course of events, this chapter also includes examples of sermons, letters, ringing pre-battle harangues to troops, persuasive orations, cunning attempts at subversion, and some notable passages of description. The occasion when Abu Rakwa, now facing total defeat and the dissipation of his large fighting force, rides out from the fortress in Upper Egypt where he has sought refuge, is one such:

As Abu Rakwa made his way out of the main gate of the castle, his face was radiant and uplifted. He mounted his finest horse and gave al-Fadl's avenging angels a look of mercy and forgiveness. Once he was level with them, he took off at a gallop with them following in sheepish silence.

Abu Rakwa's rebellion is given a prominent place in Himmich's narrative. Historical accounts suggest that such prominence is fully justified when we bear in mind the central place it occupied within al-Hakim's reign (see, for example, the article on "Al-Hakim Bi-Amr Allah" in the *Encyclopaedia of Islam*, 2nd ed., 1954 et seq.). Within the context of a novel that portrays such a disastrously complex ruler, one can almost term Abu Rakwa the "hero" of the narrative; that is certainly the way in which the historical method of the third chapter chooses to depict him.

On the question of al-Hakim's demise (or disappearance), uncertainty brings the principles of history and fiction close together. The second section of the fourth chapter of Himmich's narrative cites historical sources to the effect that al-Hakim was murdered on the orders of his beautiful and accomplished sister, Sitt al-Mulk, who assumed power for a period following her brother's "death." What is clear is that al-Hakim's mental illness had become progressively worse during the course of his reign. Many of his decrees (duly recorded within the text of this narrative) were justifiably unpopular: the banning of the pilgrimage, for example, the total sequestration of women, the killing of dogs, the requirement that Christians and Jews wear marked clothing, and the destruction of churches and synagogues. Toward the end of his reign, he ordered his troops to set fire to the old (southern) section of Cairo known as Fustat, apparently desiring revenge for the derisory comments made about him by the inhabitants of this quarter. Later he claimed that he had never given such orders. In any case, his regular habit of riding his donkey into the Muqattam Hills to observe the stars and enter a state of private contemplation clearly provided an excellent opportunity for those who eventually came to the conclusion that, whether divinely appointed caliph or not, enough was enough.

Himmich's narrative assembles for its readers a montage of different situations and sessions, and the texts—authentic and imagined, pre-modern and modern—to go with them. The resulting narrative is thus not chronological, nor indeed is the style intended to be consistent. The actual content of the texts in the different chapters varies from the apparently clear logic and style of historical accounts, to the image-laden and ecstatic utterances to be found in other chapters where the mode of expression is characteristic of a mind that is often being torn apart by the ravages of mental illness. (I re-enter this text as translator here to note that amazing juxtapositions of objects, sentiments, and images are an intrinsic feature of certain sections in the original Arabic text of this novel. In the process of translating them into English, I have made no attempt to change what I understand to be their effects.) Such a varied and categorical method of textual organization is, it needs to be added, a central feature of classical Arabic works of *adab*, the many and often enormous collections of information and anecdote which the intellectual elite (and especially the bureaucrats and scribes of the court) prepared for their own reference and edification. One must assume that in *The Theocrat* Himmich is consciously setting out to utilize such an indigenous approach to narrative structure by imitating its mode of compilation, one that allows him to assemble in discrete chapters decisions and incidents from the entire reign of a ruler whose tyranny and capricious conduct has become a byword in the region's history.

The diagnosis of illnesses and their treatment, and most especially changing attitudes to mental disease, are prominent topics for modern analysis; indeed in the works of Michel Foucault they enter the realms of literary discourse. The question as to "What is madness?" is one that many modern Arab authors have posed. Naguib Mahfouz and the Syro-Lebanese poet, Adunis, are two such. What Himmich explores in this remarkable novel shares many of the concerns voiced in the theme of the play and film by Alan Bennett, *The Madness of King George*, namely the disastrous consequences of now diagnosable mental illness on an individual ruler and his people and on the way that history deals with such eras. Himmich makes no attempt to spare his readers the full horror and tragedy of al-Hakim's reign, but his narrative's multitextual approach succeeds brilliantly in using different genres to paint a portrait of a character whose sheer unpredictability throws into relief the qualities of those who find themselves forced to cajole, confront, or oppose him.

The resort on the part of Arab novelists to history as a means of addressing contemporary issues is, needless to say, part of a much wider cultural phenomenon. To cite just one relatively recent work on the subject, David Cowart's *History and the Contemporary Novel*:

> The increasing prominence of historical themes in current fiction suggests that the novel's perennial valence for history has acquired new strength in recent years. Produced by writers sensitive to the lateness of the historical hour and capable of exploiting technical innovations in the novel, this new historical fiction seems to differ from that of calmer times. A sense of urgency—sometimes even an air of desperation—pervades the historical novel since midcentury, for its author probes the past to account for a present that grows increasingly chaotic.

More recently, the British novelist–critic A.S. Byatt has published a volume of essays in which she delves further into this linkage of history and fiction and the hybrid forms that emerge from their fusion. Interestingly entitled *On Histories and Stories*, the work explores the motivations that lead novelists in this direction. Among them she identifies a desire "to find historical paradigms for contemporary situations," an esthetic need "to write colored and metaphorical language," and an eagerness to escape the self as subject matter.

Himmich's novel then is part of a trend in fiction writing that is very much a feature of current literary interest. Yet, while he may partake in and contribute to a broader fictional endeavor, his choice of subject and his means of depicting it in narrative form are not merely indigenous to the cultural world of Arabic but also thoroughly innovative. In his case (and that of the Arab world in general) it scarcely needs to be added that the invocation of history also becomes a method whereby topics that, for obvious political reasons, would be virtually undebatable can be presented in fictional form—such as the nature of absolute power (in a region within which such governmental systems are the norm rather than the exception). In this context therefore, it needs to be made clear to readers of this translation that, in crafting this complex "novel of historical fiction," Himmich is well aware of not only what he is writing and why, but also what are the principles and methodological background to the entire endeavor. He has himself written several articles on the novel and historical writing. In them he reveals not merely the breadth of his reading in literature and philosophy, but, more specifically, his familiarity with the interesting generic blending that is reflected in current discussions of historical fiction and, as he aptly notes, in any investigation of classical *adab* (mentioned above) and its esthetic criteria. That process of "blending" is, of course, a primary feature of this novel. One of the many works that he cites in an article in the Moroccan journal, *Prologues/Muqaddimat* (Summer–Autumn 1998) is Umberto Eco's renowned novel, *The Name of the Rose*. It is therefore interesting to note that this same novel is also discussed in David Cowart's study cited above, as an example of his fourth category of historical novel, namely "fictions whose authors project the present into the past." Cowart points out that this fourth category offers the richest possibilities in writing historical fiction, since it "makes special demands on the ingenuity of novelists" (and, he might have added, of readers and, in my case, of translators as well). The "desire to mirror the present in the past finds expression most easily in a skewed or legendary or fabulous history more amenable than real history to the allegorical projection of the present." Himmich illustrates these very principles in a statement in the article noted above, when he alludes to traditional forms of narrative within the Arabic literary tradition before pointing out that "authentic writing can only interact with precedents and those forms and styles that emerge from them, not so much in order to imitate them, but rather to place them within the fulcrum of change and thus to enrich them with the added value of modernity."

This reliving of an Islamic, Arab, Egyptian past, penned by a contemporary author living in Morocco, is then a point of confrontation, as it challenges readers of English narratives with what is unfamiliar in place, time, topic, and narrative mode. Surely it is in the transfer of such differences across cultural divides that the greatest role of translation continues to lie.

As a consequence, this translation is provided with a glossary in which I have tried to provide historical, geographical, and cultural details for those who feel a need for them. Those readers of translations (of whom I myself tend to be one) who prefer not to be interrupted by such external information will not be distracted by note numbers in the text and can confront this narrative on its own terms. All dates in the text appear in their Islamic (Hijra) form. To make an approximate calculation of the equivalent Gregorian year, the reader can add 620 to the Hijra date. One other change has been made in an effort to make the text more accessible to readers of English: book titles that were of course in Arabic in the original are now rendered in English. More complete information on many of these book titles and important dates will be found in the bibliography at the end of the book. Finally, Qur'anic quotations are peppered throughout the narrative. These appear in italics and their exact location within the Qur'an can be found in the concordance after the glossary.

Bibliography

Byatt, A.S. *On Histories and Stories*. Cambridge, MA: Harvard University Press, 2001.

Cowart, David. *History and the Contemporary Novel*. Carbondale: Southern Illinois University Press, 1989.

"Al-Hakim Bi-Amr Allah," in *Encyclopedia of Islam* 2nd ed. [CD-ROM version], Leiden: E.J. Brill, 1954– .

The Theocrat

prelude to "the smoke"

l-Hakim bi-Amr Illah's beliefs were flawed. His moods could change in a flash. He would punish the simplest wrongdoing. Impetuous and irascible, he wiped out entire nations and generations and set up a reign of terror.

> Minister Jamal al-Din,
> *Accounts of Defunct Dynasties*

His caliphate was one of total contradiction: courage and recklessness; cowardice and reserve; love of learning and attacks on scholars; inclination to good works, followed by the murder of those who performed them. His most predominant trait was generosity and perhaps a miserliness of unprecedented proportions.

> Sibt ibn al-Jawzi,
> *Mirror of the Times Concerning the History of Notables*

He was at once magnanimous and kind, vicious and cunning. His belief was flawed, and he shed people's blood. He murdered many of his regime's senior officials while they were incarcerated.

> al-Hafiz al-Dhahabi,
> *History of Islam*

His demeanor was wicked and his faith faulty. Every aspect of his life
was disturbed: he would order something with a great flourish, then
countermand the order with equal display.

al-Makin ibn al-'Amid,
History of the Muslims

His behavior was extraordinary. His name was mentioned in the
Friday sermon in Egypt, Syria, Tunisia, and the Hijaz. He was interested in ancient history, and used to consult the stars. He set up an
observatory and secluded himself in a house in the Muqattam Hills.
People say that he suffered from a lack of fluid in the brain, which
caused his frequent contradictory moods. The best thing ever said
about him is: his actions were inexplicable, and his fantasies and
obsessions were undecodable.

al-Maqrizi,
Lessons and Reports Concerning Cairo Quarters and Monuments

1. He
He is: Abu 'Ali Mansur (given the honorific al-Hakim bi-Amr Illah) ibn
al-'Aziz bi-Llah Nizar ibn al-Mu'izz bi-Llah Ma'add (conqueror of
Egypt and builder of Cairo and the Azhar mosque) ibn al-Mansur bi-Llah
Isma'il ibn al-Qa'im bi-Amr Illah Muhammad ibn al-Mahdi 'Ubayd
Allah (founder of the Fatimi dynasty in Tunisia).

He is: al-'Ubaydi al-Fatimi, of Maghribi origin, but born, housed, and
raised in Egypt; third of 'Ubayd's descendants as Caliphs in Egypt; the
sixth in order of succession from his ancestors in the Maghrib.

Born in Cairo on Thursday, there being four days remaining in the first
month of the year A.H. 375 (others say it was on the twenty-third of the
month). His father, al-'Aziz, made him heir apparent to the caliphate in
the month of Sha'ban A.H. 383. He was acknowledged as caliph on the
day his father died, a Tuesday with two days remaining from the month

of Ramadan in A.H. 386. He assumed the caliphate at the age of eleven and a half (although other sources say ten and a half and six days—and there are still other versions).[1]

He: Historians are unanimous in declaring his caliphate to be one of contradictions. His behavior was unusual and his actions were outrageous ("enough to turn the hair gray"). No one, whether of high or low estate, has managed to either understand or justify them.

He: Psychologists have noted that during his youth he became afflicted with a kind of melancholia, a lack of fluid in the brain, and a flawed temperament, all of which led him to be excessively fond of killing people and shedding blood, using a variety of weapons and burning. Astrologers have had a great deal to say about him; they are all agreed that his bloody temperament goes back to the fact that he resided in the domain of Saturn and his ascendant was Mars. All of which led him to seek their favor by sacrificing human beings.

He: To his devotees he was a deity. They said that the revelation of Verse 10 from Surat al-Dukhan (The Smoke) in the Qur'an foretold his coming. With or without authorization they starting drawing devotees to him and making treaties and compacts based on a belief in his utter infallibility and the fact that divinity dwelt within his human form. They arranged gatherings and sessions, sometimes in public, at others in secret. They composed epistles and documents, so much so that they came to disagree about the precise chronology of the appearance of the newly formulated Fatimi doctrine and of the proclamation regarding the abrogation of the religious law code. Thereafter they indulged in mutual slaughter and fornication. After al-Hakim's assassination (an event instigated by his own sister, Sitt al-Mulk) in A.H. 411, their influence in Egypt waned. According to Qazoghlu and other historians, Nushtakin the Turk (he being Muhammad ibn Isma'il al-Druzi) was the only person who managed to get away and carry al-Hakim's cause to the nomads of the Syrian mountains.

In Syria he was able to propagate his creed and turn it into the religion
that still exists there in his name (Druze) and bears his particular stamp
to this very day.

During the period before the new mission manifested itself and was
openly discussed and practiced, indeed throughout the second decade
of al-Hakim's quarter-century rule, his devotees may have had widely
divergent aspirations and visions, but they still followed in their
imam's footsteps during his periods of seclusion and night travels.
Their sole task was to record the "venerable discourse" just as he
uttered it, so eloquent, subtly inspired, and crucially important. The
collected sayings would then be prepared for publication and issued
under general, yet distinctive titles, such as: *Compelling Notions*,
Glittering Segments, *Fleeting Scents*, and the like. For this purpose, the
devotees acted like disembodied spirits, tracking al-Hakim without him
even being aware of it. He used to go either to the Muqattam Hills, to the
stable at al-Tarma, to the desert by the Pyramids, or else to other places
where he would seclude himself and maintain a night vigil. The long
hours would pass very slowly. They would watch him closely, their
bodies pinned against rocks and walls, eyes and ears glued to holes and
apertures. Nothing—summer heat, bitter cold, specters in the dark—
would divert them from their task.

At the beginning of this period his devotees used to gather periodically
to assess their imam's meditations that they had collected. They would
compare notes and share the task of editing them and filling in gaps.
Then they would turn them into a complete text that both satisfied their
expectations and fired their minds and bodies. This new compilation
would then be added to the other secret texts for which a highly esoteric
kind of interpretation was used, that being a level to which only the initiated
and those drawn into the cadre of the "discerning" were privy.

Most of these texts have not survived and are now lost, but one has
survived. It is divided into sections. Devotees have confirmed that it
does consist of al-Hakim's sayings; the only role they played was to

arrange the materials and provide titles. Among its contents are the following passages:

2. I Am the Clear Smoke
History will comprehend me.

In the name of rule by the authority of God and of the Arabic language I am inclined to the ultimate and to the clash of opposites. Whoever understands me is aware that my era will inevitably be worthy of note. But for that, it would be like a mere grain of mustard-seed. With the gifts and powers given to me I have decided that it will be memorable, wracked by unforeseen events and mighty longings. When it comes to an end, it will leave behind shards of resolve and erupting volcanoes.

History only opens its ears and tomes to the most significant of events and circumstances, to those things that have the power to confound it and destroy its parameters.

History only keeps records of those who impress it and resist its twists and turns by invoking opposites. It is by nature corrupt, loving those who rupture its tedious practices and demolish its own beds.

That is why I can promise you that history will comprehend me!

The Station of "Were I"
Were I to utter anything other than what the Arab night and destiny itself utter, I would be like that philosopher armed with proverbs, the one who said: how far apart are letter and fate. So down with destiny, and may the letter show itself! How outrageous!

Concerning the Defeat of Peace
This enveloping nature is the mother of us all. It seems to me like some old debauched witch proclaiming funereal chants, distributing ashes of endings in crystal-shaped containers, gleaming and deadly; it traces the slope of flutters and sighs toward silence, the slope of all elements toward corrosion and oblivion.

As you chew over events and calamities, you should strive to collect tidings of love, joy, and safety. Should you succeed, those tidings will be like extra prayers; they and additional devotions will be one and the same.

Have you not seen that the founding essence only tells of natural disasters, blood baths, and tranquility marred by caution!

Are you not convinced that peace in history only recounts its defeats and the crushing of rose and dove!

Beware of Whiteness

Love and brotherhood are qualities of the people of paradise.

Paradise is a promise, with no part of this despicable existence.

In order to survive our lower world is based on enmity and conflict.

That was the sign of the beginning, one enmeshed in an ever recurring return.

By the name of Fatima the Radiant, you need enemies, just as they need you.

Your enemies are the measure of your power. When they appear, confront them; if they disappear or go into hiding, search them out!

Record this saying in my name: a dictum that conforms with the laws of life states that either the people will vanquish its enemies, or else it will itself be overcome and subdued.

Beware, beware! Don't let yourselves be deceived by the white or slide apathetically toward peace and neutrality. Do that, and you will be lost.

Know for certain that war has many aspects and abodes; they may come all at once or in separate bursts. War may be based on the sword or the pen, or around chattels and values.

Know for certain that every peace is a truce between two wars, and that every truce provides an opportunity to recover the breaths of resolve and to reinforce military supplies and assault troops.

I, al-Hakim bi-Amr Illah have determined that the victory of the Fatimid people will be total, indubitable, and irrevocable. The words of the poet will indeed come to pass:

Once we had pounded and overwhelmed them,

We left them there as fodder for vultures and birds of prey.

Concerning the Nature of Politics and Tyranny

Historians full of homiletic wisdom and necrophiliacs will say that I, al-Hakim bi-Amr Illah, crushed the faithful using both tyranny and despair; that I was bloodthirsty; that I was the ultimate inquisition, a total blight. . . .

If these pseudo-scholars really knew the essence of history—the way it is crafted by the power of the sword and the sheer quantity of misery and suffering, then they would understand me and would come to realize that tyranny is an intrinsic feature of politics. Beyond that, features of tyranny include wariness, caution, and a resort to preventive violence. It was a prescient sage who declared that anyone who fails to defend his turf by force of arms will be removed; a ruler who does not control his people will be the one who is ruled!

The Other Side of Politics

1.

Death is the other side of politics.

Contact with politics brings risks.

Anyone who undertakes such risks will be safe for a while, or else will lose his soul in the clash between venture and conflict.

This is why, in the exercise of power, I am inclined to dispense with everything that is contrary and competitive!

2.

Is it because Our Lord has given me power so young that you watch me so closely?

No, I shall leave no escape for that eunuch, Burjuwan the Slav, who is in charge of my administration. He will not do to me what Kafur did to the children of his master, al-Ikhshid. He came to greet me in his stinking shoes, lorded it over me, and tried to ignore me. Now tell him that the boy he nicknamed the ward-gecko has now turned into a full-size dragon, one that can wrap its tail around disloyal necks and throttle them to death.

Husayn ibn 'Ammar, the secretary of my administration, has shown me a satisfactory level of solidarity and loyalty. Toward him and all those who are after my blood I shall display the full abundance of my own duplicity and instant revenge.

3.

I have demolished the buttresses and horizons of all those who have placed themselves above me; at my hands they have been totally shattered. With great determination I have recovered my throne. I have traveled through the tunnels of my reign and my intrigues in quest of tremors and shivering. I have established my shadow wherever I went and created within my homeland a history for my swords. How happy I am at what clings to me: stories that delight me so about the volcano of my followers; a voice with prophetic impact; a happy omen.

It is fine for me to devote myself to exploration and physiognomy; it is fine to love and harass; fine too is every rift, every pass, every inundation.

I sweep things away, I dominate, then I return to the serenity of the desert that forewarns of the storm to come; I go back to the sand preface that forewarns of the storm to come.

Ribbons of Values
You ask me about the reasoning behind my penchant for destroying monuments and values. My response (take it away and reflect on it) is: anyone who does not destroy does not know the meaning of building; anyone who does not practice evil cannot do good.

The person who can only look at something from one aspect is short-sighted and unperceptive. He remains stuck in a single dimension, extolling monotony and fading into oblivion along with it.

Anyone who does not carry excess to its uttermost limit comes close to the regions of whiteness and indolence. What an idiot!

The Logic of Intrigues

Every one of us is the other's heretic!

So we are all heretics, fosterers of deviance and heresy. We are all heads, fascinated by the definition of proofs, adopting them as our own passions. We all follow the religion of emergence.

After God Himself your deity is your desires, except for those who are content to crawl and hide inside the trunk of their own shadows, covering their eyes with their hands and beseeching God to protect them from the possibility of chickens laying their eggs or of dynamic action against everything that is stagnant and cumbersome.

How Close to Me Are My Enemies!

The murder of confidants and insiders is definitely the best plan. Failing that, no despot can expect a stable rule, even if he behaves justly.

If the caliph fails to treat as enemies the people who enabled him to gain power, by adopting a neutral stance coupled with excessive caution, he will control neither custom nor authority. He should do his utmost to intimidate them and keep them at a distance; then they will not try to share his grasp on power.

There will be no peace for the caliph if he is not permanently suspicious of everyone; he must lop off his own shadow if it seems strange or ambiguous.

The caliph will never endure if he does not keep changing the list of his confidants and protectors, just as a snake keeps changing its skin.

Why Are You Not Satisfied?

The dust of the earth, that is the only thing that can fill the stomachs of human beings, except those on whom God shows His mercy! I have designated large swaths of terrain for you—Alexandria, al-Buhayra, and their environs—and filled your guts with a whole variety of things, enough to baffle the mind of the chief treasurer.

So why do you make a religion out of gluttony and greed? Why do you keep the gates of your own appetites and passions so wide open?

By God, if only you realized that each duty, each gift, each bribe I offer you out of my own abundant generosity is simply a debt I hold against you, one that ties your neck firmly to my authority and your loyalty to me. If you were even aware of that fact, you would hold a race to see who could run away from both me and my gifts the fastest. But you are like a load of rams, unaware and stupid.

Argue with Me, and I Will Take Pity on You
How extensive and fulsome are your talents for prostration and submission! In giving the matter due thought I have concluded that for you contentment is simply a substitute, a tissue on the fabric of your rancors and accumulated losses. I get the feeling that on the path to submission you bow to fates that existed before you. For you the entire burden and freedom lie in a concern with details.

Argue with me on this topic. Go on and argue, and I will take pity on you and reward you handsomely.

Learn to Be Extremists
"Do not blame me. There is no pact between you and me.
   I must clash with the enraged,
   Propel my steed away from the Tigris and Euphrates,
   And reunify the faith after schism."[2]

Within worldly limits and the framework of mundane matters, your only currency is your defeats and self-destruction; sometimes the cause is a loss of your sense of identity in a reckless dependency, and at others it is mental exhaustion brought on by an attempt to reconcile the irreconcilable.

By the lady Fatima, you will not find me offering you any alternative to this counsel: create your own essence and substance by selecting the keenest of cravings, by opposition, and by creative contradiction. Be extreme in everything; be extreme, and God forgive you all!

Hearts Closest to Me

I detest pomp in anything, not merely in worldly chattels but in language and vocabulary too.

For that reason, anyone who really thinks that I murdered Shaykh Jabbara the philologist because he knew three hundred words for dog in Arabic will find all that and more in the realm of exegesis. The hearts that are closest to mine are among the exegetes, those who compete with each other to produce alternative proofs and to expose virgin ideas to the light. They all grind and sweat, and in the end all they discover is what they started with, namely themselves—themselves just as they were and are, no one else.

You Must Be Patient with Me

Ever since I took control of events, everything about me has changed: the tone of my voice, and the way I sit, stand, and walk. My speech has altered too, and the ways I traffic in words, dreams, and reality.

Should I be too surprised when I have shouldered the burden of all of you? My dreams and waking hours are burdened by my efforts to bring your sins and continual reformulations under control.

By Fatima, all that remains is for you to seek refuge in patience and perseverance, hoping all the while that, with the disappearance of myself and the clear smoke, the signs of the luminous light may come!

By the eye that never sleeps, my autocratic rule and the usage of my trusty sword are both essential to your interest in order to cure you of, and protect you against, oppression; and so that Egypt may remain as it was and as I want it to be: a land inhabited only by a shepherd and his flock.

So fear me and do not ask to be rid of me. I am ever watchful of your deeds and intentions. Through spying and night watches I make a collection of the most malicious and gruesome of them, then I eradicate them without mercy.

My Tastes

From the biographies of prophets and messengers I have grown fond of long hair and beards, wearing wool, and riding donkeys. I intend to follow their example and to go even further, by letting my nails grow even longer, by traversing the length and breadth of desert wastes, and by giving the bald mountain of al-Muqattam the particular favor of prolonged sojourns and meditations. In that way only the most creative and comprehensive of imaginations will be able to take possession of me.

Indeed I Shall Nullify the Rule

There will be historians who will say that the deeds of al-Hakim bi-Amr Illah were inexcusable, and that my dreams and obsessions could not be explained.

A reasonable statement, not without justification, since I am the exception that nullifies the rule.

The rule consists simply of the mesh of your habits and customs.

And that very mesh is simply the product of your arguments and pygmy-like stupors!

Where Do I Get the Power to Do Evil?

When the ruler was asked from time to time why he did a certain thing, such as splitting open someone's stomach and extracting the intestines to throw to the tame animals wandering around, he replied in a confident, aggressive tone:

"If you choose to ask me about the reasons for this action and others like it, then ask your God why He has power over everything. What is the wisdom in torturing animals and children, exhausting bereft mothers, or snatching away the souls of mortals in groups and throngs?

An inability to do evil paralyzes the will of God and the power of the one who rules in His name; without such attributes he will be deprived of absolute, total power.

Every ruler in God's name (al-Hakim bi-Amr Illah) who fails to replicate God's own attributes needs to be removed from his position. His tokens and signs of authority are spurious."

Eliminating Drought

Every time your misgivings beset me or I see death spreading amongst you, I ride barefoot into the desert with a cloth on my head.

Here in the desert, whose expanses and borders are rid of you, here my anxieties diminish and I can recover my sense of self in the light of the candles of beginning and destiny. Then I can see clearly the appropriate ways to eliminate the drought in my land and my mind.

I Am the Expert Rider

I ride toward you and head for your secrets. Do not run away, do not panic! For all you know, I may have brought release after hardship, or I may have opened my beneficence to all when you were expecting murder!

Why Have I Come?

The truth is not absolute, it is free.

Truth is the making of what is most powerful and capable of repudiating immaturity and custom and giving free rein to the will for interpretation and power. There is no harm if the realms and goals of the will break away and contradict each other.

By Fatima, your destruction rests on equality of sides and the languor of that which has neither color nor followers. So seek and derive your causes from the life of opposites and contradictions.

Consider how many residents in hell crawled their way there with good intent!

How often does ease come after hardship?

How many things do you hate, when they are actually the best thing for you?

So accept and tolerate me, bitter and unruly though I am! I have come only to teach you the meanings of the hidden opposites, the secret laws of transformation. I have come only to cure you of your maladies and to propagate a fanatical opposition to what you are, what you intend, be it overt or covert; and to declare open war on all those who, in the flame of time and absence, cannot wait.

chapter one
on Enticements and Threats from the Ascendants of al-Hakim

*1. From Records of Decrees
and Interdictions*

 l-Hakim's behavior was utterly extraordinary. At every moment he used to invent laws which he forced people to implement.

Ibn Khallikan,
Book on the Deaths of Important People

Once al-Hakim had killed off Master Burjuwan—the administrator of the state, al-Husayn ibn 'Ammar—the leader of the Katama and secretary of the state, and others as well, he had exclusive control over power. From then on, barely a year or two went by without him issuing, among a flood of documents and sealed regulations, some compulsory decrees that were both strange and contradictory. One of the first such decrees, issued in the fourth year of the caliph's quarter century, namely A.H. 390, concerned "the individual nature of authority in both its overt and covert aspects." After the initial "in the name of God" and "thanks be to God," it begins as follows:

> To all you people who hear this proclamation: God, to
> whom belongs majesty and power, has ordained that leaders
> be identified by special qualities that are possessed by no

one else among the people. After reading this document, anyone who opens a debate or correspondence with anyone other than the divine presence, our Lord and Master, will be subject to execution by the will of the Commander of the Faithful. God willing, those who have witnessed this document should inform those who have not.[3]

In the right-hand margin:

My sphere is the territory you have inhabited, where women, words, and blessings are evident.

My sphere is circles and cadres where I exercise authority with exemplary violence. No ministers or gentry even dream of killing me, as they amass property and titles by pillage and plunder, live the easy life and strut about in my name and under my protection.

Be you strong or weak, beware of me and be on your guard. My only purpose in coming is to restore to the never-sleeping eye in your midst both its prestige and its rights.

In the left-hand margin:

You must always seek security from me.

You peoples who are integral to my era and my service, you may well come from different races, classes, and sects, but you are not permitted to disagree about me or about my exclusive right to grant pardon and security and to soothe hearts and minds. Until you can show contrary proof, I view you as being all against me and moving in directions other than those I wish.

Here then is my hellfire kindled by linen, sackcloth, and *alfa*. This is my hellfire, one that craves the flesh and fat of anyone who is unwilling to bring his entreaties to me or who holds back rather than entering the gate of my penance and security.

In this same year al-Hakim and his servants slaughtered many people, making no distinction between guilty and innocent, mighty and lowly, free and slave, Muslim and non-Muslim.

He forbade people to undertake the land and sea journey for the pilgrimage, since he was worried that people might escape from God's own country and Egypt thus be emptied of its own inhabitants.

During this year all fishermen had to stand before al-Hakim and take a solemn oath not to go after scaleless fish. They were told that anyone who did so and thus disobeyed this injunction would be eviscerated.

In the same year public baths were also closed, and a large number of bathers were arrested with no covering, then made to walk naked through the streets and markets!

In year five of al-Hakim's quarter century a decree against dogs was issued under his seal. Here is part of what it contains:

> Regarding all dogs, except those used for hunting purposes, rid me of them and remove them completely from all my lands and quarters. I cannot bear the sight of the vilest of creatures, the most remote from ethics of change and contradiction, the most likely to put up with the burdens of bootlicking and loyalty.

So in this year dogs were killed in thousands. Those who managed to get away fled to distant, uninhabited regions.

The occasion was also used to confiscate and slaughter all pigs owned by Christians.

This year (although some say the year before), al-Hakim got to hear a couple of verses of poetry that made him very upset and angry. He asked who the poet was and was told it was Najiya ibn Muhammad ibn Sulayman Abu al-Hasan al-Katib al-Baghdadi, boon companion of caliphs and great men. Al-Hakim demanded that he be summoned, but people pointed out that he was dead or at least one of those who had disappeared. The two lines (in the *tawil* meter) run as follows:

> I saw the morning unsheathe its sword
> As the night and stars retired in defeat

> And a red glow emerged. Then I said: Night has been murdered,
> And here is the horizon stained with blood by him who
> spilled it.[4]

In the sixth year of al-Hakim's quarter century the caliph surprised his people with the decree "The Reversal of Times and Prevention of Curfew." Part of it reads as follows:

> To prevent those delusions and disturbing dreams that
> come with the night and to uncover schemes hatched up by
> anyone against authority and me in a grab for power:
>
> I, al-Hakim bi-Amr Illah, hereby announce the reversal
> of times and meetings. From now on, work will be at night
> and sleep in daytime. I hereby forbid all travel around the
> city after sunset, all assemblies outside houses, all fouling
> of street space. Beware of breaking my time-schedule!
> Anyone apprehended and brought to me for such a crime
> will be put to death.
>
> Until further instruction to the contrary, this injunction
> will stand as is without change or adjustment.

That year, candles were lit at night in Cairo and throughout Egypt, turning night into day. One day, al-Hakim happened to pass by a carpenter working in the middle of the day. "Did I not forbid this? he asked the man. "My lord," the man replied, "when people earned their living in the daytime, they entertained themselves at night. When the opposite is the case, they entertain themselves during the day. This is entertainment." With that al-Hakim smiled and went on his way.[5]

In the eighth year of al-Hakim's quarter century his Shi'i devotees published, with his connivance, a decree concerning ancestors, requiring that insults be posted on doors, walls, cemeteries, and street corners.

In this same year a group of exoterics was paraded around the city on donkeys, after which their shoulders were fractured and they were all beheaded. In every quarter the town crier proclaimed: This is the punishment for all those who express their affection for Abu Bakr, 'Uthman, 'Aisha, Talha, al-Zubayr, 'Amr ibn al-'As, and Mu'awiya.

In Damascus a Maghribi was paraded around on a donkey, and the town crier announced, "This is the penalty for those who love the Prophet's companions." Then the man was decapitated.

This year also saw the execution of al-Hakim's order that the mosque of 'Amr ibn al-'As in Alexandria be destroyed.

In this same year there were earthquakes in Syria; cities and border regions were badly hit. Many people perished beneath the rubble.

In the ninth year of al-Hakim's quarter century, a decree was published under his seal banning the consumption of certain foodstuffs favored by exoterics. Here is an extract:

> I hereby forbid you to eat mulukhiya and all other types of food eaten by Sunnis. Through an irrevocable decree this sanction will be continued, since I do not wish you to eat at the tables of exoterics whose thoughts are only of this world, nor to consume anything that will increase your indolence, slacken your joints, and further thicken the vapors in your brains and the fancies you already have regarding your lofty status and lineage.

In this same year al-Hakim published a decree known under two titles: The Abolition of Alms, and The Suppression of Disparities. Among its contents is the following:

> By Fatima my reign will have no import if I do not strive to abolish the disparities in lifestyle and earnings that currently exist among you.
>
> Such disparities are alarming. How they trouble my feelings!
>
> Thus, since you are all part of my responsibility, I,

al-Hakim bi-Amr Illah, have decided to revert to basics so as to reveal how things really started. Riches are initially acquired through plunder and violence. People become wealthy at the expense of the weak who are exploited till they are exhausted, then die.

So I hope you are all with me in restoring to the scales of justice their due authority and glory. Anyone who thinks otherwise is no adherent of Islam or member of this community.

So let the following decree be recorded in my name: In order to achieve the ultimate goals of charity and almsgiving I have decided to abolish them. I have made this decision because their retention among you leaves the poor person a beggar while the rich continue to plunder and steal with a totally free conscience. I shall keep a close watch for anything that perpetuates these disparities among you.

Thus do I carry out my duties among you. Submit to my decrees and keep them memorized in your hearts as luminous testimony; chastise anyone who would seek to defile them or to smear them with nonsense or grime.

During the course of this year al-Hakim came across ten people asking for alms. He ordered them to be divided into two groups who were to fight each other; the winners would be rewarded. So they fought long and hard, till nine lay dead and only one remained. With that al-Hakim threw down some dinars for him to pick up. But when he bent down to collect them, al-Hakim's retinue killed him.[6]

In this year al-Hakim commanded a group of young people to jump from a spot high up in the palace into a pool; he promised a gift for each of them. The group proceeded to jump. About thirty of them died because, instead of landing in the water, they fell on a rock. Those who managed to survive the jump got their money.[7]

In the tenth year of al-Hakim's quarter century a decree was pro-

claimed throughout the land concerning the suppression of anyone raising a sword against authority. In this decree we find:

> So, you foul defilers! You oppose me with your ever
> increasing recalcitrance and proclaim my transformations
> before everyone. No, no, by my very inviolability, I shall
> make use of the highest forms of violence and the purest
> kinds of perfidy so as to bring about your defeat.
>
> Concerning Ibn Badis: he has denied my acts and
> placed distances and barriers between myself and him. But
> here are my own arms and my mosques, extended wide
> open for two jurisconsults whom he has sent in order to fur-
> nish us with some of the wisdom of Malik; in return, we
> propose to spill their blood, but all in good time.
>
> Concerning Abu Rakwa, he has frequently rebelled
> against me, created havoc in the south and reached the
> region between the two Pyramids. His campaign has cer-
> tainly gotten out of hand: now it threatens my authority. Yet
> his star is already on the wane. Prepare the strongest
> brigades of my army against him. I require you to bring
> him to me alive, so I can make a public example of him and
> have him paraded around the way I want. When people are
> bored with looking at him, slit his throat so he can sample
> my methods of torture, then bring me his severed head.
> Crucify his accursed corpse where it can rot and be eaten
> by vultures.
>
> This then is the punishment for anyone who ventures
> forth against me with the sword and dares to commit acts
> of defiance against me.

In A.H. 398 al-Hakim's mood regarding Abu Rakwa's rebellion became
somewhat more positive. He issued a series of decrees which people
regarded as showing a sense of balance, wisdom, and foresight. The first

was published in Ramadan entitled: Every Muslim may exercise individual judgment regarding his religion. After "In the name of God" and "Praise be to God," we read:

> The Commander of the Faithful hereby recites to you a verse from God's clear Book: *There is no compulsion in religion.* Yesterday with all its events is now passed, and today is now with us along with its own requirements. You community of Muslims, we are the leaders, you are the people. It is not permitted to kill anyone who has pronounced the two statements of faith or to break the bond between the two, united as they are by this brotherhood that God uses to protect those He protects and to forbid what He has forbidden regarding blood, property, and marriage. Righteousness and piety among believers are the best solution, whereas corruption and depravity are to be condemned. The events of the past should be buried and forgotten, neither mentioned nor spread abroad. Things past, practices of former times, events from the days of our enlightened forefathers—God's peace be upon them all!— al-Mahdi, al-Qa'im, al-Mansur, al-Mu'izz in al-Mahdiya and al-Mansuriya, all these are not to be broached. In those days the situation in Qayrawan proceeded in the open with no concealment, people fasting and then breaking the fast as they saw fit, with no enlightened people raising any objections as they fasted and broke fast. As the religion stipulated, Thursday saw them praying the noon prayer and the Ramadan prayer, once again with no one objecting or blocking them. The pronouncement "God is Great" was repeated five times during funeral ceremonies; no one prevented believers from pronouncing God is Great or muezzins from performing the call to prayer, nor did anyone harm those who did not. No one ever cursed any ances-

tors or sought to punish anyone for the revered names they mentioned in their prayers or for the substitutions they made. Every Muslim may exercise individual judgment regarding his religion. His resort should be to God, his Lord, and to his holy Book; with Him also is his recompense. So from today onward let God's servants behave this way: no Muslim should claim precedence over another because of his beliefs, and no one should object to his colleague's views regarding this sanction that I now issue. Following this decree of the Commander of the Faithful there comes this quotation from the Qur'an: *O you who believe, you are responsible for yourselves. Anyone who goes astray cannot hurt you if you offer him guidance. God is the point of reference for you all. It is He who will inform you of what you were doing.*[8]

This is followed by other decrees. Among them are the following:

Determining the right to practice hermeneutics:
The principles of theology involve hypotheses, leading to interpretations. As a result we hereby abolish all assemblies gathered for hermeneutical speculation and all other conduits for sectarian monopoly.

Just as I do not advocate the cause of one faction over another, I will not support the right of sectarian monopolies regarding interpretation.

Let there be competition to devise the best theology and the strongest readings and to compose the most cogent proofs. It may well be that those of you who are closest to the truth and to me—though he be a mere slave—will sow the seeds of reinvigoration and useful change in these lands.

Anyone who stands in the way of those who strive, interpret, and dispute, will be regarded by me no differently from a monopolistic tradesman or a highway robber. I have no part of him, nor he of me.

If anyone abuses my name or distorts my words, get rid of him and take him back to his seething pits and roaring follies.

Decree releasing earnings and abolishing taxes:
From al-Hakim to Husayn ibn Zahir al-Wazzan, Chief Secretary:

Praise be to God as He deserves:
I have become so that I now beseech and fear
None but my God in whom is all virtue.
My grandfather is Prophet, my imam my father
And my faith is loyalty and justice.

"All property belongs to God, may He be glorified! The people are God's servants, and we are his trustees on earth. So release the people's earnings and do not cut them off. Peace.[9]

"From today onward, all taxes on grain, rice, market tariffs, dates, soap factories are abolished. Judicial fees on wine, Ramadan alms, and complaint filings are also cancelled. I will be annulling other taxes too, once the level of the Nile improves and the river reaches its normal height."

Decree on abrogation and occlusion:
I, al-Hakim bi-Amr Illah, have heretofore decreed that you should post insults about ancestors on street-gates and mosques and that you should also daub insults on shop walls, in the desert, and in graveyards. I have previously instructed my governors to do the same thing in their various provinces.

I now totally forbid you to do so.

Up till now I have permitted fermented drinks as a way of easing your concerns and melting some of your ice-cold miseries. As of today, I forbid you to consume any alcoholic beverage even though the content be only one third. Even if the entire Nile consisted of alcohol, it would not be any more helpful to you. So dig up all vines and destroy all grapes and their byproducts. As long as you reside in my territories, make sure that you remain absolutely sober.

I have forbidden you to eat some foods favored by the exoterics, but as of today I find no difference or source of rancor between them and you. Eat what you wish and what is good for you. After all, every stomach will eventually taste death.

Decree forbidding flattery and seeking benefits:
Did I not tell you that I hated dogs?

Have you not realized that I issued a decree ordering that they be killed and that our kingdom be rid of them?

As a consequence I forbid anyone to kiss the ground beneath my feet. Anyone who does so will find me placing him in his own grave while still alive.

I have already instructed you not to pray for me in sermons and correspondence. Now I order you to make do with greetings to the Commander of the Faithful.

This then is my decision. So forget about me; take me out of your prostrations and fawnings. You will be free of my face, and yet you will find my aura even closer to you than your own jugular.

The decree is followed by a marginal note: No subject may demand of the Commander of the Faithful any increase in salary, additional position, ownership or exploitation of an estate, or any other kind of benefit beyond the demands of need and necessity.

As a consequence of these admirable decrees, the root causes of the tension and conflict that people had felt disappeared. They were able to resume their normal eating habits and pastimes. They revived their evening parties in the Qarafa Park, frolicked in the Nile waters, and played backgammon and chess. Women were able to dress up again and to sing . . .

Al-Hakim now became even keener than before to hold festivals over which he could preside. He attended the opening of the canal and the construction of its barrage, and allowed the Egyptians to use the occasion in order to celebrate and revere life in a variety of amazing ways, all accompanied by lavish banquets and the scents of musk and ambergris.

In the thirteenth year of al-Hakim's quarter century, he was seized by a frenzied desire to bolster the Islamic faith, a move that was accompanied by expressions of a vicious hatred toward the People of the Book—Jews and Christians—and other protected citizens. He composed and published a decree in which he laid out his orders and his reasoning. He called it: The Decree restoring deference to the community of Unity. Among its contents is the following:

> God is great, there is no deity but He. God is great, Praise be to Him, praise to the Possessor of glory and honor, the Creator of the universe and mankind, who alone determines death and eternity, who governs in matters of dispute, bringer of the dawn, creator of spirits, I praise Him and acknowledge His divinity and unity; I witness that Muhammad is His servant and prophet. O God, pray for Your radiant saint, Your great companion 'Ali ibn Abi Talib, bearer of the burdens of hope, destroyer of evil and the anti-Christ. O God, pray also for the Prophet's pure grandsons, al-Hasan and al-Husayn, for the pious imams and the purest of the pure.
>
> You have asked me to explain why I have ordered the destruction of the Church of the Sepulchre in Jerusalem and other churches in Egypt and Syria. . . .
>
> No, it is not because the sound of ringing bells, just like barking dogs, interferes with my intimate contacts with the

kingdom of the heavens here in Egypt and in my other domains. No, it is not that, but much worse. I can see for myself, just as you can, the proliferation of crosses around us; church towers with crosses on top and people who carry them, they have all increased in number. I now ask myself whether this land is the land of Islam and the community of Unity or a haven for Christians and other sinners? Is this country for Muslims or non-Muslims? I have started to worry that the Trinitarian faith is gaining ground over us, that Christians will seek to do us harm and violate the honor of our community and its territories.

So, in the name of prevention, start with the Church of the Holy Sepulchre; reduce it to rubble and bring its roof to the ground. Then maybe . . .

In the margins we find:

To Copts and those Muslims who join in their festivals:
From now on you will not celebrate the Feast of the Epiphany.

Anyone caught playing by jumping into the Nile will find himself consigned to the bottom of the river in chains.

From now on you will not celebrate the Feast of Norouz.

No water may be thrown on the streets, no fires lit at night, no boat trips, and no tents set up by the Nile or near the Nilometer. You may not throw wine or eggs at each other. Spare me such scandals.

In the same year decrees of the same import were issued regarding Christmas, Shrove Tuesday, and Palm Sunday. In this year, Ya'qub ibn Nastas, the personal physician of al-Hakim, died drunk in a water pool.

Just a week later an additional codicil was appended to the above decree, saying:

The Muslim is a Muslim, and the Jew is a Jew. They will not intermingle. The Muslim is a Muslim, and the Christian is a Christian. They will not intermingle.

O people of the religion of Unity, in such a critical period I am not content merely to forbid you marrying Jews and Christians and eating their meat. Beyond that I have determined that the faiths cannot be equal or co-exist. The Islam of my community is either the faith that seals the prophetic progression and abrogates other faiths that oppose it, or else it does not exist.

And so all Jews and Christians under our protection must wear a mark.

For Jews, that means wooden stars around their neck and black turbans; for Christians, crosses.

Every mark must be fully visible.

Jews and Christians will have their own baths where they can be cleansed of their particular contaminations.

They may not ride horses, but only mules and donkeys with wooden saddles.

Anyone who does not wish to wear the mark can renounce his error and become a Muslim, released thereby from all suspicion and taxation.

In this same year a decree was announced forbidding people to meddle in matters that did not concern them. They were ordered to pray at the proper times, to encourage what is good and forbid what is bad. They were also forbidden to interfere in the sultan's affairs and decrees or in the secret matters of authority.

Al-Maqrizi tells us that in this year, "Many diseases spread among the populace, and death was widespread. People were scared of al-Hakim, so he penned a number of assurances of protection to a variety of people."[10]

During the fourteenth year of al-Hakim's quarter century, i.e. A.H. 400, the caliph's religious sensitivities became increasingly perturbed and extreme. The following comes from accounts of historians for this year:

In this year al-Hakim sent someone to the home of Ja'far al-Sadiq in al-Madina with word to open it up and bring back everything inside; this included a copy of the Qur'an, a bed, and some utensils. The person who opened the house was one of al-Hakim's devotees, named Khatkin al-'Adudi. He also took with him registers of the Prophet's own family. With all this he returned to Egypt, accompanied by a group of 'Alawite shaykhs. When they arrived, al-Hakim gave them a small payment, let them have the bed, but kept the rest for himself. "I deserve it the most," he said. They all left muttering imprecations against him. Word of what he had perpetrated spread abroad, and people started cursing his name at the end of prayers without any attempt to conceal it. That made him relent, and he became scared. He ordered a House of Learning to be constructed and furnished, then had the most precious volumes sent there. He ordered two Sunni shaykhs to reside there, one of whom was Abu Bakr al-Antaki. He bestowed on them robes of honor, granted them frequent audiences, and charged them with attendance at his council sessions and convening jurisconsults and hadith scholars. He also ordered that the righteous deeds of the Prophet's Companions were to be recited there (in so doing, he lifted the prohibition on such acts). At the same time, he again permitted the Ramadan and noon prayers and altered the call to prayer, replacing the phrase "Come to the best of works" with "Prayer is better than sleep." He himself rode to the Mosque of 'Amr ibn al-'As and prayed the noon prayer there. He began to show a preference for the doctrines of the Maliki school; in the mosque he placed a silver stove lit by 1,100 wicks inside and two others underneath. The procession consisted of guards, trumpets, and cries of joy and praise to God, all accompanied by drums; this all took place on the night of mid-Sha'ban. On the first day of Ramadan he

attended the grand mosque in Cairo; all kinds of furnishing
were brought there, including gold and silver chandeliers.
The populace prayed devoutly for him. That year on the
tenth day of Ramadan he wore a woolen garment, rode on a
donkey, made a public display of his self-denial and filled
his arms with notebooks. On Friday he preached the sermon and led the prayer. He prevented anyone from
addressing him as "My Lord," or from kissing the ground
in front of him. He gave contributions to the poor, Qur'an
reciters, strangers, and travelers who sought refuge in
mosques. He had a large niche [mihrab] of silver made for
the mosque; it had ten candle holders and was encrusted
with jewels. For three years he continued this way, carrying
perfumes, incense, and candles to mosques, things no one
had ever done before. Then suddenly he had a change of
heart: he killed the jurisconsult, Abu Bakr al-Antaki, and the
other shaykh with him, along with a great number of other
Sunnis, and for no justifiable reason. All this he carried out
in a single day. In addition, he closed the doors of the House
of Learning, revoked everything he had done, and went
back to his old ways, killing scholars and jurisconsults and
so on. He continued this way until he was murdered.[11]

In the eighteenth year of al-Hakim's quarter century, a number of decrees
were issued aimed at Egyptians and, in particular, women, singers, and
astrologers, which had a debilitating effect. There follows a sample
selection of them:

> Decree against astrologers and singers:
> I have come only to refute the stars and disrupt their purity
> and predictive power. My method involves filling my king-
> dom with incidents and exceptional circumstances and
> thwarting the power of principles and expectations.

On such a basis, anyone who practices astrology or predicts by the stars sets himself in opposition to me. I will exile anyone who opposes me, or else I shall cause his star to fall from the skies. Did not 'Ali, the Prophet's own trustee, say: "Beware of the science of astrology, except whatever may guide you through the dark regions of earth and sea. The astrologer is like the magician; magicians are soothsayers, unbelievers roasting in hellfire."

My decision is irrevocable, even for those astrologers who strive to convert the pearls of heaven to my benefit and service.

Singers should be banished from my sight.

My people are innate dancers. What need do they have of people to play instruments or sing?

I have proclaimed all-out war against all kinds of debauched transvestitism and effeminate behavior. Singing belongs in that category, since it tempts and corrupts the body. As long as I live and am your pastor, singing is forbidden.

In this same year astrologers left the country, except for those who claimed to be blind or mad and a few others who took refuge in deserted towers or underground storehouses.

All musical instruments were collected and burned. No one was allowed to ride boats to the Canal; all gates leading to it and all balconies and windows looking out on it were closed.

Decree concerning the proper cloistering of women:
By Fatima the radiant, what I have to say about women is nothing but good!

How can I possibly despise them or defame them when beneath the feet of my mother lies my own paradise. My own state gets its name and its foundation from a blessed

woman, Fatima, daughter of the Prophet and wife of 'Ali,
His own trustee and legatee of their secrets?

I have indeed commanded that all cloistered women
should remain inside their houses. They are to be prevented
from going outside or looking out of windows or balconies.
I have given orders that any cobbler who makes them shoes,
any bath-owner who opens his doors to them, is to be
punished. This is not a cruel act on my part, but is meant to
prevent the anti-Christ from involving himself in a war of
sexual provocation. Such a conflict will be futile and accursed,
since it only serves to make men and women alike forget the
real war that we have all to fight against that enemy who is
ever on the watch for our foibles and slips.

In this same year the chancellery was inundated with requests from
women for special dispensations: maidservants, women with grievances,
midwives, washers of corpses, widows, yarn-sellers, and those who
needed to travel.

Some women were locked up inside public baths and suffocated.

That year a pregnant sheep was sacrificed, and, when the inside was
opened up, historians are prepared to swear on the most solemn of oaths
that the foetus inside had human features.

In this year, and, some say, the year before as well, "Al-Hakim sent a
letter to Sultan Mahmud ibn Subuktakin, the ruler of Ghazna, inviting
him to submit to his authority. The latter ripped it up, spat on it, and then
forwarded it to al-Qadir, the Abbasid Caliph." [12]

In the twenty-first—some people say, the twenty-second—year of
al-Hakim's quarter century, the caliph was afflicted with bouts of
melancholia that were sometimes severe. He secluded himself and wandered around a great deal. He started wearing sackcloth and stopped
bathing. He used to spend the night observing the stars and searching in
them for divine inspiration. These habits of his were accentuated by a
group of devotees who made their appearance at this time. They called

him "the buttress of time and most eloquent of speakers," and used books and epistles to record behavior traits and segments from his extraordinary and incredible decrees as proofs and signs of his infallibility and divinity. They demanded that he be sanctified and worshiped and secretly won his affection and his support. They started touring Egypt and Syria attracting followers to his cadre of "sages" and establishing pacts, agreements, and obligations of confidentiality and pledge. A series of intrigues and bloody conflicts broke out between this group of Sunnis. As a consequence, the devotee named Akhram was killed. Thereafter Hamzah al-Druzi took their cause with him and fled to the mountains of Syria, shortly before or after the murder of al-Hakim himself. His own followers spoke in terms of his disappearance three nights before the end of the month of Shawal in the year A.H. 411, an event to which we will refer later on.

2. The slave Mas'ud, or the Agent for Sodomite Punishment

He used to take charge of the public order for himself, riding around the markets on a donkey (he never rode anything else). When he found anyone cheating, he ordered a slave whom he always took with him, named Mas'ud, to sodomise the offender. This is a dire, indeed unprecedented, circumstance.

Ibn Kathir,
The Beginning and the Ending

Al-Hakim used to put on a white woolen garment and ride a tall, blond-colored donkey named Moon. He would make circuits of the markets in Cairo and the old city and take care of matters of public order himself. He always took along with him a tall, bulky slave named Mas'ud. Whenever he came across anyone cheating people, he ordered Mas'ud to sodomize the merchant on the spot in his shop, with al-Hakim standing close by and everyone watching till the slave had finished. For this reason

Mas'ud became the butt of jokes in Cairo. People would say: Mas'ud, go and get him! A poet of the time composed these lines:

> Mas'ud has a tool that is mighty,
> Long as a papyrus scroll,
> One that cleaves the arses of sinners
> Harder than a pearl on a nail.

Ibn Iyas, *Bright Flowers Concerning the Events of the Ages*

This Mas'ud had been one of the vast number of slaves that made the slave market on the outskirts of Cairo resound with noise. His most recent slave master, Abu Sulayman al-Za'farani, had categorized him as a tough sell, someone that needed oils and creams to make him attractive to gullible buyers. Mas'ud's face was as black as could be and incredibly ugly, so much so that, if we are to believe rumors of the time, it was impossible to entertain any positive thoughts about him even with his white teeth. In all three dimensions his body was as powerful and tall as any ghoul; if he made up his mind to kill his slave master by kicking and punching him, it would have been no harder than banging a nail.

Like everyone so endowed, Mas'ud wore his inner soul through the color of his skin and eyes. People saw his temperament as molded by sheer evil and darkness; the very purchase of him was regarded as a loss, since, like many other slaves, he was always running away. "If he's hungry, he sleeps; if he's sated, he fucks," went the popular saying, but actually it did not apply to Mas'ud. When he was hungry, he waited; if he was sated, he belched and started work again. As regards running away, he did indeed do it a lot; for that very reason, he never stayed with a single owner or slave master any longer than demanded by the limits of sur- veillance and daylight. He would wait instinctively for those moments of distraction at dead of night when he could speed away like an arrow in pursuit of careening specters.

The root cause of such behavior was not poor training or corrupt character, but rather a terrible fear of his own image as others saw him and of his smell that others termed foul. He had managed to run away more times than any other slave, so at one point he was declared legally killable inside Egypt. That particular episode forced him to spend a frantic period on the run, and he was forced to look for a hiding place. For a while he lived a life that swung between total panic and sorrow, anticipating his own downfall and the oblivion that would follow; if not that, then a mountain where he could stay clear of hunters and the blind. The last place Mas'ud stayed during this period was a deserted cemetery shrouded in silence and full of wild herbs. There he eked out a living among the rocks and tree roots. Each night he envisioned legions of the dead rising up and handing him cold and poison to drink; the angel of the dead would arrive in a black cloak of infinite length and depart with the elements. In spite of the difficulties of living in such a place and the terrifying company at night, Mas'ud came to appreciate that life among the dead was much preferable to falling once more into the clutches of the living. The eyes of the latter were hellfire, their expressions were deadly arrows, whereas the former had no eyes but merely sockets that were forever empty, neither pursuing anyone nor loading someone down with investigations and matters of conscience.

Mas'ud spent several days with no alternative but living amid the cold and mud, nourished only by the thought of his own coffin or else by looking at the women's underwear hung up to dry far away on the roofs of the houses that overlooked the cemetery. Then came the day when Mas'ud felt his guts being torn apart by an incredible hunger. He got up and walked around the city perimeter searching for food amid the garbage. He had not gone very far before he noticed that everyone around him was running away in sheer fright, making even domestic animals and fowl do likewise. When he reached a square, he realized that his body was uncovered and exposed to the army elite, so he pulled himself together and rushed back to his ditch in the cemetery. Once there he stretched out, feeling defeated and overwhelmed, someone for whom nature's only succor would be in the form of whatever herbs and grasses might feed his body and keep him concealed from the rest of humanity. He spent a few more days in this state, hovering between imminent death and labored breathing, but then all of a sudden he became aware of increased movement and the sound of human voices all around him, as though a whole group of tribes had arrived all at once to bury their dead en masse. Mas'ud was shocked and frightened. When he raised his head to take a look, he was amazed to see a peculiar, indeed bewildering, scene right in front of him: people setting up tents and lighting fires on the cemetery grounds. Only a few days passed till the entire cemetery was crammed with people and animals. These people, he discovered, were not migrant bedouin but people who no longer had homes in the city or its suburbs. The cost of living inside the city was now so high that its quarters and districts had vomited them out to the city perimeter.

Mas'ud did not bother to seek explanations for what was going on all around him. Instead he focused his entire mental capacities on a single issue: since his reliance on the dead for protection was no longer working, how could he get away from these live human beings who had invaded the cemetery? Where could he go? Mas'ud poured himself heart and soul into solving this knotty problem and explored every conceivable avenue; he thought of advantages and disadvantages and converted them into a kind of sustenance through which he could stave off his hunger and misery. On the third day of this grim period, he surrendered to a deep midday sleep, only to wake up to the sounds of a group of boys screaming because they had moved away all the branches and leaves he was using to cover himself and then discovered a living being underneath them. Elder folk arrived in droves to rescue the young children and surrounded Mas'ud's ditch in successive circles. "Look at this disgusting slave," they were saying, "who's pretending to be dead so he can run away from his master. We must tie him in chains and hand him over to the police chief!" This and other similarly brutal statements fell on Mas'ud like a fatal lightning-strike. He could stand it no longer, stood up with a huge roar, and took off through the crowd, yelling for all he was worth.

Anyone who tried to stand in his way found himself confronting a terrifying display of yelling and threats. As his voice became hoarse, people
still only managed to grab hold of the rags and tatters he was wearing.
No sooner had he managed to get clear of this mob of people than he
found himself, naked and exhausted, on the city's outskirts, confronting
a platoon of armed guards. There are many reports about what happened
next to Mas'ud in this tricky situation. The most plausible is what was
contained in the police chief's report quoted below:

> The slave named Mas'ud was surprised by our patrol out-
> side the city. He was running away from his master and
> was as naked as the day he was born. I gave our guards
> orders to surround him and use whatever weapons were
> needed to make him give up or leave him dead. How terri-
> fying this ill-starred wretch looked in the open space, using
> all possible means to avoid being hit—leaping, crawling,
> and hiding behind rocky outcrops and trees. At one point he
> hid himself to take a breather and huddled up close to the
> ground, obviously planning a getaway. Just then our men
> managed to surprise him; they pounced on him from all
> sides like thunderbolts, at which point it was all over. He
> found himself attacked and beaten everywhere and clubbed
> almost to death. When the slave showed no further signs of
> movement, our men approached him. What they saw aston-
> ished them, so much so that some of them almost fainted at
> the sight. The slave was awash in his own blood, like a
> slaughtered bull breathing his last. There he was, extracting
> the arrows that had hit him and still hurling curses and
> threats at them, spitting in the face of anyone who dared
> touch him. The major thing they discovered and which
> totally annulled any astonishment they had previously felt
> was the sheer size and shape of the man's penis; the soldiers
> were unanimous that they had never seen or heard of its

8

like anywhere. They were so amazed that they even had a
competition to see what was the best description for it; for
that purpose they resorted to comparisons with species of
wild animals, and then to confining his particulars to the
colossal size of his penis. Hardly had they finished with
their unique discovery than their commander ordered them
to carry the slave to the closest warehouse so that they
could check his file, find out his identity, then return him to
his owner.

Mas'ud was tossed into a large warehouse used for sick riding animals
and people down on their luck. To get him there they used all kinds of
violence, restraint, and intimidation. He had not been there for very long
before his fame had spread throughout old and new Cairo and into every
quarter. News of his penis made its ways through all the popular clubs
till it reached as far as the soirées of the Fatimids; echoes even came to
the ears of al-Hakim bi-Amr Illah.

Those who brought the story to the Fatimid caliph suggested that the
slave be either killed or castrated so as to put an end to all these tales.
The more sympathetic counselors advised the caliph to leave him in the
warehouse or in a charitable hostel until he died. Al-Hakim took all these
opinions and suggestions under advisement, but then rejected them out
of hand. Instead he decided—a decision he reached at dead of night—to
make Mas'ud a member of his retinue and to assign him a particular
function. When the true nature of his function was revealed to al-Hakim's
most adept devotees and philosophers, they outdid each other in welcoming the idea and in extolling the mind of the ruler who had come up
with the idea and "created it from nothing."

Not long after the idea of this special function came into being, its
inventor, al-Hakim bi-Amr Illah, moved to implement it in detail. He
ordered Mas'ud's immediate transfer from the warehouse to the palace
clinic where he was consigned to the very best doctors and gentlest of
nurses. They gave him all necessary first aid and then went on to provide

all necessary treatment. He also gave Mas'ud's former owner, Sulayman al-Za'farani, double payment as well as some decorations of honor.

So Mas'ud spent several days in the clinic receiving various kinds of intensive care and special treatment from the nurses who, following special instructions from on high, rivaled each other in giving Mas'ud massages and in teasing and arousing him. Once he was on the road to recovery, he proceeded to eat everything he was offered, and then asked for more. Everyone was amazed, and the clinic accountant was appalled. No sooner had he got out of bed and started walking and using his limbs again than al-Hakim's devotees instructed the town criers to announce in the all public markets of Cairo that al-Hakim bi-Amr Illah had given Mas'ud this special function. So they went their way and made the following announcement as they did their rounds:

> Servants of God, our Lord and yours hereby warns you all that there is no place in his lands for commodity speculators or merchants who cheat customers. Anyone who cheats in markets and food shops will discover that our Lord has authorized Mas'ud the slave to commit sodomy on him. You crooks, our Lord is riding his blond donkey among you, ever watchful. His dire punishment is yet closer to your asses than the unlawful food in your bellies. So beware! Whoever issues a warning is thereby excused!

This dire warning fell on the merchants of old and new Cairo like a thunderbolt. The general populace and people in need on the other hand greeted the news with unrestrained joy. Those who had grudges kept an eagle eye out for speculators and cheats and exposed the major violators who refused to mend their ways. The majority of merchants decided to resort to more covert types of swindling and fraud.

In the early months of the implementation of al-Hakim bi-Amr Illah's decision, the slave Mas'ud—now converted into the agent of sodomite punishment—saw continuous activity in dealing with speculators and crooked merchants. He managed to cope with the exhaustion that he felt at the end of each day by taking into account his own important status and the way he could now terrify people who just the day before had been able to frighten and despise him. He was also delighted at the special food he was given with the intention of renewing his energy and arousing his sexual appetite, things like almonds, harisa, and meat and fat from the Nile salamander.

During these early months of Mas'ud's new career, he looked happy and content, always smiling. He realized that al-Hakim bi-Amr Illah held him in high esteem and that, thanks to his own ramrod-straight scales of justice, he himself was playing a major role in correcting merchant behavior. All this gave him the clear impression that the heavens had given him a truly unique opportunity to take revenge on society as a whole, which had subjected him to all manner of contempt and suffering. He would walk around the city and through the markets of the kasba wrapped in an aura of supercilious arrogance, belching at anyone he wished, cuffing anyone he did not like on the neck, and squeezing the nose of people who made gestures at his expense under his armpit. How was he supposed to behave otherwise when he could see for himself how many merchants he had managed to injure or kill and how many had committed suicide, all because of his surprise forays into the markets accompanied by al-Hakim's demons and sergeants, or by al-Hakim in person riding his blond donkey!

Mas'ud's daily excursions into the kasba markets took in every market where foodstuffs were on sale. One of the earliest consequences of his forays was that the bar in Khan al-Ruwasin which served wine to people with problems vanished, as did all the blondes from the grain market, prostitutes who used to stand on the pavement wearing men's clothing in red, chewing gum, and making eyes at the people who came to market. These two markets, just like those in the Burjuwan quarter and on Bayn al-Qasrayn Street, were full of merchants of every kind: butchers, bakers, fruit vendors, vegetable sellers, milk and cheese merchants, sellers of frozen products, cooks, grilled meat sellers, perfumers, and others.

The only exception to this pattern was the chicken market where chicken and rice were the basic products on sale, along with various types of dove, blackbird, nightingale, and other songbirds. In all these markets Mas'ud had no trouble in training merchants who owned shops how to behave and putting a stop to their policies of overpricing and infringements of proper trading practice. Barely three months went by before market inspectors were able to report a new trend among shop owners toward upright conduct, although they did whisper that there was a noticeable decrease in the number of merchants still in business and entering the trade.

Throughout this period there remained just one black mark on Mas'ud's record, namely itinerant peddlers. How was he supposed to keep track of them and impose his unique punishment for any fraudulent practices when they acted just like Bedouin, touring the markets and operating on a 'take the money and run' policy? How could he have any impact on their control when they had organized themselves to the extent of employing young men on the make who would act as informants and sentinels? Even suppose that he did go after them, how could he arrest them all when they scattered to the four winds and took refuge in the maze of alleyways and culs-de-sac? Faced with this dilemma, Mas'ud thought long and hard. The solution he adopted involved making use of shop owners who were aggravated enough to be glad to take revenge on these roving peddlers. The way it worked was that Mas'ud allowed these merchants to chase the peddlers every time they set up stalls to ply their trade, and then block their escape routes till Mas'ud and his guards could get there and arrest them.

One day at about noon a huge din could be heard in the Ruwasin market; a fierce row had broken out between these two factions. Mas'ud soon arrived with his entourage to see what had happened and assess the consequences. There had been a serious fight involving clubs, truncheons, and slingshots, but neither side had come out on top. The brawl continued, and, when some of the combatants started unsheathing swords, Mas'ud ordered his guards to put an end to the brawl and to the shop owners' advantage, to confiscate the peddlers' goods, and force them to run away. No sooner had the order been executed than the peddlers were seen running for their lives in total panic. A group of them found themselves being chased by the hulking frame of Mas'ud, emitting hideous grunts as he ran. After a considerable time and great expenditure of energy, he only managed to grab hold of one peddler who had run out of breath and was very scrawny in any case. Mas'ud seized this poor wretch by the feet, dragged him to the closest dark alley, and started to strip off his clothes and tackle his backside. He had hardly started the operation before he sprang back in amazement.

"Good God," he exclaimed, "are you a woman?"

The woman proceeded to pull up her trousers and adjust her clothing. "Yes, I'm a woman," she replied in a tone of outraged defiance. "During the day I sell cheeses and sweetmeats. I'm a woman, and I use my feminity to earn a living at night. What's the matter with you, man-fucker?! Here's my ass, so bring all your mighty power to bear on it if you can. Alternatively here's my cunt. Fuck that, and you'll end up with syphilis. Even with your disgusting body I can see you standing there in front of me quivering all over, when I'm just a grain of mustard seed, a mere feather tossed by the wind. So go back and tell your master al-Hakim all about me, how impudent and defiant I was. Either that, or I'll tell him how impotent you are."

Mas'ud stood up with a heavy heart and turned away to leave. The woman chased after him with a whole stream of taunts. The only way he found to stop her was to give her a sudden and vicious blow to the head which knocked her to the ground unconscious. With that Mas'ud made his way back to his quarters in the palace, morose and distracted.

The next day, al-Hakim returned from the Muqattam Hills to hear what had happened in the Ruwasin market, except the details about Mas'ud's treatment of the woman. Al-Hakim summoned the registrar and ordered him to give the peddlers back their goods and to threaten them with death if they returned to the markets rather than sticking to alleyways and city outskirts. He ordered Mas'ud to be fetched.

"'Abdallah," he told his slave in joyful greeting, "I've now perused the inspectors' reports regarding your good work in the markets, and I'm very pleased. Today I'm promoting you and expanding your purview to certain other cities and fortresses in my dominions. Your next assignment will be Alexandria. You'll find lots of swindlers, racketeers, and forgers there. Take a week's vacation to prepare yourself. Now go back to your bed, and may God give you strength!"

By this time Mas'ud had come to feel a strange sense of guilt and remorse as his sensory memory recalled the varieties of backside and anus he had penetrated and the different ways in which his victims had expressed their pain, their pleas, and their screams of agony. All this haunted him in his dreams, as it played itself in front of his closed eyes like a never-ending strip the particular cases of people with narrow anal passages and hemorrhoids. In recent weeks he had taken to pushing these images out of his mind by trying to stay awake, drinking excessive amounts of coffee, and taking amphetamines. As a direct result he was feeling totally exhausted. The only thing that prevented his condition from becoming very obvious was that every day he swallowed huge amounts of fortifying drugs that al-Hakim bi-Amr Illah's assistants provided for him. Al-Hakim had decided to send him to Alexandria to carry out exactly the same task on other folk who were duping and swindling customers, and yet he could not even stand the thought; and at the same time he had no other choice apart from the very worst of eventualities and certain death.

On that fateful day when Mas'ud received al-Hakim's command, a state of total exhaustion came over his entire body, accompanied by a general debility and chronic insomnia. He lay there dozing occasionally but otherwise awake, progressing from one dreadful nightmare to another that was even worse. Droves of merchants and professionals would appear, each one devising new ways of reviling and poking fun at him; what scared him most was the thought of butchers either castrating or sodomizing him. The only way Mas'ud found of ridding himself of these appalling visions was to rush around and mouth insane threats that were magnified yet further by shouts and roars. These would resonate so much that even al-Hakim got to hear them. When he asked what was happening, they told him that the slave Mas'ud could see things that they could not; he was fighting legions of demons and other invisible creatures. He seemed to be like one possessed by the very devil. Al-Hakim commanded that he should be fed more almonds and harisa. If he did not recover his normal demeanor, he was to be beaten with sticks in the hope of dispelling his misery and recalcitrance.

But neither force feeding nor beating did anything to improve Mas'ud's condition, even a little. He actually began to lose weight. In a single week his body became even skinnier, and his bones started to jut out. People started talking about the way the slave was wasting away, while others were more scabrous in their descriptions of the way he was gradually disappearing from his groin to his sexual organ.

Mas'ud was completely worn down and mentally deranged, but even so he was forcibly dragged to the markets in order to carry out the duties expected of him. It soon became completely obvious to the guards, the people due for punishment, and the entire merchant population that Mas'ud had totally lost his potency. Aphrodisiacs no longer worked, nor did words of encouragement. Such was his condition that inevitably he became an object of general ridicule and malice.

Once Mas'ud's condition and the loss of his primary asset became obvious, he was confined to a cell close to the palace stables. There he was allowed to sleep in peace with nothing to wrack his nerves. Occasionally he would wake up, eat the scraps of food he was offered, and guffaw in bitter despair.

Running away or of even thinking about it was out of the question! For this slave, it wasn't the idea of other people's stares and swords that stirred the fires of hell. For him, hell had sunk its claws deep inside his very self. In fact, he had never experienced wars, revolutions, or natural disasters; if he had, the impact of his demise might have been easier to bear. As it was, the people around him were indolent and kept up a monotonous routine that did not give him the opportunity to reflect or to raise painful questions and suspicions. No indeed, this particular brand of hell forced him to recall terrifying incidents. Every day these memories would cause him yet more grief, and his attempts to shut them out would only make things worse. He would choke, then beg to be released from this world, with all its backsides and anuses that continued to plague him with their bloody wounds. For his accursed body all he craved was total annihilation. So it came to the point when Mas'ud used to extend his neck and beg people to use their swords and lances to cut of his head and put an end to his misery. He was so insistent in this request that he began to imagine that his head had actually been severed. That made him more apathetic, and he stopped eating. He kept threatening guards with the foul stench of his corpse if they did not agree to put him in a coffin and bury him properly.

By order of al-Hakim bi-Amr Illah, informants were not allowed to talk about the way Mas'ud met his end. As a result there were inevitably a large number of stories that circulated in popular nightspots and literary circles. One of them said that Mas'ud managed to burst his way into one of al-Hakim's council sessions with a coffin under his arm. "Lord," he said, "I seek neither forgiveness nor security. If you cannot make people live, you can make them die. Here's my coffin, so put me in it and bury it in the earth. We will meet again on the Day of Resurrection. God alone is the victor!" It is said that al-Hakim responded to the request and challenge that had been posed, and carried out his request. Another story has it that a group of high-class butchers were delegated to do to Mas'ud what he had done to them and their colleagues, keeping it up until Mas'ud died. Yet another says that the slave died after an unsuccessful attempt to castrate him, and another that the Nile waters had vomited him back. A medical examination confirmed that he had committed suicide with a hundred and one stabs to the chest.

chapter two
At al-Hakim's councils

1. A Session of Violet Oil

hen it comes to the entire succession of incredible and contradictory actions that al-Hakim took, the root cause of his
motivations was a kind of chemical imbalance in the brain.
From his youth onward he was afflicted by a kind of melancholia and
mental instability. Medical science is unanimous that people so afflicted
suffer delusions and imagine all sorts of amazing things. All such patients
are convinced that their fantasies are perfectly sound; there is no way of
changing their ways or diverting them from their chosen course. Some of
them believe themselves to be a prophet or even the Deity Himself—may
He be exalted! Among regular symptoms is a confused jumbling of
words, something that is completely obvious to those who observe and
converse with such people; any doubts on the matter instantly disappear.
Sometimes, however, this confusion may not be so obvious. The patient
will only entertain such evil notions out of sight of the general populace.
Indeed, in public he may well seem perfectly intelligent, as highly
regarded as the most illustrious members of society. It is only as a result
of prolonged exposure that the unseen contradictions become evident.

That was precisely the situation with al-Hakim. The people who kept
his company over a prolonged period came to realize the contradiction.
However, for people who stayed at a distance, it was only his actions that

made things clear. Something that illustrates the extent to which he was afflicted by this illness is that from early childhood he had a twitch that was caused by a fluid imbalance in the brain; that in itself is a major factor in the incidence of melancholia. He was treated for the condition in various ways, one of which involved sitting him in a bath of violet oil and tying him down. His penchant for staying awake till the early hours, his love of riding, and his never-ending thirst, these are all symptoms of this condition. When Abu Ya'qub Ishaq ibn Ibrahim ibn Nastas served as his physician, he persuaded al-Hakim to relax his strictures against wine drinking and listening to songs—things he had forbidden and prevented people from enjoying. As a result his demeanor improved greatly, and his mental and physical condition stabilized. When Abu Ya'qub died and he again banned wine-drinking and listening to songs, his health reverted to its former state.

Yahya ibn Sa'id al-Antaki,
Appendix to the History of Eutychius

One evening in the summer of A.H. 399 al-Hakim was in his wine salon, following the instructions of his Christian physician, Ibn Nastas. He was sitting in violet oil and drinking wine, all in the hope of ridding his mind of its fluid imbalance and curing himself of his spasms and melancholia. No sooner did he feel a sense of relief and relaxation—naked though he was except for a loincloth—than he yelled for his devotees. They came running, kissed the ground, and took their normal places. He gave orders for singers to be brought in, whereupon male and female youths arrived and regaled him with the sweetest and most delicate of melodies. Once he felt at ease and completely comfortable, he allowed the singers to leave and summoned a young male secretary. The young man arrived with paper and pens. Al-Hakim gave two orders: one for the guards to leave; the other for the secretary to take off his clothes, sit down alongside him, and get ready to write.

This summer night was like all the others during that particular season. The sky was studded with stars; the moon rose and shone, and the silence was as deep and expansive as ever. Yet deep within, this night was of a kind rarely encountered, one in which passion ferments and birth-pangs intensify. This night and its attributes were to glow only by virtue of al-Hakim's state, through the lexicon of his perception and the way insistent thoughts kept flooding over him. Such a night was only so remarkable and noteworthy because al-Hakim was determined to control his internal vertigo and hold forth about his symptoms and misgivings, all in the hope of being cured and saved and in quest of a text for recovery.

As al-Hakim started dictating his thoughts to the scribe, he was still wavering between twin delights, the violet oil and the wine that kept impinging upon his visions.

"The head," he said, "the child and its tragedy; the head split apart and its history. Two charts for compiling the trial, one of scrutiny and embarking on the caravan of travail. . . .

"Regarding the most miserable of heads, speech may often be useless and ineffectual.

"The most miserable of heads, the most outstanding, is the mournful one with a wailing-woman within; the feverish head that has broken oars and rudder, plows through the waves, and appears before God wearing hempcloth as it waits for trousers to dry in the sun, trousers that have cleft both waves and virgins and that one day were the focus of women both pregnant and bereft. . . .

"The trial of the head is in vanishing behind its own bulk, to the measure of its own shivering and gloomy mien.

"Its sign is the desert where there is neither ruler nor ruled, where it is to be seen alone plunging its torments into the sand and using negligence and delay to resist its own tumble.

"The head must inevitably disappear behind its own shadow, like an egg that abandons its own color and vanishes. Egg and head share color, the whiteness of repetition and beginning, the whiteness of concealment and discretion."

For a moment al-Hakim said nothing, then he continued, "If I were a child, I would ask for a father who would teach me to shoot at women and mirrors, and how to ride and disappear; he would bequeath me both a desert within me as expansive as fate itself and a love for refreshment through silence, biers, and absence.

"Were I a child, I would ask for a father with the rest of pre-Islamic culture in his bosom, a father who would teach me, through sense, knowledge, and poetics, how to burn down walls, though they be of silk, how to worship the sea and urinate in it. . . .

"Were I a youngster, I would dream of a father who would say to me, 'In these times love and knowledge have disintegrated, each one of them bearing its own ignorance or complaining about its she-camel, operating in its own unique fashion. And your lot is to wander in the desert wastes and turn your back on mankind, or else to devote yourself to a life of madness as you try to govern them.'"

At this point al-Hakim regained his normal consciousness, but stayed totally silent, almost as though he were in a swoon. When he started talking again, it was in short bursts. The exhausted young secretary found it utterly impossible to record them all and only managed to write down some snippets, such as:

"The desert, the desert!

"Tremulous hope and bitter words!

"I realize I'm making my way through a life where there is neither sweetness nor horizon.

"I know orphan exposure, whether on its own or with others. I know that it proceeds either alone or in mixed company, as it heads toward its pit or its own deviation before fragmenting.

"In the abode where there is neither movement nor strife, cogitation is good, planning effective. Then death arrives, fast-paced and on time, right on time. . . .

"In vain do we grow old; we only learn about life when it is all over and we are close to the end.

"Death repeats itself, but without any originality! So what? I ask myself. The wombs of women bring forth humans, and the earth swallows them up. So what, I tell myself, if this process of bringing forth and swallowing up involves behavior that is prescient, pain that is reduced, and harm that inflicts less damage? But what matters is the blindness, the space that shudders, the felicitous opportunity in a crisis. Instead of national refreshment, open space, and a change of air, there was smoke, crowd, and constricted space.

"Before the earth swallows me up, I told myself, here I am relishing the ultimate happiness, progressing toward the highest degree of certainty, moving ever forward till my head is held high and my talents are fully applied.

"I waited for her body to arrive, confident that my bride would come to me:

"a radiant gift of destiny to crystallize me,

"breasts that sigh

"chemistry of felicity and beauty.

"But not long after she came to me as my bride the whole thing turned into a disaster; her body became a mistake, chaff for the wind.

"'Patience, patience!' I told myself. So I waited till the clouds scattered, the sky was clear once more, and life came. But instead, calamity fell on me from an unexpected direction. Dangerous notions arrived, and misfortunes too. Survival there was, but it was endowed with multiple opportunities for downfall. I was unable to control this slippery slope; without lamp or axe, I had to engage in a fierce struggle to keep my head from exploding and my very face from collapse.

"I awoke one day and told the women who used to share my bed, 'By my life, it would be a wonderful idea to put you all in closed coffins and throw you into the Nile.' With that, I left them and went out into the early dawn atmosphere, there to resume my interest in smelling the scent of roses and listening to the beat of birds' wings.

"The biggest issue of all: changing this world. The very love of change, that headlong rush to sever the ties that bind self, oppression, and want to each other; the very love of change, to abolish the contradiction between life and the things that overwhelm and destroy it. However, my dear devotees, why am I destined forever to drink wine and collect varieties of grass in order to foster this headlong spirit within me?

"My ruses and medicaments will all come to naught; my drugs will lose their efficacy one after the other. I shall spend the rest of my life making countless attempts to understand what has happened, to comprehend those things that were not foreseen, to assess this sense of depression with an analytical eye, this suppressed feeling deep down that dogs human beings whether alone or in company, like a clap of thunder sometimes, and at others like a prolonged, plaintive refrain.

"Beyond what has already happened what else is there? What's happened has indeed happened! What else is there besides depression? It comes in two types: a normal type that justifies itself and is deeply enmeshed in its own essence, the rusted tedium of passing days, the travail of preserving health and peace, and the assaults of others. Then there's a second type, an exceptional kind that inhabits times of joy and clings to them like some hidden sense of fear that such times may soon disappear. Both types of depression are controlled by the sigh, something that can only be bested by the mastery of perpetual absence.

"In such cases of decline, and following the thousand and first absence, the thousand and first retreat, however severe may be the pain and difficulty, it seems I will probe my own self in order to confirm with astonishment that I am still alive and in control of you. It also seems that I will gather whatever is left of my presence and power and proceed erect through the cities and valleys of the land. As I proceed, I will ponder the fact that no one in power can take away my aura of prestige or interfere with my steadfast intent to achieve a linkage and pact between my lungs and the air. My thoughts must inevitably be drawn toward its eastern pole. Inevitably my capital must consist in keeping my head held high.

"What is most probable is that, after everything that has happened (and how I suffer over what has happened!), I will pace back and forth through the streets and alleys chanting a rousing song, with dervishes dancing before me. I am the unique atom, I shall say, so why should I care about my problems or fear death as though I were the first or last person who is going to perish?

"I shall compose fierce lampoons aimed at absence. I will spell everything in plural form and go in quest of unity and unification.

"I have been walking and still am. Walking on foot, so philosophers and doctors have it, is good exercise that provides maximum benefit to the body and bolsters its resistance to depression whether psychological or nervous (despondent psyche, tread the earth's uplands and pursue the posture of quest!). Yes, I have been walking and still am, as I contemplate writing reports of prohibitions and checks, a model for my tombstone while I am still alive. How amazing! Here I am, still seriously trying to convert to my own interest all the fates and mute trials that so dog my life.

"A few days later I had a fresh idea: maybe release might come with the diversion of a new marriage and in a panegyric to the bed; or else in learning the sounds of wild beasts; in hunting songbirds and butterflies or eating cold almonds. Maybe it lay in collecting severed heads or composing a volume on the benefits of jest.

"All this occurs whenever the water returns to its courses, calamities lessen their intensity, routine and habit return to quell the thunder and enclose bodies."

An awesome silence now descended on the place. The trembling of the devotees in their corners was enough to blow out the candles close by. By now al-Hakim was strongly affected by both the wine and violet oil; sweat was pouring off him, and blood was coursing through his veins. Suddenly he leapt up and started talking in strident tones, as though delivering a sermon or recording minutes. The young scribe fell out of the pool and stayed where he was on the ground. Even though he was utterly exhausted, he tried to record as many of his master's words as he could.

"To eradicate the concerns that reside in my vision," he said, "I took on the River Nile, as it did me; and I took on the birds, as they did me. To revive connections and relationships, I rode in a boat heading for the light, guided by the chant of the sea bird as I made my way to you, my devotees:

"With its mythic half my body is in quest of its destiny,

"I lay down the foundation stone of its birthplace,

"I place the head between two crescents of embers,

"And open the path for the devotees of conscience and secrecy.

"Then I walk the earth unsheathing my sword and power

"Against anyone who would deny me through mind or magic.

"The sun never shines on me because I am a cave,

"A grassy cave, a grassy cave in ruins,

"A prison, an ancient prison, a map of secrecy . . .

"No, the sun never shines on me, but in my heart I see a gleaming star in search of its mate, of a country and people.

"I see myself grasping the last thread, projecting birds into the heavens to shoot down, banging on doors and asking who it is that is banging.

"The sun never shines on me, but in order to despair of my own despair and restore fire to my hidden places, I roam the country. And I will come …

"By the right I have to govern and reject! I will come again, my face aglow, from hidden realms and ultimate refuges; I will come from the markets of existence and places of this world, all in order to inform the morning and you. And so, my devotees, open your hearts and embrace me; lift up your hands and support me.

"I am the one that time has brought you.

"The factors of chance and lineage, they alone intercede for me.

"I am the child of that circumstance which seeks a place in existence and fate.

"I have it in me to oppose the wind through destruction and erection in the realms of architecture and stone.

"You can write what you will about me. My tents have need of the ropes of your love and hatred, just as the earth needs sun and rain."

Al-Hakim went back and sat in the violet oil again. The young secretary joined him and continued recording his master's words. As al-Hakim careered ahead at one moment and then slowed down out of sheer exhaustion, his tone of voice kept rising, then falling.

"Show me," he said, "the kind of power I need, when people are either asleep or distracted; and all the while the march of time works its unseen machinations to procure my end.

"I blacken the whiteness of days. I sense myself leaving the realms of existence and entering the clutches of mystery, secluding myself on the pathways of resolve and entrenchment.

"Politics is all toil. Nothing amazes me more than those who are hell-bent on acquiring yet more power.

"I am tired of it all, not because my intuition has run dry or the ulcer hasn't healed, but rather because, at the best of times, my own share of its lofty intent and the flesh of my own fancies are entwined together in a common temptation.

"All I want from politics is to proceed on my way, leaving behind me heads in a state of contemplation and reflection or else frivolity and distraction. If success eludes me, then a pox on power, and perdition to all types of ruin by sword and pen.

"Every century has its own disaster.

"For this quarter-century I am that disaster.

"So transport me, the one who sits above you, beneath Cancer in the signs of the zodiac.

"Once in a while all I can perceive are darkness and blocked paths. My thoughts contort and enfold themselves on their own foundations, leading only to what is coincidental and profoundly wanting. It is then I realize that my soul is in dire need of the stars and supreme athleticism.

"The human body is all naked corruption, and the soul incites to evil. So where is the refuge to be found, and whence the escape?

"I stare long and hard into the bogs of nothingness, computing the number of bodies floating in its firmament. Eventually they fade away and I feel exhausted, or else I revert to my own navel and reside there with eyes closed and ears chained shut.

"However in both circumstances, even though I try every trick to distance my overwhelmingly powerful ego, my life is still filled with the clanging of bells which keep dancing around me and threatening me with their poison and their lethal extensions. I spend hours searching for the most effective ideas that will thwart their manifestation.

"Exempt me then from all discourse, save that which is both lively and instantaneous, that whereby utterance legitimizes the roaring of my blood.

"Let me search in the archives of the possible and impossible for something to dizzy the vision and roll the eyes, something to bring ideas carved out of earth and fire, to turn hair white and baffle minds and intellects.

"On this dark night by the light of this low-burning candle, I wonder, can you even conceive of the black notions floating in my mind, some like stinging insects, others like killer reptiles?

"By my donkey, Qamar. Did you but realize some of these dire things, you would head for exile in droves, or else you would dig yourselves in amid the thickets of silence and fatigue.

"For that very reason I intend to keep them suppressed and to strive to keep them apart from the realm of events. That is not out of a sense of pity or sympathy for you, but rather because I'm afraid that I may turn into a shepherd with no flock or God's own sword that for harvest has only wind and dust.

"In the space between myself and confession I amuse myself by dipping my hands in the blood of some of my slaves or by staring at boys' genitals. One after the other I ask them: Show me your moon. In that way I can distinguish those who will die from others who will be saved.

"There are times when I find myself overpowered by the desire to allow natural disaster to happen. The answer I give is: Just for today and no longer I give you this earth and the people in it. So launch your attack, toy with its laws and rituals; send a deluge to create it and formulate it afresh.

"How is it that my terrifying dreams spin in circles? Ever since I took up the mantle of rule by the order of God, I have been afflicted by dreadful nightmares. They beset me every single night as I try to fall asleep. Just to give a single example from among many, I see myself stabbed and falling to the ground, just like 'Ali and al-Husayn; I see myself as a severed head rolling like al-Husayn's head; I see myself failing and calling out for help, but no one moves an inch. Such is the pain and shock that I wake up and discover, much to my delight, that the whole thing was just a nightmare. But no sooner do I go back to sleep than the ravening hordes of conspiracy and extermination overwhelm me yet again, but without ever slaying me or robbing me of my consciousness. The entire dream may repeat itself in cycles, each one more horrific than the last. So picture me at the moment when I wake up, with every wrinkle on my face mirroring the varieties of terror and anxiety.

"How can I keep this face concealed from my own people? How can I walk among them without lighting my path and enveloping myself with the weapons of oppression and deceit?

"I am one of those people who, whenever they cry, weep in a veritable flood of hot tears. I cannot begin to describe it. If I tried, I would do no better than Sufi poets when they try to depict tears. So look up what people have said previously about distress and tearful eyes.

"Why do I weep? The basic reason is that I can find no alternative to violence as a way of keeping my people and authorities on the straight path; also that all my actions and adventures in the political realm are merely a drop in a bottomless ocean.

"There are secrets that I can only divulge on the day when I am close to death. So wait till I am on my deathbed, and then I will provide you with information that will expose me and dash my honor and reputation."

Dawn was on the point of appearing when al-Hakim's expression showed clear signs of exhaustion and insomnia. He stood up, looked at the young scribe's genitals, and put on his cloak. Then he left the balcony where he had been drinking and headed for his quarters in the palace. Hardly had he gone before the devotees descended on the young scribe, snatched the papers from his hands, and rushed to transcribe their contents in order to contemplate and interpret them for themselves and thereafter to utilize their findings among the circle of initiates as a mode of access to interpretation and occult wisdom.

2. A Session in Quest of Surprise

An amusing tale from the time of al-Hakim tells how a judge in Egypt was named "head-butter." The reason was that he had a cap with two cow horns on it that he used to keep beside him. Whenever two litigants came to his court and one of them tried to bully the other, the judge would don his cap with the two horns, move out, and start butting the litigant who was bullying the other one. All this made the judge very famous. Al-Hakim got to hear about this and sent for the judge. When he came into al-Hakim's presence, the caliph asked him what he thought he was doing to earn such a bad reputation among the people. The judge responded, "O Commander of the Faithful, I would be delighted if one day you came to my court, sat behind a curtain, and simply listened to what I have to endure from the common people. Either you'll see my point of view, or else you can punish me as you see fit." Al-Hakim told him he would come the next day to see what he meant. Next morning, al-Hakim did indeed go to the judge's court and took a seat behind a curtain. Two litigants came before the judge; one claimed a hundred dinars from the other and claimed that the other man had acknowledged the debt. The judge then ordered the second party to pay what he owed, but the latter responded that he was having difficulties at that moment and asked the court to order payment in installments. "What do you have to say to that?" the judge asked the plaintiff. "Make him pay ten dinars a month," he replied. "I can't do that," the defendant replied. "How about five dinars?" the judge asked, to which the defendant again said that he could not manage that much. "Two dinars," the judge suggested, and again the defendant said it was impossible. "One dinar," said the judge, with the same result. Eventually the judge got down to just ten dirhams a month, and still the defendant claimed it was impossible. The judge now asked the defendant how much he could afford to pay in order to satisfy the plaintiff. He replied that he could only afford three dirhams a year, but only on condition that my opponent in this case is put in jail so he'll never receive the amount in any case. At this point al-Hakim ran out of patience and came out from behind the curtain. "For heaven's sake, butt this fiendish wretch," he said. "If you don't, then I will." Al-Hakim was actually more stupid than the judge. The end.

Ibn Iyas,
Bright Flowers Concerning the Events of the Ages

Judicial proceedings and torts were normally resolved by personal interpretations of judges, but could also involve squabbles over influence and the stench of bribery and corruption. Al-Hakim lost no time in taking up the issue and devoting his attention to it. Perhaps the most remarkable judicial council that he graced with his caliphal chairmanship was the one that he held one night immediately after emerging from a treatment in violet oil. What made things so unusual was that the accused found themselves confronted with a banner, something that neither judges nor legal authorities had ever witnessed before—because it was entirely of al-Hakim's own devising: "Surprise me, and I will forgive you!" The point of the whole thing—as Ghayn, the chief of police and public morality, explained to the six accused who were standing inside a cage— was that, as a way of saving themselves from death, each one of them should come up with the most adept aphorisms, the cleverest discourse, and the funniest jokes, all in order to surprise and entertain the caliph.

The first defendant to come before al-Hakim was a man from al-Basra, Abu 'Ali Muhammad ibn al-Hasan ibn al-Haytham, who was renowned for his profound knowledge of physics and mathematics. The accused bowed respectfully to the caliph. "Ibn al-Haytham," said al-Hakim, "just recall the things I revealed to you in secret. You asked me what I feared most, and I told you that my single fear was too little water in the Nile. My continual hope was that at irrigation time its level would always reach seventeen cubits so as to avoid inflation in food prices and the need for taxation. In such circumstances I would be faced with famine among my own people, outbreaks of disease, and deaths in large numbers. I would have no other recourse than to make contributions from my own property and force converts to Islam to readopt to their own faith so that I could then reimpose the head-tax and bolster revenues. You came to see me, Ibn al-Haytham, and claimed you could make use of your calculations and mathematical knowledge to increase the Nile's product whether it was in flood or at lower levels. I commissioned troops of water technicians to inform you about the Nile from its Aswan cataracts all the way to its various stations, branches, and tributaries. The whole thing was a waste of time; your promises were so much hot air. Even so, we chose not to accuse you of breaking a promise. Instead we charged you to investigate other departments, but now you have started to feign madness. All the documents and numbers were a mess, and the issues ended up in a very sorry state. Just when I was on the point of deciding to take away all your responsibilities, my sources have informed me that your feigned madness was merely a ruse to avoid serving me and escape punishment. Today you stand here burdened by the weight of this cunning deceit; furthermore, my admiration for your mathematical skills is not sufficient to rescue you from the troubles you've caused yourself."

"My lord," Ibn al-Haytham replied, "a curse on my failure to curb the Nile, something that has plagued me and disturbed my slumber ever since. The river defied all my calculations and projects and simply scoffed as it demolished all my equations and measurements. It almost seemed as though it was leaving its own banks just in order to bring cascades of water crashing down on my head. All I could do in response was to whistle and get out of the way. One day I was walking and whistling just a short distance from my sleeping place in the desert, when all of a sudden I got the idea of coming to the royal assembly and submitting a request to resign from all my responsibilities. That is in fact what I did. After waiting for a while I received a letter from my lord refusing my request because of the suspect personal motivations that had led me to submit the petition. Once I had read the letter, it seemed to me that the only thing I could do was to retire with my dark beard and feign madness. Without that, all avenues to a reasonable life would be closed, leaving me in the clutches of despair and never-ending insomnia. And so I sank ever lower. I started walking around the city with a scowl on my face, never responding to salutations and guffawing as I chased equations, measurements, and integers. Now, my lord, your sources have revealed my pseudo-madness, so I beg you to remove from my path the things that block my passage and stifle my breathing."

"That is indeed amazing, Ibn al-Haytham," said al-Hakim, signs of surprise already registering in his demeanor, "but I won't let you go until you tell me why you won't work in my service."

"I'm afraid, my lord," replied Ibn al-Haytham, "that serving you can never involve failure or diffidence; it all has to be brilliant and successful. Working within the shadow of your august presence, I have come to realize that every servant naturally strives to see his star wax strong, but that, once successful, the same star is destined to fall. This is a distressing irony, one that I find unbearable; indeed I can only discuss it in the words of the poet who says:

> In you I see behavior both good and bad; by my life, you are the one I shall describe:
> Near and far, forthcoming and inscrutable, generous and miserly, upright and criminal,
> Honest and deceitful, so not even his friend knows whether to shun or flatter him.
> You are neither deceiver nor counselor; I find myself completely uncertain about you.
> So my tongue can both lampoon and extol you, just as my heart is both knowing and ignorant of you."

"You do indeed surprise me, Ibn al-Haytham," said al-Hakim with a laugh, "you surprise me very much! So go in peace! Now bring in the poet, Ibn al-Saʿsaʿ al-Qarmati."

With that Ghayn the police chief went over to the cage where the accused were being kept and brought out a handsome young man in the prime of his youth. He forced the young man to kiss the ground in front of the caliph and display signs of humility and obedience.

"Come now, young man," said al-Hakim. "Tell us about the accusation against you, the way you interpret the history of ʿAli—peace be upon him!—and the Shiʿa who make him divine."

"My Lord," Ibn Saʿsaʿ began, "you should be aware that ʿAli—peace be upon his memory—had spent two thirds of a night in prayer and recitation. Just before dawn he and his army set off to confront a group of his followers who were exaggerating his superhuman qualities and making him divine.

"Once he had reached them and had them surrounded, they bowed down to him.

"'You are our god, creator, and provider,' they all said. 'From you we take our beginning and to you we return. For you to be our Lord is glory enough; for us to be your servants is honor enough. You are as we would wish, now make us as you would wish!'

"ʿAli drew his sword and told these devotees to desist from such gross hyperbole and error. They refused and vaunted their defiance.

"'This very day I shall fill this ditch with your corpses,' ʿAli told them, 'and dire is the resort for you thereafter!'

"'If you do indeed slay us,' they replied once they realized they were doomed to die, 'you yourself will raise us up again! We testify that ʿAli is the Imam al-Mahdi, the expected Messiah!'

"When threats proved to be of no avail, ʿAli gave orders for a fire to be lit in the ditch and for their bodies to be burned. He recited the following line: 'Once I realized that the matter was anathema, I lit my fire and summoned a lark.'

"From the limits of life the humble servant now stands before you. I began my comments on this hadith by saying: Had ʿAli actually renounced such hyperbole regarding his unique essence and the glorification of his worldly record, he would have realized that the 'Ali of those who burned to death in that fire was not 'Ali himself, but rather Imam 'Ali, the expected one; and it is impossible to await what is either present or transitory. The use of the very same name for a personage who is absent is a metaphorical device demanded by the will of events. As a result, the basic, real meaning of the word ' 'Ali ' here is Man. The Shi'a were awaiting the imam named Man, and in that they were indeed radical."

"The only thing that astonishes me about your interpretation," said al-Hakim, "is your reliance on the role of imagination. You can astound us even more now by giving your imagination free rein to contemplate your death at my hands."

"I'm only contemplating death at your hands, my lord," replied Ibn Sa'sa' confidently, "in a single, utterly unique fashion. In the police record it will state as follows: 'In that the perpetrator of the above mentioned interpretation has radically supported the cause of the Shi'a who were burned, in that his words do not conform with their testimony, in that he is a well-known poet-heretic who defines poetry as the revelation of what is inspired by standing in front of a wall in the midday sun when people are taking a nap, in that this poet has extolled authority and seems devoted to it, this poet who claims that poetry is the discourse of waiting in that space which separates us from seizing power, and—in another version— that the most poetic of poets is one who senses that his poetry is an expression of essential weakness and deprivation, and so he strives for power and dreams of it. The police authorities, realizing their duties and ever watchful for the repose of the people, reserve for themselves the right to arrest and interrogate the poet until such time as he reveals the many secrets stored in his heart.' However, my lord, once I have disappeared for ever, Ghayn, the chief of police, will release a factual report to people, which will say: 'Rumors have spread abroad in the country stating that Ibn Sa'sa' the poet who had been arrested by our forces died while being tortured by our personnel. In that this is false, we have no alternative but to reveal the following information: the above-named poet's corpse was discovered where the Nile waters had deposited it. A medical examination determined that he had been killed by a dagger thrust while fighting alongside pimps and heretics.'"

"I'm truly amazed, young man," said al-Hakim contentedly. "Get out of here before my sword performs your vision for you! Now, Ghayn, bring in the Sufi with no shoes."

The Sufi did not bother to wait for Ghayn to execute the caliph's command, but rushed over to stand before the caliph, repeating the phrase, "Be kind to me, O God!" over and over again, and then, "I beg God's forgiveness; He is sufficient for me, and is good as a trustee!"

"So, shoeless one," said al-Hakim, raising his voice over the noise of the Sufi's invocations, "you stand accused of shunning me and insulting my name. Many times I have summoned you to appear, but you have resisted. As with other holy men of God, I have sought your counsel by offering bouquets of narcissus, but you have spurned them. Now here you stand before me, asking God for kindness and protection. And I am still being patient!"

The shoeless Sufi responded: "The Prophet of God—peace and blessings be upon him!—once said, 'Beware of the councils of tyrants.' He was asked, 'And who are tyrants, O most judicious of God's created people?' 'Those who govern by their own order,' the Prophet replied, 'who contravene God's laws by tyrannous deeds and self-deification, and who kill the soul that God has declared sacred. In the next world they are fuel for hellfire, and it is a dire resort indeed. O God, in Your kindness. . . .'"

Al-Hakim was furious. "That's a fraudulent hadith," he yelled. "It is unauthenticated and false. Your words are sheer nonsense; they trivialize the truth. They represent a lie and a travesty of our moral and religious practice."

The Sufi tried again. "There can be no word of truth but that the Prophet of God is its utterer. Included in that is what he has transmitted to believers following his occultation by way of dreams and visions. That is still the case today. I myself have seen him—on him be peace!—and he followed up on his previous hadith with this pronouncement (may he be exalted!): *O people, a simile is being invoked here, so pay attention.*

The people to whom you pray in place of God could never create so much as a fly even though they all combined their efforts. If that fly were to rob them of something, they could never retrieve it; seeker and sought are simply too weak. They have not given God his true value; indeed God is powerful and mighty. In my dream I heard his voice—on him be peace!—counseling me, 'Saint of God, make sure you don't adjust your words to the world of tyrants. If you do so, your words will immediately dwindle, beset by collapse on all sides. Instead, allow your imagination to confront tyranny with patience, defiance, and creativity.'"

"How sorry I feel," said al-Hakim, "for all those people who die otherwise than by my sword. Shoeless one, how much I regret the power I have to kill you. If your fondness for life were not weaker than a spider's thread, I would have no compunction about consigning you to your grave."

"How true, my lord," replied the shoeless Sufi. "If people were like me in disdaining their life here on earth and aspiring to what is more ideal and worthy in their hearts, you would have no authority over them. Your oppression and terror would have no effect."

"Leave my covering where it is," interrupted al-Hakim. "Raise it no further! Instead, since you stand here before me, reveal to us the pages of your enlightened ideas. What do you have to say about peace and love?"

"Peace is the pact whereby we all live with each other. If someone else inclines to it, then I follow in my turn, offer him my greetings, present roses and doves to him, and pray for his safety. Then I go on my way feeling secure and at ease. When I feel possessed by love, I declare it to my beloved in beautiful words marked by their grace and charm. I try to fill his heart with sweetness and to become like a tree with fruit always available. For me he is goal and helper, someone to stand by as I proceed on my way. However, if my beloved dies in my arms while I am still alive and cognizant, then I will inevitably weep sad tears, fully aware of the essence of death and that in both beginning and end there is violence and cruelty. Thus I rebel and almost recant."

Al-Hakim was clearly much affected by this. "What happens when you're hungry," he asked, "or when you feel lonely and go crazy?"

"When I'm hungry," the shoeless Sufi replied, "I intone a verse of the Qur'an and use that as food. If the verse gives forth, then I am filled; if it does not, then I hunt birds and pilfer food from ants. If I feel lonely, either I go out into the desert and yell till the wild beasts ask me how I feel, or I go out among the people and offer radical advice, or else I go and roam outside the city. When I feel crazy, my inner vision is sharpened and empowered. I turn into an eye that sees, a thousand lips that intone transcendent thoughts as I recite what I see. And, because I disclose the truth and counsel rebellion, I am forever being taken off to prison or the mental asylum."

By now al-Hakim was trembling. "And what about when you're ill and close to death?"

"In that case," replied the shoeless Sufi, "I will donate what I have earned to simpletons, read the Fatiha of existence, embrace my dear friends, and say farewell. Then I'll write on the walls of markets and alleys, on tree stumps and rivers, on gravestones and flowers in cemeteries, I'll write the instructions of water and daylight. Then I shall surrender my spirit to the elements."

"Ah, how alike we are!" said al-Hakim, sweat pouring from his brow. "How much I aspire to be like you! If only you could have come to me in my seclusion in the Muqattam Hills, you would have found me there pure and concealed, head bare, countenance transformed, stomach empty. My only companion there was contemplation of the unity of God; the absolute was my only goal. Now go back to your desert and direct your prayers toward forgiveness for all those who go astray and overstep their station."

At this point al-Hakim stood up as though bringing the session to an end. There were still a man and two women inside the cage.

"You, old man," said al-Hakim, "didn't you hear about my interdiction of drinking, transporting, or trading in wine? Didn't I run into you on a narrow bridge in broad daylight, scrambling away on a donkey loaded up with what I have explicitly forbidden? Where had you come from and where were you going with it?"

"I was coming from God's own narrow earth," the man replied boldly, "and that's where I was going."

"So you're determined to make a bad thing worse, are you?" said al-Hakim angrily. "God's earth is narrow, you say?"

"My lord," the old man replied, "if that were not the case, then you and I would never have met on that narrow bridge."

Al-Hakim gave a hearty laugh and let the man go. Now he turned his attention to the two women. "So what has brought you into these cages?" he asked.

"My lord," replied the first woman, who was very beautiful, "you have twice denied me the man who was most beloved to me. Once your men surprised and killed him out of revenge because he was my companion in loneliness, my resort in times of oppression, and my protector against temptation. The second time was when you prevented me from visiting his grave and communing with his dead body. Since you had made it impossible for me to visit him, I placed my own body in a grave next to that of my beloved. By day I used a reed to provide myself with enough air, and at night I went in search of food. I stayed this way for several days until there came the morning when one of the men who harass women visiting cemeteries trod on my reed. I emerged half-dead from the grave, and they brought me to stand before you."

Al-Hakim was astonished. "Woman," he asked, "you would do all this for the sake of a man? Who was this beloved husband of yours?"

"He wasn't my husband," she replied, her eyes gleaming with defiance. "He was my brother."

Al-Hakim was now even more astonished. "Your brother, woman! Go now to see my sister, Sitt al-Mulk, and tell her this amazing story. Perhaps my rebellious sister will take note of this tale and see the light. And you, old woman, why is your back so withered?"

"My lord," the old woman replied, "even old women have been distressed by your regulation that forbids women from leaving the house or even looking out of balconies and windows. Even old women are crushed between two flames: one is you, my lord, and the other is their own husbands who oppress them while being themselves oppressed by you. I was writing down my frustrations and anger on notes that I would place in the ladles of street vendors; all I'd get in exchange was some fruit and sweetmeats. When your decree was issued forbidding the uncovering of what was concealed, I got drunk, stole out of the house at night, and went down to the Nile where I stretched out and covered myself in a wrap. There I proceeded to drink some more and stole an occasional glance at the beauty of God's creation in the water, the plants, and the greenery. When your men showed up and wanted to identify me by removing my wrap, I stopped them. "I am fully covered," I told them in a threatening tone, "and you're trying to contravene the orders of our lord the caliph by uncovering what is concealed. So they brought me here so I could tell you my story and you could decide on my fate."

Al-Hakim was on the point of leaving. "Here I promised to pardon anyone who was able to astonish me," he said with a laugh. "From you and all your colleagues in this session I've heard more heresy and deviance than I would have imagined possible. Now I feel relaxed and forgiving, so go in peace—God forgive you!"

3. A Session on Theology with the Devotees

Al-Hakim got the notion of claiming divinity. To that end he brought in a man named al-Akhram, and attached to him a group of men whom he encouraged to engage in irreligious acts . . . . The story of his claim to divinity spread. This way he gathered around him a group of ignoramuses. Whenever they encountered him, they would greet him with the words: Peace be upon you, O One and Only, O bringer of both life and death.

Ibn al-Sabi,
Book of History—Completion of Thabit Ibn Sinan's Book of History

It was in the secret wing of the Dar al-Hikma that one night after a long break, al-Hakim reconvened his session on theology. This group was made up of major missionaries, marshals, and deputies of the community, along with a coterie of the enlightened. They used to form themselves into a closed circle ready to talk or listen, but al-Hakim preferred to huddle by himself inside his dark closet. He used to sit there looking distracted, as firmly rooted as a lofty idol.

The senior member was Hamzah ibn 'Ali, "Guide of the Respondents," whose hallmark was a broad forehead, something he relied on to convince his listeners and defeat his adversaries. He also had a capacious memory for both authentic and inauthentic Shi'i hadiths. "In the name of God, the Compassionate, the Merciful," he would intone, using a nod of his head as a means of breaking the august silence of this assembly, "all praise be to God who stands above all learning, transcends all decrees, and disdains all that can be imagined or comprehended; God's prayers be upon the sovereign of His divine mercy and deep sea of his wisdom, the Prophet Muhammad who brings good news through the Torah, the Gospels, and the Psalms; and on his brother and cousin, courageous warrior on the day of battle and repository of the secret of the night of the ascension, 'Ali ibn Abi Talib, conduit between the two rivers, Euphrates the sweet and 'Ajjaj the salty; and on his descendants, the Shi'i imams, worthy guides of God's people who preserve his faith and bring his words of justice and truth to fruition, the community of believers—may God keep you safe from the all-powerful terror and join you to those whom you love on the Day of Gathering!"

Hamza the senior missionary continued, "Our lord, Imam al-Sadiq Ja'far ibn Muhammad tells us, 'Our community of Shi'a is like bees. Did birds but realize what their bellies contain, they would tear them apart.' And this: 'Beware of revealing secrets. It will shorten your life, blind your heart, and take away your sustenance.'"

In the light of the preceding, our lord al-Hakim spoke in the ear of every missionary past or present, "Take a pledge of allegiance from every willing respondent, from every clear adherent whose loyalty and conviction you trust and whose chastity and devotion are clear. Urge them to be loyal to the pledge they have made. Do not force anyone to become a follower or pledge themselves. Only assign things to those whom you trust to preserve them. Only sow seeds in a field that will not stint its sower; for your seedlings search for the very best nurseries, then bring them to cisterns full of the water of life. Approach them with offerings of the sincere, with transport out of the darkness of doubt and uncertainty to the light of proof and clear signs. Recite the words of wisdom that you receive during sessions with believers and respondents, men and women alike, in the caliph's gleaming palaces and the great mosque in the al-Muʿizz district of Cairo. Keep these words of wisdom a secret from all save those who are qualified to hear them; only divulge them to people who deserve the privilege. Above all do not divulge the secret to incompetent people who cannot bear the burden and whose minds are not capable of comprehending what they hear. Make use of your insight to collect proofs of matters legal and intellectual, and show proof of the linkage between strong and weak. Visible entities are bodies, while hidden ones are their shapes. Hidden entities are souls, with the visible as their spirits. Shapes cannot exist without spirits, and in this haven of ours spirits only exist through shapes. If they are separated, the system falls apart, and creation is condemned to collapse."[13]

At this point the missionary, Hasan ibn Haydarah al-Farghani, "helper of the Guide," the one known as "al-Akhram" (because he had a snub nose with a split nostril) took over. He always managed to cover the reedy quality in his voice by resorting to a highly rhetorical style:

> "There has come to us from the furthest absence at the
>   glimmer of dawn
> Our lord al-Hakim, heir to the secret and the line.
> Of his goodness he has bared his head, greeted and glorified
>   his God,
> And relayed to us the word of the prophets, as musk and
>   ambergris waft from his presence.
> He has told us of blessings, of women, and of words.
> He has said: "These are the bases of life;

Whoever ignores them will perish.

He who learns them belongs to the lands of fertility and
    rebirth

And will gain the supreme bliss and happiness in the
    hereafter.

When he finished and disappeared,

We shuddered. Clouds covered courtyard and mihrab

And water in the fountain was turned into light.

In a trance of hallelujahs we all stood,

Prayed the prayer of love for our Lord the marker of time,

And asked that he return in peace."

The devotees sat there in humble silence, entranced. They asked for
more. Al-Tamimi, known as 'the emissary of destiny,' asked, "When our
lord returned from his exalted absence, what did his noble mouth have
to say?"

"Our lord came back to us safe and reassured," al-Akhram the missionary replied enthusiastically. "God inspired him to utter some noble
words: 'You can only gaze on the sun as you consign it to its resting
place in the sea or behind lofty hills. Thus it is with life.' And, 'The wisest
of men is one who in his own heart carries a sun that never sets and who
thinks about life while it is available in all its maturity and brilliance.'

"Our lord also brought forth some wonderful pieces of wisdom:
'Wisdom does not involve adapting oneself to repetition and deaths, but
rather discovering the face of God in those motivating enticements
whose general law is emanation and incandescence."

Now 'the emissary of destiny' asked another question. "Generous
missionary," he said insistently, yet humbly, "will you convey us all into
the world of our lord's conversations with His Lord? All of us desire it
to remain a secret, and we will preserve it as such."

"I have heard our lord with my very own ears," responded al-Akhram,
his eyes gleaming. "I've recorded some of his divine confidences,
including the following:

'Within me is the wind's own girdle and songs of love
    for the sandy temples,
And fleeting bubbles.
O You who pass by my distress,
I have no secret within.
Nothing keeps me from you, O my God, nothing distances
    me from You.
This world is an arena that You have paved with watch-
    towers and informants,
That you have roofed over with a gloomy, barren trellis.
O You crusher of limbs, whither can I flee with my
    nakedness?

My calamity takes shape in the evening.
Faced with me all ancient deities have collapsed
And turned into dust and ashes.
My calamity takes shape,
So I have turned to You, O guardian of my power.
From You I await a prophet of great repute,
His eyes the color of cement,
One whose mind will combat fates and thunder in the
    heavens,
And whose hands all around us will kindle the fires of
    resurrection and eternity.'"

As al-Akhram recited these words, the group sat beside each other totally
entranced. It was at this precise moment that the missionary, Muhammad
Isma'il al-Druzi, 'the mainstay of the Guide' as he was known, inter-
vened. A tall man possessed of an eloquent turn of phrase and powerful
mind, he now recounted some of his experiences. "I myself heard our
lord—blessings on his name—after returning from his thousand and first
quest into the unknown, 'My devotees, whenever I consider establishing
new theologies, I find it extremely difficult to investigate the topic of the

Creator, the eternity of the world and its emergence from nothingness. In dealing with these complex issues and their subfields all I come up with are bland ideas and proofs that in their balance cancel each other out.'

"Our lord continued, 'We should study God's very self, as though it were possible to analyze its essence and investigate its attributes. All theology that does not acknowledge its defeat and unfeasibility approaches the Most High from a false perspective and fails to render Him honor.

"'The theologian worthy of the name is one who, when he treats God's attributes or is driven by curiosity to consider their modalities in detail, does not hesitate to guffaw with laughter at his own folly.'

"Our lord—praise be to Him—also said, 'I've observed theologians going so far in their disputes concerning God's attributes that they started hurling shoes and stones at one another. Whatever may have been the outcome of these squabbles, I hope they will allow me, as a long-standing servant of the faith, to record discreetly to the credit of God the powerful, the living, the knowing, and so on, the great attribute of subtlety.

"'Indeed how subtle is my Lord! He is the eye that never sleeps. It is inconceivable that he should see me beset by disasters and various categories of crisis. However, from the pinnacles of His lofty wisdom, he feigns a lack of interest in me and turns away so as not to restrict my actions. This is one of the signs of that subtlety whose savor and meaning He alone enjoys.'

"Such is my Lord's sense of fun that he decided to joke with me: 'They say that Sufis are children sitting in God's own lap. Do you see what they do there? What do al-Hallaj and Rabi'a al-'Adawiya have to say to each other when they meet? Do they recite poetry and inspirational sayings to each other, or is it rather jokes, followed by caresses and kisses?'

"Before saying farewell—may he be thanked!—my lord gave me this advice: 'Muhammad,' he said, 'neither greet nor say farewell to people without telling them to do well by the light.'

"I asked my Lord for the rationale behind his advice. He said, 'If mankind did not set up imaginary pyramids around the light, to the extent that they are beneficial, he would not settle on any opinion or establish definitions of truth and what surrounds it. It is by the light then, in other words through the illusion of discovery, stripping bare, and revelation, everything that points to the infinite, everything that sharpens and confuses the vision, it is by this light that ideas can breathe freely, requesting fruition for their interests and ease and relaxation for their veins.'"

Now Hamza the missionary spoke again, "In that God has given the Commander of the Faithful a noble wisdom, made him heir to the role of imam, consigned to him the role of making known the legal bounds of the religion, of informing those believers who seek refuge under his care and enlightening those respondents who cling to his veins, he therefore proclaims the establishment of an enlightened mission among his saints. Its shadow will extend over his followers and faithful adherents, nourishing their minds with its clear message and sharpening their intellects with its sheer clarity. Its subtleties will train their thoughts, and its learning will rescue them from the perils of doubt. Knowledge of it will lead them to paths of satisfaction and point them toward the spirit of paradise, the sweet breeze of affection, and bliss eternal by the side of the Generous, the Provider."[14]

"You marshals, deputies, and elite devotees," went on Hamza in a homiletic tone, "you flames of the beneficial memory and glowing conscience, the great mission has been entrusted to your shoulders. So now go forth, interpret with mind and passion, and spread the word wherever is most appropriate and however will best convince others. Now depart, and a thousand farewells go with you from our lord and myself!"

When only the senior missionaries and al-Hakim bi-Amr Illah were still left in the secret wing of the Dar al-Hikma, the latter broke his stolid silence. His followers went over to him and sat in front of him, listening like children to what he had to say.

"Among my most loyal devotees, Hamza, al-Druzi, al-Akhram, and al-Tamimi, there is no priority or preference as far as I am concerned. Whether some of you choose to deify me or others claim that Adam's soul is transferred to me by way of 'Ali's soul, you will only find me adopting whoever among you comes closest to action and success.

"Those of you who deify me and are granted success I will clothe in splendid robes, and mount in my procession on a saddled horse. I will bless him in secret and offer him welcome. However, if anyone advocates my divinity in vain, unaided by strength or will, then eradicate all traces of his droppings from my court, spare my people his false claims, and rid me of his folly. Leave it to al-Kirmani to refute his preachings and to guarantee him misery and hellfire."

Al-Hakim continued his thoughts. "My devotees," he said, "if you wish to advocate my deification, start in the mountains of Syria. That is virgin territory, and people there are quick to commit themselves to causes. But, apart from that region, it will be difficult to convince people of my divinity; instead it may provoke much discord among them!

"My devotees, I have this desire to hover god-like over the details of people's daily lives and to stay above their petty affairs! But there are so many of them, and they are so corrupt! They have hampered my impetuosity and soiled the clear sky of my disdainful retreat. Today I find them tiresome. I immerse myself in a world where they have transformed the surface into muddy swamps; all its charms are now iron bars."

Al-Hakim gave a yawn. "My devotees," he chanted, "plant me and give me roots! Talk about me as the books of the prophets do in the Bible. In calling people to me, urge them to make me unique, to weave all around me the threads of their wanderings in dark realms of absence and return. For all those people who stretch out their necks to me in prayer and glorification, I am indeed one who sees.

"My devotees, call to me those who are barefoot and naked. Chain their hearts to my garments. Anyone who dies in my cause will enter paradise in all its glory, strolling through all its parts and relishing what he loves and desires."

A prolonged silence now came over al-Hakim. He looked completely exhausted and feverish. Al-Druzi hurried over, used a cloth moistened with rosewater to wipe his forehead, and then returned to his place.

"Any deity," al-Hakim resumed, "who renounces his absence, disappearance, and total transcendence is no deity, but merely an idol or totem.

Anyone who comes and talks to people, gets close to them and involves himself in their mundane squabbles is no deity either, but simply a wizened old woman. Such a person deserves to be defamed and stoned.

"So, my devotees, do not emphasize my deification to excess while I am still alive, ruling the people, determining their fates in this world and the next, and keeping a watchful eye on their every move. Once I have gone, once I have disappeared, urge people to weave from the ashes of my extinction whatever fancies and delusions appeal to them in the firmaments of absence and divinity."

Al-Hakim's fever steadily intensified, and he kept feeling boiling hot and then shivering with cold. He began to lose touch, but in his lucid moments he could still talk: "I'm like a deity with broken limbs, the kind that you can only find in pieces in rocky fields or desert sands. Oh, my devotees, how often I pass by, and so do my own funeral and wedding! How often in the wake of night I will vanish from my subjects, and all so that the sea may remain!

"These then are my words and my teeth, both collapsing inside my mouth. It will be for those who come after me to kindle the fire in my locations and corners and to toss my commands and covenant into the recesses of oblivion, all so that the sea will remain.

"O servants of God! Be like the sea, vast and giving. It is promise and menace, thunder in quest of soul's repose and happy outset. At every moment ask the sea for opinions, not the dead. . . ."

Al-Hakim continued to mumble some unintelligible words, but then lay down on the ground shivering with fever. He asked for some paper so he could record his last will and testament. The devotees rushed over to cover him with blankets. They refused his request and decided instead to move him back to the palace and hand him over to his private doctor. That is what they did. Each one of them then left to begin the process of interpreting the sayings and visions of al-Hakim that they had just heard and then of making a selection based on their own instincts and the provision of proofs, all with the goal of gathering souls to the cause.

chapter 3

The εarthquake caused by Abu Rakwa, Revolutionary in the Name of Allah

A bu Rakwa lived in Barqa. His cohorts frequently conducted forays into the lands of Upper Egypt. That upset al-Hakim, who fell into despair and came to regret his past deeds. However, the army and doyens of Egypt all rejoiced at this news. When al-Hakim came to hear about it, he became even more worried and started apologizing for his former behavior. Many people, including al-Husayn ibn Jawhar, the Commander-in-Chief, sent messages inviting Abu Rakwa to invade Egypt. So Abu Rakwa moved from Barqa into Upper Egypt. When al-Hakim heard the news, he became still more panicked, and his state of mind went from bad to worse.

Ibn al-Athir,
The Complete Work on History

The desert region of Barqa was inured to a life of poverty and hardship, with sparse, sandy terrain stretching away to the south. The tribal oases were sparse and widely scattered—Jafra, Awjila, Jaghbub, and others. Palms only produced dates. Grass only grew thanks to the scant off-flow from a watercourse fed by springs and inaccessible subterranean wells (something that only happened on average every other winter). The tribes of the region, among them the Banu Qurra, had learned to endure this hard existence. With considerable fortitude they would withstand the lethal desert sand storms and the unbearable lack of sustenance, not to mention the destructive attacks launched against them by Fatimid armies. The Banu Qurra only managed to survive and parry the blows of fate because of periodically successful raids launched against their tribal neighbors, the Luwata, Mizana, and Zanata; the spoils from these raids enabled them to eke out the leanest of livings. Each member of the tribe was used to enduring a life of hardship. Peace would only come in the form of a blend of risks and precautions. One conflict was barely over before another started; that was the pattern that furnished their only lifestyle and solutions. However many motives and causes may have been involved—attack, revenge, or defense, war was always war, a universal law governing humanity. In all this war was the only victor!

One day in the month of Muharram in A.H. 395 a strange-looking man in Sufi garb appeared at the Banu Qurra oasis. He was grasping a thick stick and carried a coffeepot on his back that he used to wash himself before praying. He used to pray, go into seclusion, and meditate a great deal. People described him as a man in his thirties, tall and thin, with olive-brown complexion, a flowing beard, and prominent eyebrows. His expression suggested vigor, seriousness, and piety. During the first days of his stay in the tribe's guesthouse he was much honored and respected, but he only spoke in gestures and signs. When he did compose sentences, it was only to curse all tyrants, beg for mercy on his forebears, and ask for God's forgiveness. For a long time the tribe remained puzzled by their guest's identity, origin, and purpose, but then their shaykh, named Abu al-Mahasin, chose a quiet, moonlit night to sit down with his guest and join him in his ruminations and protestations. It took a great deal of patience and much effort, but eventually the shaykh managed to get his guest to talk and give him some information. As morning was almost breaking, he emerged with praises and thanksgiving and spoke to his tribesmen as follows.

"Good news, fellow tribesmen! This man is a gift to us from God. His nickname is Abu Rakwa, but his real name is al-Walid. He is a descendant of Hisham ibn 'Abd al-Malik ibn 'Abd al-Rahman al-Nasir, scion of the Umawi family. He was exiled from Spain when the tyrant courtier, al-Mansur ibn Abi 'Amir, placed the young heir-apparent, al-Mu'ayyad

Hisham, under guardianship and married the boy's mother, Subh. He then set about killing the other members of the ruling dynasty in Cordoba. Many of them were murdered, but others managed to escape. One of them was our honored guest, Abu Rakwa, who at the time was twenty years old. Since then he has spent an entire decade of his life travelling to Egypt, Syria, Yemen, and holy Mecca, seeking knowledge and teaching the young the word of God and His Prophet—peace be upon him! It is indeed good news that he has joined our company after being ejected from Kinana territory by their governor."

No sooner had the shaykh finished speaking than Abu Rakwa appeared at his side. Kissing Abu al-Mahasin on the forehead, he proceeded to address the awe-struck tribesmen in a quavering, emotional tone: "Hail to you, proud Arabs of the Banu Qurra! What your revered shaykh has divulged to you about me is the truth. Furthermore, since you are all keen to know every detail about me, I will not conceal from you the secret particulars of my situation. Before I depart at sunset today, you shall know everything . . ."

With that Abu Rakwa paused for a moment, as though to recoup his energy. Abu al-Mahasin and all the tribesmen present sat down. Then Abu Rakwa started an eloquent address in a gentle, lilting voice:

> Tyranny and treason expelled me from Spain.
> I have become an ascetic, O people! Today I have no
>   wives to impregnate.
> My only possessions are my coffee-pot, my cloak, and my
>   stick; I use them to protect my honor and the last
>   shred of my personal protection.
> As an ascetic I roam God's earth, passing my time in
>   prayer and teaching children.
> I have presented the other life to the peoples of Egypt
>   and Syria,
> My heart being open to them like a blossom.
> Have I not advised them to be patient and forbearing?

"Patience, patience!" I told them. "Even though your skin
     be flayed and the outrages of the tyrant al-Hakim
     spread abroad,
have I not proclaimed sweetness in word and deed?!
I have glorified love, and before the people
I have been extolling the exchange of flower petals
     and concealing rocks.

…

Thus I have occulted the life of power
And fraternized the exultations of seasons and dew.
I have welcomed glad tidings and expressed my joy;
I have climbed rocks,
I have pledged allegiance to the sea,
I have told people: You beloved who remain,
There is nothing so sweet as to intensify
     my great longing for you all.

…

I have said what I have said; I have made claims.
Time has passed, and another time has come
Bringing with it a cursed era of one who rules by tyranny,
     with chains and wires on feet and neck,
introducing things inconceivable to eye and ear:
     tiny coffins, destruction,
     women in prison, men whose souls gush out
     on sword blades,
terrified faces, wordless inquisitions,
the River Nile overflowing with the blood of victims and
     the heads of the innocent.

…

By the light of what the eye has witnessed:
The seed of all peace is but a false promise;
The windmill of waiting no longer draws any wind,
resolve is flagging, and suffering is all that remains.

By the light of what the eye has witnessed, we must confess:
Faced with such misery, in the most forceful sense of
    that word,
The schemes of the hermit are mere folly and deceit.
We must confess:
All my words about strategy in the face of such miseries
    are crippled,
My ideas about abstinence in the face of power have failed,
And my head has become utterly useless.
My eye still bears the dusty tears of the eternal
As I contemplate the foaming blood that bursts from
    the history of inquisitions and wounds without number.

When Abu Rakwa had finished, he fell to the ground exhausted. His audience was thunderstruck. It felt as if they had just heard something they had been anticipating for a long time; or as if a set of pearls had long been hidden away within their innermost feelings, in the recesses of their memories and very beings; all that was needed was for someone to open them up and array them neatly in the realm of their current consciousness. As they sat there feeling such sensations, a young man named Shihab al-Din ibn Mundhir, fully armed and renowned among his tribe for his courage and eloquence, stood up and said, "Peerless counselor, our life here is not as we would like it to be! Seasons of lack and burning hot days have brought us low. We have gone into exile, with rocks for our beds; in years of drought we have wandered aimlessly. We have headed for streams and valleys, saying, 'Maybe there is salvation in water.' Down poured the water and destroyed our crops. Some folk said, 'Maybe there is salvation in sun and sand,' yet we became parched and exhausted. We fell into despair. At the very edge of disaster we found an escape in raids on other tribes. Some battles we won, others we lost. Yes indeed, O peerless counselor, our life is not as we would wish it! With every death, every famine, we are enveloped in silence. If we so much as raise our heads, the army of al-Hakim takes us prisoner and burns everything. As you can see, only despair remains, just like an axe digging ditches and hollows throughout our terrain.

"We beseech you by God, you who are descended from nobility and like us realize full well the hard yoke of oppression and tyranny, do not forsake us when the sun goes down today or in future days, do not forsake us when you have come to purge our minds and eradicate all memory of our mourning. Do not forsake us now that you have shown us the way to transform our despair and trauma into a great boon."

Many voices were raised to echo Shihab al-Din's thoughts, as one word or another was repeated. The import of them all was the expressed desire that Abu Rakwa stay with the tribe and discuss its present and future situation with the chiefs. At this point the shaykh of the Banu Qurra stood up, silenced the crowd, and addressed them all in a forthright tone, "By God, men of our tribe, if you want Abu Rakwa to stay with us and adjudicate our dispute with the Zanata tribes, then I'm with you. But if you expect him to bring you all victory against your closest enemies, then let him be! Leave him out of your obsessions and strategies and let him go on his way."

Expressions of disappointment and opposition greeted this speech; some men even looked angry. As soon as Abu Rakwa noticed their reaction, he quickly interceded, "The revered shaykh is absolutely right. By Him who created the heavens and changes circumstances, I have no intention of remaining among you if it is only some sinister purpose that draws your hearts toward me. I will not join you in any project to bring you victory over your imagined foes, those fellow inhabitants of these desert wastes who share with you a life full of hardships. I am firmly convinced that you and they are partners in misery and deprivation; the only reason why you fight each other is because you are so alike, each one of you trying to erase his own weakness by erasing that of people who find themselves in the very same plight or worse. You attack each other, totally forgetting the one who is the cause of all the misery and making much of his tyrannical power. I want you all to realize that there flows within the veins of your tribe, of your enemies—the Zanata tribe, and of others as well, a single kind of blood. There is no question of similarity or difference; that blood is the blood of piety and faith. Your only enemy is the person who has burned you and sucked you all dry, then tossed you into the desert wastes where food and drink are so scarce."

What was foremost in their minds was the memory of the accursed fire that al-Hakim the Fatimid had unleashed against them all. With that thought burning inside, none of them had any trouble at all appreciating what Abu Rakwa was referring to. Their expressions showed clearly enough that they both understood and accepted what he was saying. Abu Rakwa seized the opportunity to add, "Noble Arabs! Are you happy to see al-Hakim dispatching his devotees into Egypt and Syria to disseminate slanderous and demeaning images of you to people far and wide? They claim that you are all tyrants and rapists, the very dregs of the Arabs, people who earn a living by raiding caravans on the pilgrimage route to Mecca; that you shed the blood of women and children; and that no sooner do you settle anywhere than you destroy everything, greenery and shrubs, and start spreading apostasy and destruction. They keep repeating these calumnies and worse. How much longer are you going to allow yourselves to be despised like this and to go on living in this terrible environment with such a reputation? How much longer are you going to waste your time fighting stupid and unjust wars against people who are just as weak as you are? Do you really want to let this desert keep on piling its life of poverty and suffering on top of your heads? By Him who has the power and the authority, I shall return to my own haunts if you do not change your ways and seek to achieve in this world the justice, glory, and divine unity that God has promised."

Abu Rakwa's words struck at the very souls of his listeners; his import hit its target cold and clear. Words of admiration and blessing filled the air. In an atmosphere charged with awe and outbursts of hope and promise, the shaykh of the Banu Qurra quickly gave his support to what Abu Rakwa had said, anxious as he was to make him feel part of the community, saying, "Tribesmen, what our distinguished guest has just told us is absolutely true! It is a sign of sheer cowardice and malice for weak people to keep attacking others who are just as weak as they are; any victory gained by one weak tribe over another is vain stupidity. From today there will be no more wars against our indigent peer tribes; instead we'll concentrate our attention on what really matters. Most important of all is for us to demonstrate to mankind that we are Arabs with pride and dignity. It is no part of our nature to commit obscenities, be they overt or covert, nor to condone illegalities such as highway robbery on pilgrims to God's house or shedding the blood of minors and innocents. No! Our most important task now is to join with our peers in cutting off all types of tyranny and injustice and to carry the fight to the core of Fatimid rule. Then we will pull out evil by its roots, and, in so doing, earn the bounty of this world and the reward of the next. Praise be to God who has sent the sage guide and imam, Abu Rakwa, to us at this particular moment."

Barely had Shaykh Abu al-Mahasin finished speaking before the young man, Shihab al-Din ibn Mundhir stood up again and spoke, "Abu Rakwa, for us it will be the greatest of good fortune to support you and march behind you. Today you are our only guide, while we are your only source of power. However, before we make a pact with you and give you our pledges as imam, answer us this question in God's name. Don't you think you are rushing things and moving ahead too quickly? For the peace you advocate, you are relying on our hands alone, without consulting the views of those who have been our foes."

Abu Rakwa responded to this sound objection in a calm, confident voice, "God honor you! Don't you realize that before I came to stay with you, I spent some time with the Zanata tribe? While I was there, I taught their children and listened to their complaints about the rule of those renegade Fatimids. I could see for myself how much they have suffered under the fierce tyranny of al-Hakim. On more than one occasion their leaders and sages spoke to me about their feelings toward you. I was thus able to confirm their view that the ongoing wars against you were a futile waste of time and effort, something they only did with the utmost reluctance and with hearts full of sorrow and bitterness. So, may God support you with His light, you should all know for sure that, if you were to opt for peace at a mere stroll, they would join you at the run; if you asked for a limited truce, they would seek a permanent one. So don't be so certain that your very determination is fruitless, nor so supercilious that your gain comes too easily. You Arabs of the Banu Qurra, if you really want an irrevocable peace with the Zanata tribe and others who share with you an adherence to the true religion of Islam, then as of tomorrow I am prepared to serve as a messenger to lay the groundwork for a truce and to work out specific terms and objectives. If on the other hand you are scared of possible outcomes, then you will have to let me sally forth deep into the desert where I can let the sands pile high above me."

The shaykh of the tribe and Shihab al-Din exchanged glances of agreement and support. They both went over to Abu Rakwa and embraced him warmly. Voices of acceptance, support, and welcome were raised, amplified by the ululations of womenfolk and yells from children. All this constituted a unanimous call for an irrevocable truce between the tribes and a preparation for acknowledging Abu Rakwa as imam. All this coincided with the muezzin's call for noontime prayers. Everyone hurried to line up in rows behind their illustrious guest. They invited him to lead the prayer, and after some insistence on their part, they got their wish. The prayer that they all performed was marked by an aura of devotion and humility that they had never experienced before. They had hardly finished, greeted one another, and embraced before a group of them made preparations to slaughter a female camel in honor of Abu Rakwa and as a way of hallowing his felicitous advent. However, Abu Rakwa himself stopped them. He told them they should hold off doing that till the day when a real truce was signed between themselves and the neighboring tribes. Once he had convinced them, he made do with a piece of bread, a handful of dates, and a glass of fresh milk (all of which constituted his regular daily meal). When he had finished, he praised God and excused himself. He went to his tent and stayed there for a few hours, praying and performing extra devotions, reading the Qur'an, and writing out accounts of the Prophet's life for meditation.

Toward day's end the sunset was creating amazing light patterns that attracted Abu Rakwa's attention. He sat there watching them through the tent flap and made use of them to forge one insight after another till night fell over the desert. Everyone, young and old, felt a special sense of involvement, an absorbing kind of release. This night seemed to them to be different from others, yet more serene than the doves of Mecca, and steeped in the sweet aroma of paradise itself. The heavens were studded with pearly stars; how close they looked and how sympathetic to human beings! The radiant full moon lavished on people's hearts the fondest of hopes and premonitions! The very desert winds seemed to have agreed upon a truce and enveloped the assembly in a breeze that was soft, gentle and joyous. The tribesmen all gathered around the tent of their imam, forming circle upon circle. There were circles for children who frolicked and played games, each one of them more lively than a moon-struck gazelle. There were also circles for womenfolk who kept laughing and chanting their favorite songs. The men, middle- and old-aged, took turns in filling the air with sound, sometimes religious chants and at others songs of chivalry and defiance accompanied by dancing.

Everyone took part in the celebration for as long as their enthusiasm and energy allowed, and things continued well into the night. Activities only began to flag somewhat when the men noticed that Abu Rakwa and his horse were nowhere to be found in the encampment. Soon afterwards Shihab al-Din ibn Mundhir appeared with a document signed by the absent imam. It said the following: "My beloved ones, I did not wish to take formal leave of you since that would have interrupted your fun and celebrations. I am going to see my Lord to ask His help and counsel. I will be away no longer than my longing to see you again can tolerate and than my desire to see peace between you and your enemies demands. To God alone belongs success, and He is a good trustee." As soon as this note had been read, the celebrations came to an end, and everyone returned to their own shelter to sleep or wait. A total quiet fell over the encampment, only broken by the barking of dogs and the pacing of guards.

Next morning people woke up to a sense of lack. Several days passed. The feeling of anxious anticipation they all had was exploited by a clique headed by a certain Hamad al-Madi. They started insulting Abu Rakwa, casting aspersions on both his origins and sayings and turning people against him. Hamad al-Madi himself seized every possible occasion to address the assembly in a way guaranteed to provoke their anger. Saying for example, "My fellow tribal kinsmen, by God I no longer recognize your faces, nor do I detect any prudence in your sages. You seem to have lost all common sense and shrewdness, so much so that you're fumbling around like someone trying to collect firewood in the dark; you're all as stupid as someone trying to chew water! You watch a mirage and assume it's real; you adopt a vagrant and treat him as salvation and everlasting good. What is the matter with you, that you should react in this fashion to this stranger with his phony asceticism, eloquence, and piety? You've acknowledged him as your imam when, by all the right of our blood ties, he's no more useful than a merchant of illusions. The light he emits is highly dubious; it will be the cause of your downfall. The soft breezes of his aspirations and mission will prove to be gales with the direst of consequences. What power do you possess to be drawn into a fight with the enormous Fatimid army? If you undertake such a task, you'll look even more stupid than butterflies immolating themselves in fire, yet more blind than bats at noon-time. Beware, beware! By the blood that we share, your only escape from these pretensions is by ejecting this snake charmer and reverting to your blessed actions and petty wars."

Hamad al-Madi's words were having a more powerful impact on the tribesmen with every day that extended the wait for Abu Rakwa's return. Were it not for assurances given by Shaykh Abu al-Mahasin and Shihab al-Din, they would have all revoked their allegiance and broken the ties of obedience. But then one Thursday, just as Hamad al-Madi was haranguing people in the market, a thick cloud loomed on the horizon; before long it turned out to be a group of horsemen led by Abu Rakwa. They had hardly reached the camp and dismounted before it became clear to everyone that the group included the notables of the Zanata,

Luwata, and Mizata tribes. The Banu Qurra regarded their arrival as a good sign and greeted their guests fulsomely. Meanwhile Hamad al-Madi and his clique hurried away ignominiously to their tents. The time for noon prayer arrived, and everyone performed it with Abu Rakwa as leader. They then sat down to share the prepared meal before the guests went away to have a rest in anticipation of the peace negotiations the next day, it being the first Friday of Rabi' al-Awwal A.H. 395.

Next morning the visitors and the shaykhs of the Banu Qurra gathered in the imam's tent. They performed the morning prayer behind him, then had breakfast and listened to some verses from the Qur'an. Once a spirit of harmony, humility, and exaltation had pervaded the group, Abu Rakwa appeared, sat on two cushions, and started talking in a mellow, affecting tone:

> "I praise God who provides my blessings and fills my pot
>   with water.
> I have now washed and purified myself,
> High, high above my solitude I have burst into flame
> Hoping to bring hearts to unity and spread happiness,
> To work as a member, with a dream of progress
>   and community . . .
> Like you I have termed this flame that burns us well-being.
> All of us have soaked our fever in the river-valleys.
> We have all wished—Oh how much we have wished!—to
>   celebrate our loved ones who remain;
> We have made musk of our words and illumined
>   dark corners!
> We have all wished for tears of joy and homes rejoicing.
> But how can this be when the thorn sticks to our flesh,
> When wounds are the norm and a life of poverty?
> How to proceed when true life has become
>   an impossibility? . . .
> What you and I witness is true:

The very veins in your bodies and those of your children
    are slowly drying up,
And eyes still bulge when al-Hakim's executioner
    flays them.
And what of their life? Did the people of Islam but realize
    how their lives were spent,
The oil in their jars would turn into blood and tears would
    flow on their lips.
Ah! In your lands the sigh is truly the essence of life.
Here a river-valley traverses your domain with paltry waters,
While the seasons bring their harbingers of danger
And the spindly ditches produce nothing from their soil.
Everything you say is correct:
The time is corrupt, and food is beyond the reach of
    the oppressed.
True enough, and the love between you has nothing to
    support it.
Mankind is in dire straits, and further migration is futile . . .

So here you are, trapped between barren earth and
    armed men,
Moving from one strait to another,
From the clutches of destitution to the grave . . .
True enough, but true also are the tales you tell of
    defiant bodies:
those who, amidst the refuse, the fig-branches, and
    vagrant trees,
manage to conquer death and go in quest of new morns.

With that Abu Rakwa fell silent for a while. It was obvious that everyone had been much affected by his words. The tent in which the assembly was being held had been encircled by the young men of the tribes, all
of them with high hopes. Abu Rakwa now started talking again, although

this time it was in a determined tone aimed at bringing matters to a firm and swift resolution, "My brothers in piety and tolerant faith, you are all well aware of the efforts I have made among you. Your only course now is to douse the embers of your enmities and unite in a campaign against the forces of tyranny and injustice. So what are your views, and what do you suggest be done?"

The shaykh of the visiting tribes—an august warrior—stood up, gave the entire assembly a look full of affection and amity, and then addressed Abu Rakwa, "Man of courage and virtue, you have spoken the truth. As far as we are concerned, your blessed efforts are enveloped in glory and success. We people of the tribes in whose name I now speak at this illustrious gathering will make mention of your name generation after generation for your discriminating ideas and laudable conduct. How could it be otherwise when you have managed to bring about between us and our neighbors, the Banu Qurra, that one thing that we ourselves have failed to achieve and have despaired of ever attaining: unity instead of discord, a spirit of brotherhood in piety and faith in place of a tribal fanaticism based on ties of blood. Once we have abandoned our stupid wars against each other, we can make preparations to launch a sacred campaign against cruel tyrants. May God grant you a just reward!"

This shaykh returned to his place accompanied by a chorus of voices of approval and blessing. He was followed by the shaykh of the Banu Qurra, "The illustrious shaykh of the Zanata has spoken well. You people, all praise be to God who has guided Abu Rakwa to us and used his sound ideas to direct our course of action! Praise Him too for bringing an end to our enduring feud, by depriving us of what has led to conflict and showing us the way to unity and agreement. We praise Him also for enabling us, through our new spirit of unity and aggregation, to fight in the cause of right, undaunted by tyrants and oppressors. The best opinions are those that emerge from consultation. What Abu Rakwa has asked us to do is to review our methods and resources now that the outline of our objectives have been defined."

For some time Shihab al-Din had been fidgeting restlessly, eager to display his views and talents. As soon as Abu al-Mahasin had taken his seat, he stood up. "Brothers in our tolerant faith," he said, "dwellers in peace and concord, we render boundless praise to God. Our joy at this spirit of unity knows no bounds. What greater goal can there be than to combine in focusing all our wrath on the root cause of our suffering and ignominy rather than on each other! But we will never get to appreciate the benefits and merits of this goal of ours if we do not commit ourselves to implement it. What we must do is to put the idea into concrete form by giving due thought to modes and conditions of implementation. We must put our trust in God and rely on the enlightened guidance of our courageous leader."

Abu Rakwa realized that now was the time to pose the implicit questions that were on everyone's mind: fixing territorial targets and the relative balance in the distribution of booty.

"Good men," he said, "for me the ultimate joy and happiness lies in your absolute conviction that my only objective is to elevate the name of God and to make justice and right triumph over tyranny. If that is what you want of me, then I am with you all through thick and thin. I will fight with you, I will bless your ranks, and will watch over you as you embark upon all the elaborate activity needed to prepare your forces for action. I see that you regard your new unity as a boon, and intend to consolidate it by undertaking a campaign in God's cause."

From among the Zanata there rose a gruff voice that demanded clarification, "Dear saint of God, God's cause to which you call us is infinite. So give us some specific principles and goals."

Abu Rakwa's reply was firm and authoritative, "We shall move by way of Barqa, with Egypt and Syria as our goal."

These words spread among the people present, "We shall move by way of Barqa, with Egypt and Syria as our goal!" At this point Shihab al-Din stood up to underline the point, "You people, what our leader says is right. If you decide to make do with Barqa, your period of power will be no more than a summer cloud. If you really want your unity to radiate outward and your power to be converted to state authority, then you will have to deal with Egypt and Syria. You must eradicate the rule of the Fatimid tyrant and in its place set up a just regime based on the laws of God."

"Champion guide," asked a man from the Banu Qurra, "let us suppose that, with our swords united, we manage to achieve the goals we seek, how will we divide up and administer the country?

Abu Rakwa realized that, in responding to this tricky question, he had to show some initiative, "On this topic I can see no alternative but what reason dictates. The land belongs to God. Should we be granted victory, then the land of Egypt will belong first of all to you and me. We will need to rule it justly and through consultation, guided only by the twin lights of forethought and consensus. Syria will be governed by whomever we delegate from among the people campaigning along with us."

Almost all those reacting gave support and consent to this idea, with little sign of doubt or opposition. But then someone from the Zanata said, "Abu Rakwa, why aren't you telling us about the thing everyone wants to know: booty. Give us some details—God grant you His support! Tell us specifically how much we'll get so we can work out the terms for unsheathing our swords and have a clear idea of our role."

Abu Rakwa's reply attempted to soften the sharp edges of the question itself, "God Almighty has said, 'You seek the offerings of this lower world, when with God there is booty beyond measure.' The Prophet Himself—on Him be peace—said, 'Wealth is in the soul.'"

The same man shot back, "God's booty is only of use to us in the hereafter. Regarding this lower world, God also said, 'Consume of your booty what is licit and good.'"

Abu Rakwa's reply was still conciliatory, "'Consume of your booty what is licit and good, and fear God.' O people, God has spoken the truth. The distribution of booty will only be done by portion. A fifth will go to the poor, the indigent, and the homeless, and a fifth to the treasury. The rest will be for you, licit and good, with no distinction among those who have fought. Booty will only be taken from those who have fought against us and who still take up the sword against us. Those who seek peace with us and are innocent of any wrongdoing against us have nothing to fear for either themselves or their property. Any person who plunders, robs, burns a tree, or destroys crops is no part of us; we will not hesitate to punish such people. These are my words to you, so take note."

The response to these words was all agreement and assent. The shaykh of the Banu Qurra seized the moment to bring the matter to closure. He invited everyone to recite the Fatihah, and they did so in all humility. Then they all stood up and went outside the tent shaking hands and embracing each other.

The women meanwhile had been busy outside preparing plates of food. The men of the guest tribe brought over a camel, made it sit on the ground in front of Abu Rakwa, and asked him to bless the occasions by slaughtering it. The imam performed the ritual ablution, prayed two prostrations, then slit the camel's throat while all around people intoned, "God is great." Before midday the guest tent was crammed with visitors and distinguished guests, all eating and drinking to their hearts' content and exchanging jokes and stories. Once they had finished, they hurried to perform the noon prayer behind Abu Rakwa, then returned to their tents to relax and take a nap.

For quite some time a profound silence descended on the encampment. A strong wind blew over the recumbent bodies as their stomachs struggled to digest so much food. In spite of it all, spirits soared high and far, as they dreamed of all the boons of Barqa, Egypt, and the other cities that had been part of the promise, and envisioned all the booty, visible and invisible, that would be theirs across the infinite miles of their journey. They would own fertile fields and the River Nile enveloped with its own blessings; gold, silver, marked horses, and sheep; power, glory, and stature. If the muezzin had not chanted the afternoon call to prayer, their spirits would have pursued this series of visions, ignoring both time and the need to rouse themselves.

After a while the visitors made ready to leave. Warm, sincere handshakes, accompanied by embraces, were exchanged between the tribesmen and their guests. They committed themselves to meet again soon and, above all, to progress toward cooperation and victory. As this farewell ceremony with all its strong emotion, was at its height, Abu Rakwa approached the shaykh of the Zanata tribe, produced a roll of documents from his sleeve, and handed it over to the eldest among them.

"May God sustain you all," he said, "this is the text of the peace agreement between you and the Banu Qurra tribe; I have penned it myself in a sincere spirit of fidelity. As you can see, I have appended a document that is a secret between us and you: it contains details of what we have committed ourselves to, a campaign to eradicate tyranny and wrongdoing. Have all your sages read it, then send it back duly signed with the seals of honor and dignity so that we can send you a copy signed by the Banu Qurra. As soon as this procedure is completed through God's own power, the next month of this blessed year will be upon us. By then our discord will be at an end, our ranks will be united, and we will enter Barqa safe and successful. Now return to your fellow tribesmen, conveying the good news and escorted on your way by peace and good fortune."

As soon as Abu Rakwa had finished speaking and embraced the guests one by one, they all mounted their horses and rode away to a chorus of farewells, leaving the Banu Qurra feeling exultant and overjoyed. Once they had left, Abu Rakwa spoke, "Praise be to God who has brought us thus far. Without His guidance, we would not have taken the right path. Tribesmen, from now on you must be in a maximum state of readiness for the great day. Muster as many forces as you possibly can and make comprehensive and detailed plans. I am with you and one of you; I am willing to take part in coordination and organization and to assist you with the more complex aspects of strategic planning. Should you need my help, then ask me in the evenings during the course of the current month. In the mornings send me your children so that I can teach them God's word and appropriate parts of the Prophet's sayings and deeds; after all, learning things as a child is yet more enduring than inspiration carved on rock. From tomorrow send me your children so that I can wear on my neck the symbol of their education as a task to serve as intercession in my favor on the Day of Resurrection. Now I need to spend the rest of today on my own in order to purify my own soul and seek my Lord's guidance."

From then on, life for the Banu Qurra continued along the path that their imam had laid out for them. During the months of Rabi' al-Awwal and Rabi' al-Akhir every day brought good news. The Zanata and their allies sent back the documents of peace and the accord concerning the campaign, all duly signed. The Kutama in Tunisia offered to take part in any war against the Fatimid ruler, al-Hakim. Preparations for the campaign moved ahead in fine form. Even though Abu Rakwa was involved in teaching, reading, and cogitation, he managed to stay in touch with every piece of news, receiving it from the shaykhs with smiles and expressions of gratitude and blessing. Something else that he heard or noticed was the way that Shihab al-Din excelled in training the young men how to use every kind of sword, to engage in close combat and simulated fights, and to construct traps and ambushes.

One night Abu Rakwa invited him to his tent and had him sit close by. "Shihab al-Din," he said, "I've noticed that you're working very hard even though the war has not started yet. Are you eager for a leadership role?"

"Great leader," Shihab al-Din replied, his voice a mixture of diffidence and conviction, "I find myself separated from what I desire by a distance whose only resolution is death."

"And who has established such a distance and set guards to watch over it? The tribes?"

"Who else has the power to subdue any miscreant if he's one of their number! If I aspired to be their leader, I would need to be you!"

"Need to be me?" Abu Rakwa repeated in amazement. "Explain what you mean, young man!"

"Your grasp of things is quite broad enough to realize what I mean. But if you need me to be more explicit, then you should know that you are what I lack. These tribes never aspire to lofty goals unless a religious guide enters their lands from the outside, someone who is able to speak to them in the language of their innermost feelings, preach to them about piety and purification, promise to dispel affliction and grant imminent victory, and call them to a life of good works and a transformation of the principles of this ephemeral world. It does not matter if the person comes in the guise of a hermit or claiming some noble lineage. What really matters is that he arrive at the right time, impelled by auspicious circumstance."

For the first time Abu Rakwa felt he was in the presence of a real colleague, someone who was talking to him like a kind of mirror, an image of his own self. He kept listening to the young man, staring at the sand in front of him as though it had been turned into a translucent lake.

"My brother and leader," Shihab al-Din continued, "I am not questioning either your asceticism or your lineage. How could I when, for me at least, truth lies only in what can be verified, and thus provides settlement and profit! As far as the Banu Qurra are concerned, your advent has provided them with a universal boon at a moment when they were just inches away from perdition."

From time to time Abu Rakwa took a plate of dates that was close by and offered them to Shihab al-Din. Eventually the latter became somewhat irritated by his host's generosity. "Do you want me to keep talking," he asked, "or to chew dates?"

"Certainly not, by God!" Abu Rakwa replied. "I just wanted to supplement the sweetness in your ideas with sweetness of a different kind!"

"How can I refuse your sweetness when I have not questioned either your lineage or your asceticism? Now watch what I'm going to do with these dates to show you how much I respect you."

So saying he started swallowing the dates one after another; he would have finished the entire plate if Abu Rakwa had not snatched it away.

"I don't need any such proof," he said. "I trust you completely."

Shihab al-Din was deeply touched and struggled to continue. "I had not planned to open my heart to you," he said, "till I had entered the battle and, along with the tribe under your aegis, achieved a great victory in the regions of Barqa. However, now that you have anticipated things in this meeting of ours, I will show you all the arrows in my quiver. A while ago I said that what I lack is you; more precisely, you need me just as much as I need you. If we pooled our resources and reached an agreement, we would make a combination that was unbeatable: I with my never-failing sword, you with your trusty shield; I by joining territory to territory, you by watering and fostering them; I through curbs and threats, you through promises of a life of ease. So are you prepared to make me part of your ocean of understanding and take me with you on your quest?"

"Woe to you, young man!" Abu Rakwa said. "You're racing ahead of events at top speed. What you're talking about is secular rule!"

"If we plan to expand, what other resort is there?"

"Maybe. But why bother discussing it before the appropriate time? Have we won all our battles and resolved all our residual problems already, so that all that's left to worry about is secular authority?"

"Such general authority is crucially important. If that's what we really want and need, then it's better to dream about it before victory rather than after. Aren't you the one who said, 'We shall move by way of Barqa, with Egypt and Syria as our goal'? How can we traverse regions and reach our goal if we don't show people how we intend to rule and administer justice? By Your Lord, let's make a pact, you and I, something we can swear on and aspire to, then we can proceed to make space for our dreams and proceed to implement them."

"Suppose I agree to a pact, what will you tell your people?"

"You ask me such a question, when you know the secrets of things better than anyone! Here you are talking to me as though my relationship with my tribe were like slippery mud and I had no right to show myself among them. Enough of flattery! Just look at yourself through me. You will see that each of us is a twin of the other. What we both want is for these tribes to abandon their marginal status and their caves and to give up all thought of discord and strife. All they want is to march behind us and have us as leaders to guide them and implement our lofty goals."

"If only I had your drive and enthusiasm, I could envisage a task yet more challenging than merely putting an end to the regime of al-Hakim the Fatimid!"

"But the very essence of our plan involves bringing our tribes and allies into the cities and implementing still broader projects. . . ."

"That's true, my twin!" interrupted Abu Rakwa, with a pat on Shihab al-Din's shoulder. "You are indeed that spark [*shihab*] that is lacking in me, the fire that can rid me of my doubts and indecisiveness."

"How can anyone such as you, great imam, experience either doubt or indecisiveness?"

"Anyone who doesn't possess such traits has no right to be an imam; indeed he has no faith. I wonder if you have given any thought to what will happen to us if things don't go our way and we are defeated? If you had any idea of al-Hakim's tyranny as I do—the vicious relish he displays in killing anyone who opposed him and even those who submit to his rule; if you were fully aware of all that, then you too would keep in mind the things that I truly fear: *wadi*s flowing with blood, mounds of severed heads—God forbid!—with al-Hakim's devotees chanting his name and inviting people to worship and deify him. As I envision all that, I ask myself whether I have the right to push these tribes toward the very perdition of their souls. How will I be able to answer them if tomorrow they face the Day of Judgment and say, 'You promised us victory, not loss. You have crushed our hopes—may God in turn crush yours.'"

Abu Rakwa's eyes glistened with tears, and his voice choked with sobs. Shihab al-Din felt as though the earth was shifting underneath him. Even so he managed to control his troubled emotions.

"Dear brother," he replied in amazement, "how can someone with your faith, someone who seeks the triumph of God's word over the wrongdoers, have such doubts about victory?"

"It's not the tribes that worry me, but rather the treachery of my followers and supporters."

"If by that you mean Hamad al-Madi and his clique, I'm watching them like a hawk. If you prefer, I'll eliminate them tomorrow one by one."

"Al-Madi is merely a foretaste of treachery to come. Don't do anything to him now, so we can see how he fights in the upcoming battle in Barqa."

"Excellent idea! Even better, put all these doubts and fears aside. Place your complete trust in Him who is sufficient for your needs! As far as our tribes are concerned, if they win, they will gain in this world and the next; if they lose, all they'll be sacrificing will be their chains and times of utter misery. I cannot envision them taking you to task on Judgment Day, while they dwell in heaven and enjoy the fruits of what God promises to all those who fight for His cause."

"Exactly so, Shihab al-Din! Either we win, or we'll die. True? If we lose, we won't be the first people duped by a mirage. Now what type of command is it that you wish?"

"You possess the status of imam and all spiritual powers, seen and unseen, connected with it. I'll take charge of the government. I'll run things under your inspiration and use as many or as few assistants as the situation requires. Give me your hand and let us seal our pact!"

"If we get as far as Egypt, I will grant you this division of duties. I will remain as imam to provide you with supervision and counsel. I will only accept true followers in these roles, and I'll be keeping both eye and sword at the ready if I detect in you any tendency toward exclusive control or untoward conduct."

The two men stood up, shook hands, and embraced each other warmly. They went their separate ways in the expectation of another secret meeting before long.

By the end of Rabi' al-Thani the Banu Qurra had completed all their training and preparations and were eager for battle. The shaykhs decided to pay an exploratory visit to the Zanata tribe. They sent an advance group ahead to warn people they were coming and asked Abu Rakwa to go with them. He welcomed the idea and rode out with them. No sooner had they arrived than they found themselves warmly welcomed; the elders of the tribe assured their visitors that they were fully prepared. Abu Rakwa sensed that now was the time for him to seize the moment and bolster his followers' enthusiasm.

"Tribesmen," he said without elaboration, "today we're on the threshold of a great event, as we depart for Barqa. We are going to wrest it from the claws of tyranny and injustice. Even greater will be that preordained day when we conquer Egypt itself, the source of all the pestilence. So prepare yourselves and preserve your energies for that great day—may God Himself support you all! Let none of us seek victory or martyrdom save on that decisive day. As for Barqa, I have begged God to grant it to us as a gift. Twice in dreams I have witnessed us entering it safe and sound through the power of the Almighty, all without spilling a drop of our own blood or that of those who oppose us."

The assembled company looked at each other in amazement.

"But what if they unsheathe their swords and try to fight us?" people asked.

"That's very unlikely," Abu Rakwa replied, shouting over the host of voices that were all asking the same question. "If that happens, kill just a few of them. We will do better to capture them alive and exchange them for the Kutamis who are prisoners in al-Hakim's jails."

"Why should we bother about the Kutamis and their prisoners?" asked someone from the Banu Qurra tribe.

"By doing such a good turn we will win over to our cause the Kutamis in Egypt who are working for the Fatimid government and army. At the same time we will be able to prove that we are accepting help from the Kutami tribes in Tunisia. All those who oppose al-Hakim, openly or covertly, will be our allies on the decisive day. We will pave their path toward us with roses and affection and provide them with all the help and support we can. Is that clear?"

No one moved or said a word, as though they were all reassessing the situation. Then the voice of Abu al-Mahasin arose behind them like a clap of thunder. "What's the matter with you all? Why are you all dumbstruck when you should be welcoming what you've just heard! Say what you're thinking so we can see clearly where we are."

Two groups spoke up, one after the other. "In Barqa we should be shedding as much blood as possible, so that al-Hakim the Fatimid will panic."

Another voice said, "How are we supposed to convince our fighters that we're going to enter Barqa safe and sound, when Abu Raqwah's dream is all we have to go on?"

And, "We're strong and well equipped. We don't need the Kutamis. As far as we're concerned, the more people involved, the smaller the booty."

Now Abu al-Mahasin spoke again, but this time his tone was mute and tired, "Oh dear, I see that nothing's changed! I feel so sorry for Abu Rakwa, standing there and seeing you still stimulated only by the idea of bloodshed and booty. There you all are, trivializing complex matters and cheapening things that cost dearly. Isn't it about time you changed your attitudes? Don't you feel the need for loftier virtues?"

Abu Rakwa and Shihab al-Din exchanged pleading looks. The latter realized that Abu Rakwa should be the one to speak.

"Tribesmen," he said, "the thing that distresses me is that some of you still don't really understand what I have in mind for you all. So, before you follow me into battle, I want you all to be well aware that my goal is not what you imagine. I have no intention of competing with al-Hakim the Fatimid in bloodshed, something forbidden by God, nor in gratuitous acts of violence and murder. It is no part of my purpose to expose you all to injury and destruction. Your souls are in God's hands, not mine. God who will grant you victory wants you to win, not to lose. So lend me your support in what I aim to achieve. For us Barqa is just a transit point; Egypt and Syria are our goals. Do not forget what we have agreed. Do not invest in the transitional stage energies that you cannot muster for the final goal. About Barqa I am only sharing with you the information that I have. I myself have traveled through it; I have tilled its fallow soil along with vagrants and others who suffer under the Fatimid tyranny, and I have sown among its folk some seeds of expectation, hope, and a longing for deliverance. Today Barqa is an easy crop to pick; I picture you enveloping it in a warm embrace of peace. However, it will require real conflict to conquer Egypt, but those wars will not be like any you have experienced before. By God, your only means of success will be to enter the territory in numbers to rival the Fatimid hordes and to use the same weapons and skills. They will have horsemen, infantry, and lancers, and you will need the same. They can wage war on land, sea, and in trenches, and you must be their equals. They have supporters and allies, and you must have them too. If you are aware of all these facts, then you'll be even more eager than the Kutama tribe to form an alliance with them and accept their proposals. On the borders of Egypt and within its boundaries they will be our very best helpers and supporters."

Abu Rakwa had hardly finished speaking before shouts of support and agreement could be heard, strongly encouraged by both Abu al-Mahasin and Shihab al-Din. The imam looked relieved and happy.

"Praise be to God," he said, "who shows us the best path to our welfare and salvation in both this world and the next! Now in His name I hereby proclaim the first day of Jamadi al-Akhira in this blessed year as the day we will invade Barqa the auspicious, safe and victorious. Those of you present here should inform those who are not."

These words were a cue for the Banu Qurra to say farewell to their partners. To the sound of fond farewells they all agreed to meet on the great day. Mounting their horses and led by Abu Rakwa, they sped joyfully away to their own encampment.

At dawn on the agreed day, all Abu Rakwa's followers gathered at the southern entry to Barqa as a single force under joint command. They hastened to implement Abu Rakwa's directives by investing the city and sending agents to infiltrate the city with propaganda. By the end of the first day the besieging forces had been bolstered by soldiers running away from the army of al-Hakim the Fatimid and also by large numbers of citizens. The next day the stranglehold on Barqa's troops and its commander, Yanal al-Tawil the Turk, was tightened. Abu Rakwa himself led an assault on the city in an attempt to get the defenders to abandon their lines and fortifications, but he was unsuccessful. He called off the attack and returned to camp disillusioned because his plan had not worked. He retired to his tent to rest and think things through. On the third day, the Banu Qurra and their allies started to get restless and annoyed because they had been ordered just to keep watch and not to attack, whereas Hamad al-Madi was secretly inciting them to action. Abu Rakwa was still cloistering himself in his tent, but word of these developments reached him in the form of protests and tough questions. Abu al-Mahasin helped matters by intervening to cool tempers; he threw his entire weight behind a recommendation for restraint and patience until such time as Abu Rakwa broke his silence and made some new proposals. Just before nightfall people noticed that Shihab al-Din was not in camp. Cries of protest and disapproval were heard, and the atmosphere turned tense. Hamad al-Madi seized this golden opportunity.

"Men of the Banu Qurra," he said, "are you supposed to be real men or not? Here you gather behind an imam who vanishes when the going gets rough and let yourselves be fooled by one of your own. Is this supposed to be a campaign or a huge joke? If it's Barqa you want, then unsheathe your swords and attack it. Don't sit here waiting, hoping, and barking. But if you're scared of the outcome and realize the kind of vengeance that al-Hakim the Fatimid will exact, then return to your tents and abodes. As far as I can see, that's the best plan."

Barely had Hamad al-Madi finished before a redoubtable cavalier from his own tribe started cuffing and kicking him. "You vile wretch!" he yelled, "you provocateur and coward, you look so despicable when times are good and strut obstinately around when things turn bad!"

This cavalier would have killed al-Madi if Abu al-Mahasin had not rushed over to stop him.

"My fellow tribesmen," he said, "I have just talked to Abu Rakwa in his tent. He tells me that Shihab al-Din has neither turned traitor nor withdrawn. Abu Rakwa has sent him on a mission, the happy results of which will soon be known. Please be patient. As for you, Hamad al-Madi, you've made your choice. You are not of our number, nor we of yours. By dawn tomorrow you and your group will imitate Umm 'Amr's donkey and disappear."

With that a degree of tranquility was restored among the troops, and they were more prepared to wait. As they were getting ready for sleep, they heard their guards announcing the approach of three men, with a fourth in front carrying a torch and a white cloth. With that Abu Rakwa came out of his tent.

"Good news, my fellow tribesmen," he shouted, "good news! God willing, that will be Shihab al-Din, bringing us Yanal, the enemy commander, alive. Before the morrow you will enter Barqa safe and sound!"

They did not believe him till they saw Shihab al-Din for themselves. With that all their doubts vanished.

"Tribesmen," said Shihab al-Din, "Here I am returning to you. With God's own support I have carried out our imam's idea by arresting the garrison commander, Yanal al-Tawil the Turk. I was helped and guided by this Kutami soldier; he disguised me in clothes like his own and was one of the first to join our number."

With that Abu Rakwa went back to his tent, followed by Shihab al-Din with his captive. They both had to decide what to do with this man who would be able to surrender the Fatimid positions inside the city without any bloodshed.

"I'm sure you would rather stay alive," Shihab al-Din said to Yanal.

"As long as I'm a prisoner of yours," he stuttered in dismay, "I've no desire to stay alive."

"If you send instructions to your soldiers to lay down their arms, we'll release you."

"The only way to convince my soldiers to do that would be to send them my fresh-cut head. If you prefer to release me, al-Hakim will have me killed."

"Issue the order, and you can stay here under our protection."

"A huge gap separates you and me, one that's loaded with perils."

"How so, you obstinate man!"

"You're Maghribi and I'm a Turk. Like Turks, you all want power and authority. I cannot envisage coming out victorious on your side, but rather with my Turkish colleagues who are on their way."

"Ill spoken, you purveyor of bad news! Do you want my hand to take the initiative and slay you now?"

"I wish you had done so already! Shall I slap your master or spit on him so you can dispatch me quickly?"

Abu Rakwa now broke his silence. "I saw no slaps and spit in my dreams," he said with a frown. And with that, he grabbed Shihab al-Din's sword and struck off Yanal's head right in front of the people standing by the tent's exit. Everyone stood there thunderstruck, Shihab al-Din most of all.

"Did you really do what we have just seen?" he stammered. "How could you use such unprecedented violence to cut off his head with your own noble hands? By God, I never expected such behavior of you. From now on I'll make sure that our acquaintance only involves non-aggressive issues."

Abu Rakwa wiped the sword and handed it back to its owner. "I shall behave this way and even more so with anyone who closes doors in my face and leaves me no way out. Now take this damned head back so the Fatimid soldiers in the garrison can see it. Take with it a proposal for them to consider: either they surrender or anticipate certain death."

"What you and we desire will come to pass before morning breaks."

That was Shihab al-Din's response as he staggered his way out of the tent to carry out the imam's instructions. He consulted the shaykhs, and they suggested asking for two volunteers to carry out the task along with the Kutami soldier who would serve as their helper and guide. Many men volunteered, and it fell to Shihab al-Din to choose two who were both strong and astute, one from his own tribe and the other from the Zanata.

Only a few hours went by before they returned accompanied by the Fatimid soldiers; they were holding their arms above their heads and carrying a white flag as a plea for safe passage. Their surrender came at dawn; the news spread through the camp just as the sun's rays were beginning to appear above the horizon. Everyone gathered around the imam's tent, and an infectious joy pervaded the scene. One group banged on drums and played the flute, another chanted and sang, and a third danced and played with swords and canes. This total chaos only quieted down when they all noticed Abu Rakwa getting on his horse and yelling, "God is great!" They all repeated, "God is great!" many, many times in a ringing unison and then stopped to listen humbly to what he had to say.

"Tribesmen," he said, "all praise and thanks be to God who has realized my vision and granted us our first victory as a gift (may He be exalted!).

Today we are yet greater than yesterday, "Men who have fulfilled their pact with God." Barqa is our transit point, and we will now enter it in safety and devotion, neither raiding nor pillaging. Barqa will be a mirror of us, the place where we will show to those near and far the true extent of our justice and piety. Enter the town in groups. Once settled on its reddish soil, organize yourselves to offer the people help and assistance. Behave properly, take good care of its oil supply and its rusty earth. As far as possible, prepare yourselves for the decisive battle against the Fatimid tyrants in Egypt. Any prisoners who agree to join us and fight are free; those who don't will be used as hostages to be exchanged for the people in al-Hakim's prisons who wish to join us."

Cries of support and compliance were heard from the warriors, then everyone mounted their horses and headed for Barqa, with Abu Rakwa and all the shaykhs at their head. When they reached the city's quarters and squares, they received a fulsome welcome from the populace during which everyone expressed their utter delight at being freed from slavery. Abu Rakwa was at the head of the procession. He was greeted by the men of the town with enthusiastic paeans of praise, while women ululated and scattered sweet-smelling rose-petals. It was a truly emotional scene, and even Abu Rakwa could not hold back his tears. He leaned over to Shihab al-Din.

"These people are enveloping me with feelings of devotion that I don't deserve," he said. "They're giving me a task I can't perform. Where are we going to stay?"

"We'll stay in a place befitting the imam," Shihab al-Din replied, his face wreathed in smiles. "That's the governor's residence, of course!"

When the procession reached the governor's residence, Abu Rakwa dismounted and hurried inside followed by his retinue and the shaykhs. He settled in the closest furnished quarters, sat down, and addressed his retinue in the following terse fashion: "Worthy shaykhs," he said, "Spend the rest of this wonderful day relaxing and recovering your strength. Tomorrow—God willing!—organize our army's activities both inside and outside the city. The next day we will all pray the Friday prayers together; we'll give thanks to our Lord and renew the pledge we've made in the cause of justice and equity for our Muslim people. God's peace be upon you all!"

From the company arose the shout of a redoubtable shaykh. "And peace be upon Abu Rakwa, our noble imam, and welcome to this blessed town! You have called us to good works, and we have responded; to a life of probity, and we have given you our support. The shepherds of this city have prepared for you and your companions a cup of Barqa milk and trays of dates as a celebration of your blessed advent. Do not send them away till you have tasted what they are offering."

A senior servant came forward and offered Abu Rakwa some dates and milk, of which he took just a little. The rest of the company descended on the dates and milk with considerable relish. Abu Rakwa got up, went over to the shaykh who had welcomed him, and asked his name and status.

"My name is Zaydan the Mazati," the man replied respectfully. "As you know, great imam, the Mazata tribe are Arabized Berbers. This city of Barqa is my birthplace and residence. I have only left it once in order to perform the obligation of pilgrimage. I serve as the community's mufti for the Hanafi rite and celebrate God's name in spite of the efforts of al-Hakim the Fatimid and his Shi'ite disciples."

Abu Rakwa was clearly much affected by the shaykh's words. "My dear august man of law," he said, "may you be blessed, along with your knowledge and wisdom! My dearest wish is for you to stay close by me and to assist me in making God's word victorious, in revealing the truth and vitiating the false."

The shaykh started showing Abu Rakwa to his bed. "Through God's will," he said, "tomorrow I will show you the tomb of Ruwayfi'—may God perfume his grave. There I will pledge to you my support and loyalty."

In the early hours of the first Friday morning of Jamadi al-Akhira, Abu Rakwa accompanied the Mazati shaykh to pray at the tomb of Ruwayfi', the companion of the Prophet. There he heard the shaykh hold forth in emotive tones about justice and the unity of God and the need for a campaign against tyranny and injustice. The shaykh then pledged Abu Rakwa his loyalty and allegiance. The two men stood up and headed toward the mosque which they found packed with worshippers. They performed some supererogatory prayers together, then sat down to talk about matters suited to the location, prophetic accounts and Qur'anic verses.

Just about at midday the preacher delivered a sermon in which he substituted Abu Rakwa's name for that of al-Hakim the Fatimid, extolling the former's religious virtues and praying that he would be both victorious and steadfast. Hardly had the preacher finished before Abu Rakwa sat in the pulpit. An amazing silence descended on the assembly, only interrupted by the sound of his voice which resonated around the porticos and courtyard of the mosque.

"Praise be to God! We praise Him, we ask for His aid, we ask for His forgiveness, we turn to Him in penitence. In Him we seek refuge from the evil in ourselves and from the evil of our deeds. Whosoever is guided by God cannot be led astray; whoever He leads astray will never find anyone to guide him. I witness that there is no God but God alone and He has no associate, and that Muhammad is His servant and His Prophet."

"Servants of God!! *Remember, when you were few in number and oppressed on earth, fearing that others would overwhelm you. God gave you shelter, granted you victory, and provided you with good things, that you might be grateful* (the true words of Him who alone has the power and discretion). So recall the name of God frequently and bring Him into your debates. He can remove the causes of dispute and rivalry and unite your hearts and ranks. Mention often the name of Him who possesses all majesty, who commits not even the smallest shred of injustice. God the Almighty serves as your sustenance and strength against the forces you fear; He will provide the steadfast spirit needed to hold our ground and resist. I myself mention His name morning and evening, standing, sitting, and reclining. In Him I seek refuge from the dark night of Fatimid tyranny, with all its murders and scandals. In Him I seek refuge as I humbly and submissively beseech Him to bring it about that true religion should prevail rather than schism. And what greater schism can there be than the corrupt line of the Fatimid dynasty who want to use their mouths to snuff out God's own light and to replace it with their own illusionary regulations and lunatic statements about stars and creation? Their sole quest is to pollute the realms of reason and sincerity. They have no other goal than to subdue the country and its people in a display of their own tyranny and whims. How can there be any greater apostasy from God's true faith than that of al-Hakim the Fatimid who has turned himself into a god, tyrannized people with his cruelty and murder, and governed them through his own obsessions, thus imposing his own mental state on their destiny!

"Servants of God! This al-Hakim the Fatimid is a complete abomination. He forgets God and the way He dealt with 'Ad, Thamud, and the Egyptian pharaoh. You see him murdering friend and stranger alike, jurisconsult and Sufi, anyone, in fact, who dares to raise his head in protest or requests some largesse. How many unfortunates have been ruthlessly killed by his criminal hands? This is supreme folly! Neither advice nor preaching can prevail against such tyranny; how could it when pig-skin is never to be tanned?

"Servants of God! Those in whom I confide know well that I challenge both servility and insult, in that I show a certain amount of hunger but a great deal of rejection. I only pronounce what God orders me to do, and He is the best of pronouncers: 'My prayer, my devotion, my life, and my death, all these are for God alone, the Lord of humanity.'

"Those people who encounter me in towns, then turn back and leave me, are fleeing their tomorrow, in that I am reminding them that such a morrow will be full of fear and death. In these regions and others under al-Hakim's control, no one is asking about their future destiny. No year brings any boons, the whole of humanity has no life, and sustenance comes in crumbs.

"Servants of God, are we then to remain forever beset by this massive conspiracy and the likelihood of blockade, living by sheer precedent as close as can be to perdition, wasting our lives on disasters, abandoning the laws of God and the rights of humanity, and satisfying our religious instincts with rituals and trivialities?

"A ruler and his Shi'ah have drugged you; and they have
   done it well!

Within the dream-realms of liberty they have planted the
   poison of treason and nonsense.

They have positioned themselves above you, over the
   tents of your own lethargy.

I have come to know them; in every aspect I have taken
   an opposite stance.

Haven't you seen with your own eyes how they destroy
   the bounty of this land,

Frequenting havens of pleasure and ease, inhaling
   luscious scents,

Snatching and flashing through touch and illumination?!

Haven't you seen them in all those fields that they have
   taken from your soil,

Belching as they extol the Giver of all benefits and gifts,

And living a life of sin and lechery in the midst of both
   you and God's signs?!

"If only you saw and were aware, all the warriors among
you would race to enter the fray against tyranny; they would
gather the poor together and say to them: 'Behind you lies
death; in front of you is the enemy.' They would send out
a suicide mission against him and light the path for the
generations to come, all in obedience to the Creator's own
words: 'Fight against the leaders of disbelief. There is no
faith among them, as though they might come to an end.'

"For that reason I have embraced your spirit of unity;

I have embraced it and gathered around.

With my entire being I have begged the Lord of Might
   and Majesty, saying:

The time has come for the one who rules contrary to God's
   own book and the practice of His prophet to disappear,

for the destruction of the one who holds sway in Egypt,
    subjecting its people to annihilation and his vile moods.
It is time for the dark night of Fatimid rule to end.
The River Nile can free the land from the grip of
    this calamity.
O God, give us power to assemble the scattered fragments
    of this community,
Aid us in emerging from the vaults of gloom and impotence.

"As for you, illustrious Maghribis of time-honored memory, by Him who created the heavens and changes conditions, I can only envisage you as the nemesis of every stubborn tyrant, steadfastly opposing all thoughts of submission and disparagement, and making ready all the forces you can muster in order to extirpate evil and disaster and to fight God's enemy and yours. Were I to say or promise anything else, I would be talking nonsense. That is why I have urged all the living elements of the community to rise up in one massive unity. I term it the flame of the sea. 'Surge forth, O flame of the sea,' I tell it, 'surge up amid ribs and inside eyes and heads. Muster the brave youths of our community, fire-birds alight and ready; women, row upon row, in revolt, and men standing firm together.'

"O Lord, You know what we desire and crave: for the rule
    of Your law among us and the rights of humanity that
    strives in Your direction;

"O Lord, do not lead our hearts astray now that You have
    guided us. Grant us Your mercy.

"O Lord, open up for us and our people the gate of truth;
    You are indeed the best of openers.

"O Lord, it is on You that we rely, to You that we return,
    and to You that destiny leads.

> "O Lord, forgive us our sins, pardon us for our evil deeds,
>   and grant us to dwell with the righteous.
> "All praise be to your Lord, Lord of Power beyond what
>   they describe. Greetings to those sent on a mission, and
>   all praise be to God, Lord of the worlds."

As Abu Rakwa intoned his intercessions, the men responded "Amen" in unison, sometimes lengthening the vowel sounds, at others shortening them. Then the muezzin gave the call to prayer. Everyone performed the prayer behind Abu Rakwa, lined up humbly in droves that managed to fill the mosque space and the terraces to the side. Once the prayer was over, Abu Rakwa was keen to proceed immediately to the governor's residence, but on the way out, he had to make his way through crowds of people. They were all eager to see him, shake his hand, and offer up prayers on his behalf. He made his way through the throng, smiling and clasping hands, all of which took a long time. Shihab al-Din was following close behind, hand on sword and checking carefully in every direction. After a good deal of time and effort Abu Rakwa and his entourage made it to the governor's residence. No sooner had they arrived than Shihab al-Din upbraided Abu Rakwa.

"Imam," he protested, "how can you rub shoulders with that huge mob when we are not sure of their loyalty? How can you risk your life that way when we are only just at the start of our long road?"

Abu Rakwa was still sweating and out of breath. "We've passed the first test," he said. "People have put their trust in us, and we in turn must trust them back. As one of our saints once said, 'There's safety to be found in taking risks.' Oh, how dearly I would love to retire to the desert, confide in my Lord, and seek His counsel regarding the events and duties he has obliged me to take on!"

"You can do all that," Shihab al-Din protested, "once you've eaten and had something to drink."

"Even if God grants us control over the entire earth, my eating needs won't change. Tell the people in this residence to erect my tent on the roof, and have some food sent to me there."

"Your tent? You've just entered a governor's residence, and now you decide to put a tent on the roof? I find you truly amazing! Don't you realize that, when it comes to matters of authority, it's a take it or leave it situation? You've entered this city victorious, you've expunged the Fatimid name from the Friday sermon, and cursed al-Hakim and his ancestors. Now all you need to do is adopt an official name, appoint a chamberlain, and mint some coinage."

"Tell people to call me 'the revolutionary in God's name' if they wish. Ask the senior supervisor of this residence to bring in anyone who wishes to meet me, should he wish to do so. Strike coins in my name, if you like. All I want is a tent on the roof. This residence belongs to God. Anyone who has nowhere to live can reside here, starting with the dervishes and invalids who made it possible for us to capture this town."

Shihab al-Din slapped his hands together in frustration. "So be it," he said as he went out. 'We'll do it your way!"

For two whole months Abu Rakwa did things the way he wanted. The only time he came down from his tent on the roof was to lead prayers or dispense justice in complex disputes. Once in a while he would check up on both civilians and soldiers to make sure that the reports he was getting were accurate. He felt optimistic about the way people were living and enjoying more rights, but at the same time he was worried about unruly elements in the army who were tired of waiting and not fighting; they kept making derisive remarks about the paltry raids they had conducted and the small amount of booty they had collected. Toward the end of the week, just when he was thinking of ways to keep his fighters calm and happy, Abu al-Mahasin and Shihab al-Din arived with news that al-Hakim's army was approaching to the east of Barqa, close to Dhat al-Hammam.

"God be praised!" he yelled. "Here's news to warm my heart and relieve me of the anxieties that have beset me for the last few days."

"You're right, Abu Rakwa," agreed Abu al-Mahasin. "Like every army, ours is meant to fight; it'll only fight to win victories and gain booty. Now we must make it ready to plunge into the very conflict it was meant for. In that cause may God assist us!"

"Thus far," Shihab al-Din commented with determination, "our army has only had to combat boredom and undertake minor tasks. Till our forces can score a genuine triumph against a strong army such as the one now facing us, we'll never be content."

Abu Rakwa stood up. "So we're all agreed then," he said. "There's no need for more talk. Go to our people and muster them and our allies for battle. Tell them to fill in the wells and to be prepared to make flanking movements and conduct a series of rapid assaults. And make sure neither of you comes to see me on important business without bringing along one or two Zanati shaykhs as well."

Barely an hour passed after their receiving this command before Abu al-Mahasin was back again with two Zanati shaykhs.

"Imam," he said, "everything is in excellent order. Preparations are complete, and infantry and cavalry are lined up in rows. Now all we're waiting for is your order to begin. We all beseech you not to take part in this battle in case something terrible should happen and we should lose you!"

"Woe to you all! Have you gone mad? Are you all unanimous about something that is not at all what I would wish? Don't you all realize that someone who stays at the back cannot be an imam? Have you forgotten that the lives of all of us are in God's hands?"

Abu al-Mahasin tried to calm the imam down. "We're unanimous, Abu Rakwa. We're still at the very beginning of our long road to Egypt. There's no harm in your agreeing to these terms. We've agreed to it because the Zanatis have given us a good reason. They've charged these two shaykhs to tell you about it. Now I'll leave you with them. God willing, I shall return with news of victory."

Barely had Abu al-Mahasin left before Abu Rakwa approached the two shaykhs with a smile. "So, Hammu," he said amiably, "what's this all about? And you, Yahya? All's well, is it not?"

"Yes indeed, imam," replied Yahya somewhat awkwardly. "What we want to tell you is that we Zanatis are particularly concerned about your safety and welfare. You represent the source and guarantor of our union with the Banu Qurra. What made us even more anxious is our fear that a tribal secret of ours might be uncovered, something without which we would never have been able to resist our foes in the past. . . ."

"What secret are you talking about?" Abu Rakwa interrupted in amazement. "Are you taking things back to the old days of diffidence and mistrust?"

"Abu Rakwa," Hammu explained, "we have a unique knowledge of surface and sub-surface water resources in the Barqa region. When it comes to keeping such resources hidden, we have methods that are still unknown to others. It's these methods that we want to use today in the desert area between us and Dhat al-Hammam; that way we can make the enemy feel incredibly thirsty before the fighting even starts. Even so, we beg you to preserve your own life for these tribes that you have managed to unite in purpose and served as both witness and trustee of that very purpose."

Abu Rakwa rubbed his hands together in resignation. "People worry that I'm going to be killed by a stray arrow, whereas I might well die in my own bed by order of Him who controls all souls. But what can I do when everyone's agreed that I should stay away from the fighting? Let every warrior do his utmost. I'll be standing on the bluffs overlooking the desert and watching the battle from close by. I will be watching with pounding heart, as I look forward to a glorious victory brought by you and God Himself."

So Abu Rakwa stayed in his tent. He sat there on his rug, calming his worries with fervent prayers to his Lord, beseeching Him that little of the warriors' blood be shed and that large numbers of enemy be captured. However, soon afterward he was escorted by a squad of guards to a hill overlooking the battlefield; there he stayed pacing back and forth. His head kept throbbing as he watched the armies pound each other in a maelstrom of noise and fire. The only way he managed to calm himself somewhat was by focusing his attention on his own troops as they out-shone each other in felling enemy forces. Some of them were breaching enemy ranks and encircling them, while others peppered them with weapons from secure positions; still others led them toward water which was a mere mirage and then easily took them captive.

As Abu Rakwa watched the ever changing scene, Shihab al-Din, Yahya, and Hammu rode up with the tremendous news that their warriors had decisively defeated al-Hakim's forces. They had also cut off their lines of retreat so that only a few had managed to escape.

"We made them feel the bitter taste of thirst," said Hammu enthusiastically, "something they'll never experience again till the day they're sent to hellfire. When we came at them with our swords, their tongues were as parched as the very desert sands, dangling from their mouths as they tried to lick up their own sweat."

"God forgive you!" Abu Rakwa commented by way of reproof. "Tell me instead that you've fought with honor. The Zanata fought bravely, didn't they, Shihab al-Din?"

"Most certainly, Abu Rakwa," Shihab al-Din replied, realizing the imam's import. "The same applies to all our warriors to whom God Almighty has given a clear victory. There is a great deal of booty. Competent men are now assessing amounts and preparing to distribute it. The enemy lost a thousand dead and wounded, and there are more than two thousand prisoners, including Yanal the Tall, the Turkish commander."

"Yanal the Tall?" Abu Rakwa asked. "How many Yanals do they have? Isn't he the one we killed before entering Barqa in triumph?"

"The Yanal who had the singular honor of being killed at your hand were merely a poor soldier. He managed to fool us by adopting the guise of the real Yanal so that the latter could escape, and—God curse him— he succeeded."

"We'll deal with that after you've told me how many dead and wounded there are on our side."

For just a moment Shihab al-Din frowned, but then he noticed Abu Rakwa's anger rising.

"Just a few," he said, "a hundred and twenty warriors, all of whom are guaranteed a place in paradise. Fifty-one wounded, among them . . ."

"Who?"

"Abu al-Mahasin, Imam. He was treacherously struck from behind. He's lying on his bed being tended by the very best doctors."

"Your mercy, O God! Take me to him at once, then go and issue orders that all wounded are to be carefully supervised and all prisoners properly treated."

Abu Rakwa rushed after the three men as they made their way toward Abu al-Mahasin's quarters. When he reached the door of the tent, the chief doctor told him that Abu al-Mahasin's condition was very grave. "We've done everything we can to stop the bleeding," he told the imam. "Ask for God's mercy on him, Abu Rakwa!" Abu Rakwa told everyone to go about their business, then sat down alongside Abu al-Mahasin. He placed one hand on his forehead and the other on his chest.

"This isn't the time for us to say farewell, Abu al-Mahasin," he said, stifling his tears. "We still need you badly for the decisive battle."

"God forgive you, Abu Rakwa," interrupted Abu al-Mahasin. "Aren't you the one who said that our lives are in God's hands?"

"I ask His forgiveness, the best of guarantors. You are right, O noble Muslim. Forgive my fear of losing you, you who are such a stalwart supporter of our cause and give us the benefit of your sage opinions."

"I praise God for granting us this victory and for making me one of the first martyrs in our cause. I have only ever wanted to fulfill the Prophet's wishes, to fight in the cause of God; to fight, then live, then fight again and live again. I am destined to die, and your consolation must be with Shihab al-Din once you have tamed his impetuous nature, with the Zanata, the Banu Qurra, and others who will join the cause. Surround yourself with such folk and relish their sense of unity and fraternity. You are bound to achieve your goal and bequeath to future generations the best of what is past. To God we belong and to Him do we return."

After Abu al-Mahasin had said those words, he recited the statement of faith. The two men then embraced, and with one last gasp Abu al-Mahasin was gone. For a moment Abu Rakwa stood there with tears flowing, then with bloodshot eyes he left to greet people outside. "Get some people to help you bury our dead warriors as they are," he told Yahya. "Others should wash the body of Abu al-Mahasin and his dead comrades. God willing, we will say prayers over them."

Following Abu al-Mahasin's death a day or two passed. Abu Rakwa chose to stay in his tent, receiving numerous reports from his assistants. Once in a while he went out to confirm bits of information that he kept hearing about the good mood of not merely people in general but particularly his warriors; they were bursting with enthusiasm and champing at the bit for the major confrontation to come. They kept asking him over and over again about this battle, but he would always reply, "Finding patience among all of you is rarer than a mosquito's brain! As long as you insist on adopting a weak position, you'll never even get a date from a crow."

"And what exactly is that weak position, God preserve you?" they asked.

"Excessive haste," was the reply.

With that they left him alone and went on their way. "Our imam certainly knows the way things are!" they told each other by way of explanation.

In the ensuing months events piled up on one another. Abu Rakwa was not used to the pace. Every month brought with it new situations. These he pondered carefully, using them as inspiration for a whole series of recorded thoughts. One Ramadan night in A.H. 396 he was engrossed in his reading and note-taking, when a heavily armed man managed to sneak his way into his tent. He greeted the imam and sat down close by.

"Forgive me, Imam," he said, "for visiting you in this way. When you hear why I've come, I hope you'll forgive my intrusion."

Abu Rakwa was not in the slightest bit afraid. "I trust it's good news, young man," he said. "But tell me first who you are and where you're from."

"I am 'Ali ibn Husayn ibn Jawhar from Sicily."

"Are you the son of al-Hakim's chief general?"

"Yes, I am indeed, Abu Rakwa," the young man replied, "and I am here as his emissary to you. I didn't march to Barqa. However, I was actually there ahead of you, looking after my father's interests and pretending to serve al-Hakim as commander of its garrison. When you entered the city victorious with your army, I hid for a few days in an underground grainstore. That gave me time to think about my situation and plan an escape. The day I disguised myself as a beggar and got out, I vowed to assassinate you and then escape back to Cairo."

"How could you do that when there's so much hatred between al-Hakim and your father? In whose interest would you be committing such a dastardly deed?"

"If I'd done any such thing—heaven forbid!—it wouldn't have been to curry favor with al-Hakim. I loathe him just as much as everyone does. The reason would have been to eliminate all the doubts and rumors being put about by al-Hakim's spies to the effect that my father is secretly in league with you and encouraging you to enter Egypt."

"So what prevented you from carrying out your foul deed?"

"It was that sermon you gave, Imam! Your words hit me fresh and true; they convinced me that you are indeed the true religious leader and guide. When you finished, I left the mosque still in disguise. I was cursing myself. To kill you, I told myself, would be akin to murdering righteous people—something that is totally forbidden. I took a horse from one of my former aides and rode to the site near Cairo where my father was encamped so I could tell him about your virtuous deeds. Now here I am back again with a letter from my father, along with an attestation from his son-in-law, 'Abd al-'Aziz ibn Nu'man, the chief judge. In the letter he salutes you and urges you to conquer Egypt and overthrow the tyrannical rule of al-Hakim. He promises you the support of the Sicilians and Kutamis and all other soldiers under his command."

Abu Rakwa took the letter from his visitor and studied it carefully. "It's late at night," he said, "and you look very tired. Leave me with your father's letter and choose a room for yourself to get some sleep. Tomorrow, God willing, you will attend a meeting with our warrior leaders to prepare for the conquest of Egypt. Now, 'Ali, go in peace."

"As you command, Abu Rakwa. Tomorrow I'll await your command to attend the planning meeting that augurs a great future."

The visitor left as surreptitiously as he had come in. Abu Rakwa started to read Ibn Jawhar's letter. Then he snuffed out the candle and went to sleep.

Early next morning (a Thursday), Abu Rakwa learned that the imprisoned commander, Yanal the Tall, had been killed by Shihab al-Din after a bitter argument. The imam immediately thought of summoning Shihab al-Din and severely reprimanding him for his action, but he decided against it. With the cause of unity and the imminence of a decisive battle in mind, he stifled his anger. However, while he was still pondering the whole matter, Shihab al-Din entered his tent, nervous and red-faced, and greeted the imam.

"No doubt you've heard about what happened early this morning," he said. "My excuse for what I did to Yanal the accursed is that he would get away from us again and become another Hamad al-Madi, a thorn in our sides and a barrier to our forward advance. All I meant to do was to hobble him, but he insulted your status as imam, then spat at me twice in the face, saying: "One for you, and the other for your phony imam." The insult was too much, and I lost my temper. I gave him a sword. For a while we parried, but then I managed to impale him in the stomach and split his head in twain. He fell to the ground drowning in his own foul blood."

"Hamad al-Madi certainly is a thorn in our flesh," said Abu Rakwa, trying to calm things down. "You're right about that. Have you any idea how to crush this thorn?"

"By making sure we don't delay our advance."

"So we must make haste and move toward the decisive engagement. Isn't that so?"

"Yes indeed, Abu Rakwa! At this point time is a formidable weapon in our hands. We can either make full use of it to achieve our goals, or else waste it, in which case we'll be the ones who'll be eliminated."

"What about the rest of the prisoners? What do you think we should do with them?"

"They're all leaning toward your cause. They'd prefer to bolster our numbers rather than go back to Egypt where they're sure to die."

"Nevertheless release all the wounded who want to return home. Now go back to our camp and tell the shaykhs that after today's evening prayer I shall await them in my tent. We will discuss our forthcoming battle. Don't forget to invite Hammu and Yahya. Now go and find Shaykh Zaydan the Mazati."

Shihab al-Din had only been gone a short while before the Mazati shaykh entered the tent to see the imam. He warmly greeted Abu Rakwa, and in return was welcomed and honored by his host. The two men sat on mats, sipping cups of green tea and chatting about a variety of issues: Sunni jurisprudence, Shi'ism and Isma'ilism, and whether the Fatimid ruler al-Hakim could be legally anathematized. Once in a while the two men disagreed on a point. For example, the Mazati shaykh, who by inclination adhered to the Hanafi school of law, expressed his regret that Sunni Islam should be divided up into schools and sects.

"Abu Rakwa," he said, "the imams of Islam are men just like us. We have to interpret the law just as they did. Since Abu Hanifa Nu'man himself made that statement, I agree with it. It is the disciples and followers of those imams who went wrong. When they all split up into different sects and schools, they allowed the unity of the religion to be compromised. Worse than that, they introduced heresies and innovations by indulging in varieties of sin and unbelief and sowing discord. I ask you, Abu Rakwa, is it conceivable that there should be a single truth, and yet those who receive it are divided into a number of different schools?"

"The truth is indeed one, Zaydan," Abu Rakwa replied, "and God's messages are unchanging. However humanity is numerous and varied, and its circumstances are continually in a process of transformation. That explains their division into different religious communities and creeds. Every community is subdivided into sects and groups. There are different modes of interpretation and schisms. All that is God's practice with His servants."

"If that's your view, then why don't you leave al-Hakim the Fatimid Caliph alone?"

"Because he won't leave us alone. But, even if fear and religious piety did cause him to leave us alone, it would still be the solemn obligation of every Muslim to fight him and his dominion. How can we possibly ignore the fact that he has ruined the lives and destroyed the souls of countless human beings whom God has honored; that he has transcended the limits of interpretation into the realms of schism, and from there into murder? He has become insane enough to deify himself and become enmired in the direst perdition. No, no, by Him who is Lord of East and West, there being no other god but He, I will fight al-Hakim till God's servants are rid of him and restore to them the signs of justice and honor. Should I fail, then God is my steward who will wreak His promised revenge on heretics. *Whoever associates with God anything, it is as though he has fallen from Heaven and the birds snatch him away, or the wind sweeps him headlong into a place far away.*"

"Yes indeed, Abu Rakwa, your struggle is indeed the right one. May God come to your aid and grant you victory. I pledge all the support that my own dwindling powers can provide for you, sometimes giving you my own opinion and at others listening to your moments of joy and concern."

"May God bless you and give you long life, illustrious shaykh! Now let's talk about Barqa for a while."

"If al-Hakim's army left us alone and ended the conflict, we could be the happiest of people in our own territory. It's a blessed land. God has provided it with qualities found nowhere else. In some parts you can find oil that is an antidote for scabies, cough, and skin rash. Everywhere is tinged by a gentle red color; I notice, Abu Rakwa, that your own clothes bear some traces of it, as happens with all its inhabitants. You only get rid of it when you leave the region of Barqa."

"The red color is most welcome! Let it be red till victory!"

"And then there's the green that surrounds us on all sides. That mountain that you see enveloping the city has a thick forest of juniper trees, and the slopes provide rich pasturage where our flocks can graze safely as they praise their God."

"Yes indeed, Zaydan, ever since I took up residence on this roof , those very junipers and green pastures have always been with me in my hours of solitude."

"The verdure extends as far as the open spaces to the north where there's a profusion of fruit trees, citron, quince, and walnut. They provide us with different kinds of fruit throughout the year."

"Dear colleague, if we weren't going to embark on the crucial confrontation with al-Hakim the Fatimid, I'd ask you to take me to those open spaces tomorrow so we could spend the day there relaxing and strolling around. So let's make that a promise for the future if God grants us victory!"

"Should God grant you victory, Abu Rakwa, it's a promise. And if not, then you have an even greater reward dwelling in the gardens of eternal life."

"True enough, Zaydan! And what of the other boons of this land?"

"There's good, fresh animal meat, pure honey, tar, wool, and cotton. They're all taken away for al-Hakim's troops, either for a paltry price or else by sheer plunder and aggression. The tribes of the Barqa region, Bedouin of the Banu Qurra, Berbers of Zanata and al-Hakim, and Arabized Mizata Berbers, had no name for their common enemy nor for the fruits of their land till God sent you to us in order to unite us in His religion and to grant His word triumph over the forces of tyranny."

With those words the shaykh stood up to take his leave. Abu Rakwa stood up too and escorted his guest to the tent entrance, clasping his arm.

"Don't forget that walk we are going to take, Zaydan, if God grants us victory. Beyond that I promise that you will serve as prayer-leader whenever I have to be away. Also don't forget to come to the meeting of tribal shaykhs this evening."

Zaydan nodded his head in agreement as he patted Abu Rakwa's shoulders and wished him all success.

Shortly after the evening prayer the tribal shaykhs started gathering at Abu Rakwa's tent. They shook his hand and sat down in their places; they were sipping cups of tea and exchanging small talk and compliments. The last to arrive were Shihab al-Din, Hammu, and Yahya, accompanied by 'Ali ibn Jawhar and Shaykh Zaydan the Mazati. No sooner had they greeted the imam and the assembled shaykhs and taken their places than Abu Rakwa addressed them all, "Greetings, illustrious lords," he said, his facial expression a beacon of good news. "By God, this is indeed a great night! As you all know, we're gathered here to consider the final measures to be taken before our worthy warriors enter Egypt. They will arrive as conquerors, not raiders; they will bring glad tidings of justice and unified faith, not of tyranny and oppression. More than ever before we are now embarked on a decisive campaign during which we are going to rely completely on Him who alone possesses the glory and majesty. Dispatches keep arriving from Egypt filled with accounts of people's complaints against al-Hakim the tyrant, of pleas that we come and rescue them, and of heartfelt prayers for our victory and success. The field marshal of the Fatimid army, al-Husayn ibn Jawhar of whom you have all heard, no doubt, has sent us his son, 'Ali, whom you have all met, charging him to assure us of his loyal and steadfast support for our cause. He has also sent a letter. I have read it, and I want you all to hear its contents so that you can all gauge for yourselves the kind of conspiracies al-Hakim is hatching against us and the preparations he is making for our arrival. After the traditional invocations of God's name, here is what he has to say:

> Imam, now that you have crossed the borders into Egypt, you can see for yourself the tyrannical rule of al-Hakim and the ways in which he toys with the country and its people. And yet everything you have seen and heard so far is considerably less severe than the details of what remains concealed from view. You have known the Egyptians to be good folk; they resist tyranny whenever they can and rely on patience and humor when they cannot. But today, confronted by al-Hakim and all his Turkish troops and slaves, they find themselves powerless. Even their jokes only bring them vengeful attacks from the tyrant and misery and suffering as a consequence. Dear Imam, it is hard for me to sit and watch the Egyptian people resorting to silence and lassitude as deliberate strategies. It is all for fear that

the slightest display of disapproval or levity may reach the ears or eyes of al-Hakim's spies. They have managed to infiltrate houses and quarters alike, to such an extent that this poisonous atmosphere of espionage can even infect different members of a single family. If they are forced to live even for a short period in such circumstances, they will all become completely paranoid—God forbid!—and that is a terrible fate!

Imam, the entire Egyptian people, crushed and terrified as it is, now eagerly awaits the end of this disastrous period, an end that will come through your actions, all with the will and help of God. They regard your blessed advent to Egypt, armed with the twin weapons of power and speed, as the agent of their salvation. We Sicilians, along with the Kutamis, are raising people's hopes for your success and bolstering their courage by trusting in you and in Him to whom is the power and majesty. But, I beg you by God, do not use the slogan of "deliberate speed" to veil your eyes or fetter your hands. In the present circumstances moving too slowly may turn out to be an irresponsible act. If that happens, then so much the worse for you! Don't imagine that al-Hakim the tyrant is ignoring you; to the contrary, you have his full attention. Recently, he's been spending all his time and energy on devising ways to bring you down. The only people he meets are those who wish you ill. All his mental energies are concentrated on tricks and ruses. For example, totally contrary to his normal practice, he has started displaying signs of a fake sense of justice and fairness in his decisions. God fight him, he has even stopped sentencing people to death. Beyond that, he has started importing mercenaries from Syria to protect himself against you; he gives them all sorts of gifts, thus depleting his own resources and those of the treasury. What I am most

afraid of is that weak-hearted people, those who have
despaired of ever achieving any kind of release or happiness,
will be taken in by his trickery. To avoid this disaster, something that would result in a yet more generalized distrust and
a full-scale catastrophe, I'm sending my own son with this
letter. I beg you, by God, to lead your warriors to us without
delay. With our aid you can achieve that great victory that
God has promised against the forces of the tyrant. From
today we will be awaiting the arrival of your army by the
western gates of Cairo. We will prepare the terrain, provide
food and ammunition, and recruit as many cavalry and
infantry as we can muster. Victory can come only from
God; in Him we trust and to Him is the return. His peace
be on you and on your companions and followers.

"Alongside the signature of al-Husayn ibn Jawhar is that of his son-in-
law, 'Abd al-'Aziz ibn al-Nu'man al-Qayrawani, the Chief Judge of Egypt.

"My people, now that you have heard the contents of this letter, do
you feel the need for more discussion? Shall we proceed from one session
to another, using due deliberation as a convenient way of turning caution
and anticipation into sheer delay? Time, as I'm sure you're all aware, is
a double-edged sword: when we use it well, it serves to our advantage;
but, when we waste the chances and benefits it offers us, then it turns
against us. So then let us act wisely by using it to our advantage before
it abandons us and gives our foes the benefit. Have I made my point? Tell
me what you think about our current situation: should we be setting out
tomorrow with God's power and aid, or the day after?"

A profound silence fell over the assembly, as though everyone was
agreeing with what Abu Rakwa had just said. However, it was a time for
action, not talk and discussion. It was 'Ali ibn Jawhar who eventually
broke the silence, "Dear colleagues, your silence is a genuine blessing.
By God, it shows that you have all realized how serious the situation in
Egypt really is. This short letter which my father has sent is all you need;

there is no call for prolonged debate. Now you should all be rushing to prepare your riding animals and embark on this great campaign before this golden opportunity slips from our grasp. People are relying on you. The Sicilians and Maghribis are waiting with their two thousand men, all burning for action. It is God alone who grants success and power."

"God bless you, 'Ali," Abu Rakwa said in a tone that blended gratitude with resolve, "and likewise your father and your fellow people! Now then, how many fighters do we have and how much ammunition?"

"Imam," responded Shihab al-Din immediately, "we have six thousand fighters in Barqa and its environs—Banu Qurra, Zanatis, Mizatis, Luwatis, with two thousand cavalry and the rest infantry. A small troop has been fully trained to hurl rocks and fire arrows, while another one specializes in diverting the enemy with skirmishes and feints. Apart from those, all our fighters are good at hand-to-hand combat and set-piece battles."

"Imam," continued Hammu, "the ammunition situation is, thank God, excellent. Every warrior carries his sword, dagger, and shield, cavalry and infantry alike. We have enough swords and arrows in reserve for several days of fighting. If we stick to our current policy of moderation, there won't be any shortage of food or water."

"What about al-Hakim's army?" someone asked from the assembly. "What do we know about their numbers and ammunition. Tell us about the foe we face before we actually confront him—may God reward you!"

Everyone looked at Abu Rakwa, then at 'Ali ibn Jawhar. It was the latter who responded.

"Men," he said in clipped tones, "the Fatimid army without our allies, the Sicilians and Kutamis from the Maghrib, is like a straw tiger; its various subdivisions are at odds with each other. The only motivation they have is money and largesse. The contingents of Turks, Byzantines, slaves, Hamdani youths, and Bedouin louts, only exceed you in their weakness. On a decisive day of battle such as this, neither ammunition, nor drums, nor trumpets will be of any use to such an army, devoid as it is of either creed or faith."

'Ali ibn Jawhar's words were greeted with cries of approval and praise. They continued until someone else asked the following question, "Can you tell us about the march toward Cairo where this battle is to take place? What's the terrain like? Then we can assess how tiring the journey will be."

At this point Abu Rakwa produced a map from his sleeve.

"I've already asked that question of those who are well acquainted with the route from Barqa to the outskirts of Alexandria," said Abu Rakwa as he was spreading out the map. "I agree with their view that we should stick to the coast, then head south toward Cairo where, aided by God's power, we will engage in our first battle. Our journey toward our goal will not take longer than a month and will not involve any hardships. This map which Shaykh Zaydan of the Mazata has kindly provided for me shows the most important stages in our march to Alexandria. Take it, Yahya, and read out what it shows."

Yahya stepped forward with a yawn, took the map, and pretended to be looking at it. "Imam," he said, "I know by heart every single detail of the route to the outskirts of Alexandria. We'll go by way of Qasr al-Nadama, then to Taknist, Maghar al-Raqim, Halima's well, Wadi Makhil, the well of the Square, Jinad al-Saghir, the well of 'Abdallah, Marj al-Shaykh, then to 'Aqaba, the shops of Abu Halima, the ruins of al-Qawm, the palace of al-Shammas, the road of the Hammam, the well of 'Awsaj, the churches of al-Harir, al-Tahuna, Hinniyyat al-Rum, Dhat al-Hamam, Thuniya, and finally Alexandria. That's the shortest and most direct route. There are twenty-one stages, and it is about five hundred and seventy-two miles. That's not written on the map. God knows best."

"Young man," said Shaykh Zaydan the Mazati, sounding tired, "God has indeed taught you to assess things correctly. The distance from Barqa to Alexandria is exactly as you have described it. It's not a hard trip as long as drinking water, above and below ground, is available at the staging posts. God is the provider of benefits, and He is our helper. From Alexandria to Giza in the environs of Cairo itself, it's all plain.

The distance is no more than two hundred and fifty miles. Isn't that right, 'Ali ibn Jawhar?"

"Yes indeed, sage shaykh," 'Ali replied by way of confirmation. "The only thing I can add is good news: your ranks will be swelled by allies and supporters wherever you travel and alight during your journey to Cairo."

Abu Rakwa now looked round at the assembled group, giving the impression that he was keen to finish the session. "So now you can all bear witness to the fact that our Mazati shaykh's wisdom extends to measuring distances as well. As God wills, and He is the best of providers. My people, if we've asked all the necessary questions, then let's leave the conclusions we may draw to the inspiration of the battlefield itself. Now I ask you all to recite the Fatiha before we pray. Then we will all part in anticipation of our meeting again at dawn tomorrow, when our forces will set out on this holy campaign."

With that everyone recited the Fatiha in a spirit of humble devotion, then went back downstairs to perform the evening prayer. After that they all went to their beds and slept with their families and relatives.

Next morning, having said farewell to families and loved ones, Abu Rakwa's army was ready to set off on its march. No sooner had Abu Rakwa mounted his camel and surveyed the ranks of warriors that he started to intone "God is great," to which the entire assemblage responded in kind. Then he commanded people to mount their camels and horses in alternation, to cooperate and to conduct themselves in good order. Finally he himself moved to the front and gave the signal for departure. With green flags fluttering over their troops, and the ululations of women, the cries of children, wounded, and infirm bidding them a fond farewell, the whole army began to move off. Once they had left Barqa, they passed the time either singing fight songs and religious chants or resorting to silence and simple conversation. Thus they traveled from stage to stage, ten hours a day or more, only dismounting to pray or for a much needed rest.

For the first few days Abu Rakwa was unable to mount his camel or horse without feeling an odd sense of alarm. He kept having terrible visions, betrayals that demolished all his carefully laid plans and secrets; his entire army defeated and rent apart; his men in the thick of battle falling dead and wounded as they confronted enormous armies extending further than the eye could see. In order to ward off these discouraging visions he used to seek refuge in God; he would dismount and walk for hours, all the while chanting Qur'anic verses. Once remounted, he would chat with 'Ali ibn Jawhar about Egypt and its physical environment or else yell out to Shihab al-Din, "Is Hamad al-Madi really such a thorn in our feet?" to which Shihab al-Din would reply, "He is indeed, Imam, but—with God's might—we'll extract the thorn and chop it off."

After covering a little over half the total distance, the marching forces entered Kinana territory. There they exchanged blessings and thanks, especially when the people of the region welcomed them with greetings and jubilation instead of resistance and antipathy; rather than recalcitrance and stones they offered the visitors dates and milk. All these positive signs calmed Abu Rakwa down, and he began to feel much more upbeat. With all his misgivings and worries behind him, he started shouting to 'Ali ibn Jawhar, Shihab al-Din, and others as well, with questions such as, "Can these favorable signs be false promises? As we proceed on our way, can it all be a dream or are we actually awake? I beg you all, by God, you soldiers of charity and mercy, answer me." The entire assembly would respond that the signs were indeed true; it was indeed all real, not a dream. It was Shaykh Zaydan of the Mazati who took things even further. "Conjecture has no role in this matter," he said. "The entire basis of religious belief lies in complete certainty. Don't flay the bear till you have caught it." "How right you are, Zaydan," said Abu Rakwa by way of confirmation. "The opinion of a shaykh is worth more than the visual testimony of a young man."

About one month after the warriors had set out, their platoons reached the valleys of Alexandria. In order to avoid conflict with the city garrison, they followed Abu Rakwa's instructions to turn rapidly south toward Cairo. Some twenty miles from their goal they set up camp for the night, the aim being to get some rest and make necessary preparations. Next morning, Tuesday, they decided to divide the army into two detachments: one of them, commanded by the imam himself, would attack and occupy al-Giza; the other, commanded by Shihab al-Din, Hammu, and Yahya, would smash al-Hakim's army in al-Fayyum. The two detachments would then reassemble at the Pyramids before entering Cairo itself. "This way," Abu Rakwa explained, "we'll be able to weaken the enemy's vanguard and rear first and then confront him in his own back yard." That then was how things were decided, accompanied by praises to God and promises to meet up and move on to victory. The men in each detachment proceeded confidently toward their target, each one prepared to sacrifice himself for the cause.

The sun had hardly set on that renowned Tuesday before Abu Rakwa's army reassembled, as prearranged, at the Pyramids. News of victory spread among the warriors. The imam asked for information about the number of dead and wounded. "A hundred and thirty martyrs," Shihab al-Din replied, "and sixty wounded. Those are our losses in men, a mere fifth of the enemy's losses." "However," Hammu continued, "one of those who fell was Yahya, may God have mercy on his pure soul." Abu Rakwa gave thanks to God and called for mercy on the souls of the martyrs. He then asked about the new contingents that had joined the army.

"Great Imam," 'Ali ibn Jawhar informed him, "the Maghribi and Sicilian soldiers that my father promised you began the battle pretending to fight against your fighters, but they soon joined them and turned their swords on the enemy instead. They played a major role in these initial victories of ours. I am now serving as their commander under your orders, all on behalf of my father who is currently hiding in some unknown place within the gates of Cairo."

By now Abu Rakwa had received information from his aides that it would be impossible to storm Cairo because of the height of the walls and the fact that the gates were closed.

"We will never forget the role the Maghribis and Sicilians have played," he said. "As you can see, we have defeated al-Hakim's army under the command of 'Ali ibn Fallah. However, the battle is not yet won. We still have to capture Cairo where the root of the problem lies. What do you all think?"

"Great imam," said Shihab al-Din with Hammu's support, "I think we have to subject Cairo to a terrible siege so as to force al-Hakim and his army either to come out and fight us or else raise the flag of surrender."

"I think he's right," Hammu went on. "We don't have the means to scale or breach the walls of this impregnable city, and we certainly don't want to expose the inhabitants to a communal slaughter with the direst possible consequences."

Abu Rakwa looked somewhat distraught. "And what about you, Shaykh Zaydan?" he asked. "Why aren't you giving us your opinion? Tell us what we should do."

Zaydan hesitated for a moment. "Great imam," he said with a frown, "the best decision is whatever everyone agrees on, and that needs to be based on good information. Neither I myself nor, I suspect, you know very much about what the enemy is planning. Since that's the case, how am I supposed to make a decision and pretend that it's based on some kind of sound reasoning? 'Ali ibn Jawhar, you know more than anyone else about this terrain. Supposing we maintained the siege and there were no fights or squabbles amongst us, how long could the city of Cairo hold out against us?"

'Ali ibn Jawhar responded immediately, as though he had had the reply ready for some time. "To be quite blunt," he said, "I don't believe besieging Cairo will work to our advantage. Al-Hakim is protected by loyal servants and has nothing to fear from his unarmed and debilitated populace. His coffers and granaries hold enough food and goods to last for a few years. If we conduct a prolonged siege, the primary danger for us will come from Syria. Al-Hakim is offering rewards and incentives to foreign troops, Turks, savage Bedouin, and even Byzantine mercenaries. That likelihood is confirmed by all the information that I've been getting from our trustworthy allies. We may have defeated and scattered al-Hakim's army in Upper Egypt, but they are now regrouping in the desert by al-Fayyum under the command of al-Fadl ibn Salih, and he's renowned for his strategic skills and cunning. The incredible number of reinforcements arriving daily from Syria is making this army steadily stronger. Beyond all that, we face yet another danger if we start a long siege: our own ranks will be infiltrated by informers and spies, not to mention people who will spread false rumors, discord, and dissent. That's my opinion, and God knows best of all. It is you who have the authority to decide."

'Ali ibn Jawhar had barely finished speaking before a din was heard outside. Abu Rakwa asked what was going on. Suddenly a group of men approached, surrounding a man who was dressed exactly like them. They told Abu Rakwa this man was a spy, and he had been caught red-handed. On him they had found documents and purses full of coins and gold pieces. Shihab al-Din seized the documents and purses. Abu Rakwa meanwhile told the soldiers to return to their positions, then ordered the spy to state his own name and mission, and that of the person who had sent him. For a moment the spy stood his ground, not saying a word. But then Hammu threatened him with his sword.

"I am one of Hamad al-Madi's men," the man replied. "I've been working for al-Fadl ibn Salih for some time. Al-Madi ordered me to infiltrate your army and pass on information. I've managed to do that and have recorded everything I've seen in these documents. The purses are intended to bribe your soldiers, persuade them to betray you and join al-Hakim's army in the al-Fayyum desert. That's all I can tell you about my mission. Now do with me what you will."

"So you're just like that cursed wretch, Hamad al-Madi!" said Hammu in a tone that blended malice and insult. "You're from the Banu Qurra, aren't you?"

"You're wrong," the man replied. "I'm a Syrian Bedouin. I've taken part in many wars by disguising myself and trading information. If you are interested, my name is . . ."

"We're not interested in your name," interrupted Abu Rakwa, "just tell us everything you know about al-Hakim's army. If you do, we'll spare your life. If what you tell us is useful, we'll set you free. If you can identify spies and traitors working among us, we'll give you back your purses before you leave."

"Imam, you can have all the information you and your colleagues want. Al-Fadl's army has close to ten thousand soldiers; the numbers keep increasing, as does the ordinance to back them up. The strategists have all agreed that time is on their side and they can afford to let you languish outside Cairo's gates, while you dream of launching an assault and discuss methods of mounting a siege. It's their view that every day that passes enhances their position while yours gets progressively weaker as you wait and lose hope. They're planning to send out spies to infiltrate your ranks and persuade your soldiers either to desert and join al-Hakim's army or go back the way they came. In addition to finding out as much information about your troops as possible, I was also commissioned to look for men who would be prepared to kill you, Abu Rakwa, for a substantial reward. There may well be people like me and other traitors in your midst, but I have absolutely no information about them. I am not so malicious that I would betray innocent people for my own benefit."

Abu Rakwa took two purses back from Shihab al-Din and tossed them to the spy.

"Untie this man's hands," he told some soldiers, "give him a horse and some provisions, and let him go back whence he came. As for you, spy, go back and tell your masters that we remain steadfast. It is our intention to besiege Cairo till we win it or die in the process."

Abu Rakwa's aides looked astonished and perplexed, all except Zaydan. "Bravo, Imam!" he whispered to Abu Rakwa as soon as the spy had left. "War is all treachery. That spy seemed happy enough with what he got. He'll be able to convince his masters that we plan to stay here, exactly in accordance with their own assumptions and calculations. But now, friends, our own path is clear, and the plan is in place. The spy for al-Hakim's generals has managed to provide us with the information that was missing from 'Ali ibn Jawhar's report. Do you all agree that we should leave al-Giza and take out troops early tomorrow to the al-Fayyum desert? Once there, we'll be able to surprise the enemy and clip their wings before they have a chance to bolster their numbers any further."

"Victorious imam," the aides responded in unison, "that is clearly the best plan."

"So then, let us all put our trust in God. Take a brief rest, then prepare for tomorrow."

Tents were erected, and some of the fighters who were either exhausted or wounded made use of them. Many soldiers in the field took brief catnaps, with local men from the Kutamis keeping a rotating watch. Abu Rakwa himself sat down on a palm-trunk, having expended a lot of his own energy in persuading his companions to leave him alone and get some rest.

The imam was well aware that on a night such as this he would not be able to sleep; the situation was critical, and there was no lack of things to keep him awake. In difficult times such as these all he could do was suppress all noxious thoughts by reciting Qur'anic verses or contemplating the stars in the heavens. Once in a while he would close his eyes, not so much to try the impossible by getting some sleep, but rather to search his memory for a previous episode of chronic insomnia. However, he could not recall one, and that made him realize why, from now on, he would never be without a dagger or sword in his hand. "Here I am then," he muttered several times in a bitter tone, "gradually becoming even more scared of revolution than I used to be of getting rich. I can smell the presence of traitors in our midst, yet I can't trace a single one of them! Like any caliph and amir, Abu Rakwa is falling prey to delusions, doubts, and panic. He realizes that safety valves can explode at any moment when exposed to the combined pressures of the unknown and critical situations." The imam found himself obsessed by these thoughts one after the other, and each one was worse than its predecessor. He decided to squelch them all by standing up and pacing around the area. He kept chiding himself for nursing such melancholy ideas and cursing the evil in his soul. For a while he managed to maintain this frame of mind, but then he started yelling out loud, "Ye people! Wake up, soldiers of God! Prayer is better than sleep; rise up to salvation! Rise up to fight for a cause where there is no slumber! Men, rise up to salvation!"

The imam's shouts woke up all the soldiers and animals. His aides tried to calm him down, but he rounded on them. "Weren't you the ones," he yelled, "who wanted to move quickly to the decisive battle? By God, sleep interrupted by worries and anxieties is useless. After today our only rest will come with victory. Order our fighters to muster and prepare their riding animals. God willing, we will head for the field of battle immediately after the dawn prayer."

The imam's aides did not dare challenge his call for a swift departure. With heads bowed they ranged themselves behind him like all the other soldiers and performed the dawn prayer with dispatch. As they prepared to move off toward the al-Fayyum desert, an amazing aura of silence descended on the troops, only broken by the padding of feet and muted voices. As they advanced, Abu Rakwa forced himself to lighten his expression so as to encourage his troops. He made a big effort to squeeze shoulders and smile encouragingly at everyone.

The forces were now just a few miles short of the battlefield. Abu Rakwa ordered a brief halt so they could snatch a brief rest and recover their strength. Shihab al-Din made use of this lull to take the imam aside. He reluctantly informed the imam that some soldiers had already deserted to the enemy camp. Before he had even finished relaying this information, Hammu came rushing up.

"Seventy deserters, Imam," he said. "I've confirmed those numbers, and I know each one of them by name."

Abu Rakwa rubbed his hands together. "So those purses have done their job with weak-willed hypocrites!" he sighed. *"A little enjoyment, and then they will face a dire punishment."*

"They are all from the Banu Qurra," said Hammu, continuing his detail. "Seventy hypocrites, God shame them!"

These insulting words made Shihab al-Din very angry. "That's isn't totally accurate," he argued. "For sure, some of those deserters include people tempted by Satan himself; they're the minority. As for the rest,

I've dispatched them myself to infiltrate enemy ranks and get information. They'll try to influence our brothers and fellow Arabs in al-Hakim's
army. Only people from our tribe could be entrusted with such a task.
The Zanatis certainly could not do it . . ."

At this point Abu Rakwa interrupted. By now Shaykh Zaydan and
'Ali ibn Jawhar had joined the group.

"A pox on all your squabbles and arguments! Is this a time for rows
and insults, or for pulling together in the common cause? Every fighter
should realize that faith is on our side and money is on theirs. We'll see
which one is more marketable. Should we win, it will be the fulfillment
of our desires. If we perish, then we are God's and to Him do we return."

"You have spoken the truth, Imam," said Shaykh Zaydan. "At times
such as these, people who try to proceed in the midst of discord and
doubt come to a gruesome end. We must move boldly forward, relying
on our swords and steadfast will and on Him who alone possesses the
might and majesty. Now 'Ali ibn Jawhar has some good news for us."

"Great imam," said 'Ali ibn Jawhar, his voice wavering between happiness and caution, "some of our informants who managed to infiltrate the
enemy camp have now returned. They've told us that the enemy knows a
good deal about our numbers and equipment. The leaders of the Arab
troops who are currently fighting for al-Hakim have promised to join our
forces at the decisive moment in the battle. Now all we need to worry
about is Hamad al-Madi's spies and the unforeseen tricks and stratagems
that al-Fadl ibn Salih, the enemy commander, has up his sleeve."

Abu Rakwa remounted his horse and drew his sword. "*They schemed
and God schemed, and God is the best of schemers.* Mount your horses
and arrange the army in platoons so they can attack in waves. Then we
can restrict the terrain that the enemy can use; they can either fight the
big battle or surrender. Tell the Arab leaders to come to us tonight so we
can shake hands and promise them Syria as their own land in return for
reinforcing our numbers and granting victory to the cause of truth. Now,
follow my lead as we achieve what God has promised to those who fight
in His path."

With that, Abu Rakwa's army advanced in tight formation and covered the ground between them and al-Fadl's camp in short order. They ranged all over the battlefield; the glint of their swords had a debilitating effect on the enemy troops. Once in a while Abu Rakwa penetrated the enemy ranks, engaged with the enemy's best fighters and killed them, then returned to a safe place where he would consult with his aides and hear their reports. The third day of Dhu al-Hijja was barely over before victory was tilting in favor of Abu Rakwa's forces. However the exultation that Abu Rakwa and his companions felt was tempered by a sense of alarm whenever they heard about the mercenary soldiers al-Hakim had employed to bolster and rescue his army. It was obvious that they badly needed the Arab forces to keep their promise by joining Abu Rakwa's forces without delay.

"On the appointed night, al-Fadl summoned the Arab leaders to break their fast with him. He made it clear that he had been fasting himself and forced them to wait a while. Then he had the food brought in, and they all ate and talked. Al-Fadl had sent a battalion toward Abu Rakwa's forces, and the two groups had fought. News of this reached the camp. The Arab leaders were all anxious to get back to their troops, but al-Fadl prevented them. Instead he sent word to their Arab colleagues that they should mount and go into battle; these latter had no idea of the pact that the Arab chiefs had already reached with Abu Rakwa. So they went into battle. . . . Al-Hakim sent an open letter to al-Fadl, stating that Abu Rakwa had been defeated, and another secret one with details of what the actual situation was. Al-Fadl now made a big show of delight at the defeat of Abu Rakwa, in order to calm people down.

"Meanwhile Abu Rakwa had headed for a heavily wooded area known as "the bog," with al-Fadl in pursuit. Abu Rakwa hid among the trees and proceeded to attack al-Fadl's troops. Abu Rakwa's army now started pulling back so as to entice al-Fadl's soldiers toward the ambush. However, when the troops in the wood saw their colleagues retreating, they assumed they had been defeated and joined them in their retreat. They were mowed down by al-Fadl's soldiers, and many thousands were killed."[15]

The marshy woods were strewn with the corpses and wounded of both armies, and warm blood nourished the soil. The rest of Abu Rakwa's army was now confronted with a significant obstacle, one that required the conflict to be shifted into more open space. The fighting raged on with no relief, but eventually Abu Rakwa managed to break out and ordered his companions to withdraw with him. Some of them managed to do so, but others were either killed or taken prisoner during the ambush.

Abu Rakwa and his followers sped southward toward Nubian territory. There they stopped for a while to regroup, take stock of what had happened, and decide what needed to be done next, but everyone was so completely exhausted that they could not think clearly or talk for any length of time. Just before sunset on the last of these grimmest of days, Abu Rakwa was still staring at the faces of about a hundred of his surviving followers. He looked for any signs of hatred or anger, but found none. To the contrary, all of them quietly and firmly advised him to return with them to Barqa. Once there, they could regroup and prepare for a new war against al-Hakim the Fatimid caliph. He listened to their advice with a smile.

"Heaven forbid, beloved friends," he said, "that I should return to Barqa defeated! The forthcoming campaign against Fatimid tyranny is entrusted to your hands. Choose another imam from among you who can take from me whatever is useful and benefit from the mistakes I have made."

As night fell, Abu Rakwa asked for pen and paper and started writing his last will and testament. It was as though he were saying farewell to the world and human beings and expediting the final episode in his rich and full life. Hardly had he penned the final word before Hammu and Shihab al-Din rode up, exhausted and out of breath. They dismounted and embraced Abu Rakwa, who hugged them back and praised God for their survival. Abu Rakwa mentioned the names of Shaykh Zaydan, 'Ali ibn Jawhar, and others as well.

"All of them have either fallen as martyrs," Hammu interrupted, "or else been taken prisoner by the enemy. But now, Imam, we must return to Barqa. We have to move quickly before al-Fadl's troops catch us unawares. There's no need for us to die that way."

From a bag he was carrying Shihab al-Din now produced a severed head covered in blood. "Here, Imam," he said, " is the head of Hamad al-Madi, that accursed traitor. I cut it off with my own sword. We can display it round Barqa and its environs as an example to all renegades and dissemblers. I think it best for you and all of us to return to Barqa as quickly as possible. Once there we can assess our situation and make preparations for another battle against al-Hakim the Fatimid. What do you think, Abu Rakwa?"

The soldiers were all lined up, ready to leave. Deep in his heart Abu Rakwa realized that, by going with them, he would inevitably be causing their deaths, all as part of a losing battle against the forces who were rushing to take him prisoner. Even so, he managed to put on an optimistic air.

"Dear friends," he said with a confident smile, "now it's up to all of you to continue this campaign, an unending fight for the cause of truth. Return to the people of Barqa and convey to them my greetings and love. Pledge them to victory with or without me. That in all its brevity is my testament to you. Let it be read out to the young people in Barqa, and let them interpret its message as a victory for truth and justice. It will serve as a token of loyalty between you and me, and between me and them. It's the foundation stone, so use it to erect an edifice of those very values and principles that have brought us all together. Take it with you, and may safety be your companion! For my part I will now seek refuge with the king of Nubia till the crisis is past and the shock of it all diminishes somewhat. The king is a merciful and decent man who honors guests and respects the requests of all those who seek protection and safety in his domains. I ask God to protect you from all evil; He—may He be exalted— is hearer and answerer."

With that Abu Rakwa embraced Shihab al-Din and Hammu; they all exchanged hugs and kisses. The two men were so totally overwhelmed with emotion that they were unable to speak. Abu Rakwa then embraced every single soldier. That done, he mounted his horse and set off for Nubia. When he had disappeared from sight, his surviving companions mounted their horses and headed speedily toward Barqa.

As Abu Rakwa was making his way toward his destination, he managed to overcome his exhaustion and detach himself from his bodily needs. A faint echo was all he heard of his own heartbeats and the clopping of his horse's hooves. With reddened eyes he stared at the brilliant colors on the horizon and communicated his yearning for a swift arrival. When he reached the borders of Nubia, he was welcomed by the crown prince who greeted him with great honor and invited him to stay till the end of Dhu al-Hijja. After that he hid Abu Rakwa in the Abu Shanuda monastery where he spent the first two months of the new year fighting off his sense of loneliness and despair with sleep, prayer, and fasting. At the beginning of Rabi' al-Awwal his host came to see him.

"Honorable guest," he said in an emotional, yet humble tone, "my father passed away at dawn today. He has left me a throne under threat, since I cannot risk a war against al-Hakim the Fatimid. Messengers from al-Fadl are at the gate of the palace demanding that I hand you over. They swear that their lord is only interested in your safety and in helping you get back to your homeland safe and sound. Honorable sir, tell me what you wish to do."

The new king had hardly finished talking before Abu Rakwa was preparing to surrender himself to the party that had come for him. "*The imminent is imminent. Only God can disclose it,*" he intoned before going out to them. "*Every soul tastes death. You will receive your rewards on the Day of Resurrection.* God have mercy on your father, young man, and give you the benefit of his memory and good works. Now I go to meet those who have neither faith nor morality. My best wishes to you. Farewell!"

As Abu Rakwa made his way out of the main gate of the castle, his face was radiant and uplifted. He mounted his finest horse and gave al-Fadl's avenging angels a look of mercy and forgiveness. Once he was level with them, he took off at a gallop with them following in sheepish silence. In such a fashion they reached al-Fadl's headquarters in an oasis shaded by lofty palm trees. Al-Fadl's soldiers greeted him with deference and took him to their commander's tent which was opulently furnished and carpeted with expensive rugs. Al-Fadl accorded him an elaborate welcome at the entrance, then sat him down on a plush sofa. Upon the clap of his hands servants appeared with plates of dates and cups of milk. He invited his guest to take his fill.

"We welcome you among us, noble shaykh," al-Fadl said. "From today you're our guest. You have but to ask for something, and we'll grant your wish."

Abu Rakwa gave al-Fadl a dubious look, followed by a sardonic smile. "So, Fadl," he asked, "what's the meaning of this lavish welcome? I'll take some of your nice food since I'm quite sure you haven't put any poison in it."

"How could I do that when your life is worth more to me than anything?"

"It'll be better for you to sell me to your master alive," said Abu Rakwa, his mouth stuffed with dates, "than to throw my corpse at his feet. You're even more worried about me than I am. You're afraid I might take away al-Hakim's privilege by taking my own life. But you can relax! Rest assured that I have no intention of wresting my own allotted time from Him who has all lives and times in His hands. Tell me what kudos and benefit you'll get when you hand me over to your master as he so desires."

"I beseech you, by God, revered imam," replied al-Fadl, "do not think ill of me nor of my master, al-Hakim bi-Amr Illah. You may have hated the Commander of the Faithful, but perhaps he will come to love you. While you have shunned him, he may still decide to befriend you; even though you've waged war against him, he may still bestow his bounty on you."

"If indeed your master is willing to treat me kindly even though I have done him ill, then he may also do you harm even though you have given him the great boon of victory."

"What do you mean, Imam?" asked al-Fadl in alarm.

"I'll answer you when you've told me how much money al-Hakim has spent on mercenaries in order to defeat me."

"He's spent everything. He's exhausted the state treasury, then emptied his own coffers and those of his family and retinue—untold quantities of money, gold, silver, and jewels. But how could he do otherwise, Abu

Rakwa, when you came within an ace of destroying his throne? You forced him to make a dire bet, something he had never experienced before: either behave like a ruler or perish. When you confronted him with images of imminent perdition, he was forced to hire mercenaries from east and west, Arabs, Slavs, Sudanese, Byzantines, Turks, and others. He had to lavish presents and gifts on them and provide enough to satisfy the most voracious appetites. This unstemmed flow of expenditures would all have been in vain if your army had not entered that marshy terrain and become enmired in its bogs and impenetrable forests. Today you might well utter a curse on money and ambushes alike!"

"A curse on the enormous sums you spent on agents and mercenaries of every conceivable color! A curse on soldiers whose only religion is greed and gain and whose life consists of one long contravention of God's laws! What you have just told me, Fadl, responds to the question you asked me earlier."

"Explain what you mean, Abu Rakwa."

"There's no particular divination or prophecy involved. I am simply deducing from what we both know about your master that he won't give you the chance to celebrate and boast about your victory over me. He'll spare no effort to insure that you do not gain any prominence at his expense, especially since he believes that credit for the victory doesn't belong to you but rather to all the money and gifts he had to lavish on troops. That's the way all cursed tyrants behave."

"Once you have been disposed of, death may well await me too. But what's the point of accepting your prediction when I'm surrounded by al-Hakim's most loyal slave soldiers whose never sleeping eyes watch me night and day?"

"Then let us go where God wills. He alone has the power and the might. He is sufficient for us, and good is the Trustee!"

Al-Fadl stood up in response to Abu Rakwa's invitation and ordered the formation of an escort to return to Cairo. The order was carried out, and the journey started. The pace was slow, since al-Fadl wanted to show off his prisoner in both cities and countryside and to vaunt his own pride and self-importance. After some three months of travel the procession neared Cairo, with al-Fadl at the head on his horse, Abu Rakwa behind on his camel, and slaves bringing up the rear with shouts and threats.

On that unique day in the middle of Jumada al-Akhira A.H. 397 Abu Rakwa rode into the city of Cairo. As he made his way through the streets, his eyes could not take in the full horror of what he was witnessing: thousands of heads in every alley and square; an endless succession of prisoners being killed after being subjected to "all sorts of torture at the hands of the populace who clubbed their necks, tore out their beards, and beat them so hard that many of them had fractured shoulder blades. The whole thing was dreadful to behold."[16]

Abu Rakwa leaned over to talk to al-Fadl. "So, al-Fadl," he yelled in a coarse voice tinged with fury, "is this the way your master treats Maghribi prisoners? I tell you, sooner or later, through God's great power, the end of this ill-starred regime of al-Hakim will come about at their hands!"

"This is the way," yelled al-Fadl at the top of his voice, "that my master is punishing your followers for the outrages they have committed. They are to serve as a warning to all deviants and pretenders."

With that he took an enormous swipe at Abu Rakwa that knocked him off his camel and broke his nose. He ordered slaves to grab him, clap him in irons, and put him in the line of people to be tortured.

While they were carrying out his orders, Abu Rakwa managed to surprise al-Fadl by spitting in his face.

"You've changed your spots, you son of a bitch!" he roared defiantly. "By God, you'll be killed too, and by the very person you're trying to serve by killing me. Both of you have set up a legal system based on murder and destruction. You will inevitably get everything you deserve, just as God has promised."

The columns of prisoners awaiting execution passed by one after another. Abu Rakwa, dispirited and utterly exhausted, his face splattered with his own blood, joined one of them. In his moments of consciousness, he managed to recognize many of his followers and tried to touch and talk

to them, but he was pushed away in a hail of blows and cuffs. He happened
to spot Shaykh Zaydan stumbling along behind him, with blood pouring
from his head and soiling his ample beard. When Abu Rakwa realized
the shaykh was now blind, he yelled out to him.

"Are we to be blamed, Shaykh Zaydan, because we decided to wage
war against evil? What we didn't realize was that the forces of evil are
more powerful than we imagined!"

"No, no, Abu Rakwa," replied Shaykh Zaydan with all the voice he
could muster, "we will earn a handsome reward; the boons we will
receive last longer. It's merely our earthly bodies that these enemies of
God's truth are subjecting to ruin. Our souls will wing their way to the
paradise of God Almighty."

"To the Pious One we go on the Day of Resurrection," chanted Abu
Rakwa. "It is with God that all grievances are gathered."

"If I die a believing Muslim, I don't care," chanted Shaykh Zaydan in
response. "From any side my death was for God."

Shaykh Zaydan was hit so hard that he fell to the ground. He let out
a groan. Abu Rakwa paused to berate the slaves. "You sons of bitches,"
he yelled, "how dare you hit this revered shaykh? You can see he's old
and infirm. A pox on you and your master!" With that he was subjected
to a hail of blows that cracked his shoulder bone. When al-Fadl realized
what was happening, he told the slaves to keep Abu Rakwa alive till they
could exhibit him to al-Hakim the Fatimid close by his palace in Cairo.
Even though Abu Rakwa had been subjected to such punishment, he still
managed to grab opportunities to talk to the people of Cairo who clustered
around in places. As al-Maqrizi describes, "He would ask the people he
met what their name was, then recite the Qur'an and call down God's
mercy on his forebears."[17]

By midday all the devices of terror and defamation were in place for
Abu Rakwa and the heads of his companions to be paraded in front of al-
Hakim the Fatimid's balcony.

"Cairo had been completely decked out for the occasion. There was an
old man named al-Abzari who, whenever a renegade was brought out, used

to make a clown's cap for him and decorate it with colored tassels. He had a monkey that he had trained to take a whip and scourge the renegade from behind. For that he would be given a hundred dinars and ten pieces of velvet. As soon as Abu Rakwa had passed through al-Giza, al-Hakim ordered him to be brought in. Abu Rakwa was put on a two-humped camel, and al-Abrazi put the clown's hat on him and then rode the camel behind him. Surrounded by soldiers and preceded by fifteen decorated elephants, the procession set off with al-Abrazi's monkey whipping Abu Rakwa from behind. This is how Abu Rakwa entered Cairo, preceded by the heads of his companions impaled on stakes and poles. Al-Hakim was seated on his balcony by the Gate of Gold, while Abu Rakwa was surrounded by Turkish and Daylami mercenaries riding caparisoned horses and fully armed. It was a memorable day. . . ."[18]

During this amazing spectacle, al-Fadl stayed close to Abu Rakwa, thinking all the while about the dire prediction that the latter had given him earlier, something that made him feel extremely depressed. Then he got the idea of secretly killing the imam before he ever reached the presence of al-Hakim, as the latter had demanded that he do. If the two of them engaged in a debate, he reasoned, there might well be some surprises; previous understandings might well be cancelled. He kept chewing the whole thing over, then reached a decision. "It's better for me to kill Abu Rakwa now," he told himself. "I must kill him before he reaches al-Hakim's threshold." With that he ordered one of his retinue to deliver the fatal blow, and the command was carried out. He grabbed the perpetrator and killed him too. When Abu Rakwa was carried to the palace, he had already breathed his last. Al-Hakim was furious and asked al-Fadl what had happened. The commander informed him that a young soldier had treacherously murdered Abu Rakwa; the culprit had already been caught and killed.

"I had promised myself," said al-Hakim with a sigh, "that I would first argue with him, then kill him. One of the two is now impossible, but the second is that much easier. Come close, al-Fadl, and give me your dagger."

"But he's already dead, my Lord. There's no point in killing him again."

Without uttering a word al-Hakim took al-Fadl's dagger, leaned over Abu Rakwa's body, and slit his throat so that blood oozed out. Standing up again, he wiped his hands on al-Fadl's uniform, and gave him back his dagger. "Your weapon is blunt, al-Fadl," he said. "Don't rely on it in a crisis. Either get it sharpened, or else get another one." With that, al-Hakim departed, intoning as he did so, "Let this be a lesson for all worthless imposters and opportunists. *When they angered us, we took revenge on them*; *Verily humanity oversteps its reach by thinking itself sufficient.*—my Lord, He who has designated me his agent among mankind, has spoken the truth." Before leaving, he issued orders to the slaves. "Take the rebel's body," he said, "and hang it from the ear of the Sphinx, so the changing seasons can turn it into chaff to be blown away by the winds."

Al-Fadl remained riveted to the spot, silent and morose like a statue. Then he collapsed. "O Abu Rakwa," he muttered, "how right your prediction was." With that his slaves carried him to his home, where, as historians all agree, "he fell ill. Al-Hakim visited him two or three times and gave him many estates. He recovered, but a few days later al-Hakim had him arrested and gruesomely murdered."[19]

Just a few hours after Abu Rakwa's death the news reached Barqa. A week's mourning was decreed. Everyone, men and women, young and old, was in a state of alert. They all gathered in mosques and public squares to pray for the souls of their martyrs, and listened in humble contemplation as the contents of their imam's will were read and interpreted by Shihab al-Din and Hammu.

"At the very moment," it said, "when I set myself to speak in praise of God for all his benefits and trials, then the world collapses in my eyes and I prostrate myself. My children from Barqa and all oppressed lands, I shall rise again and tell you the truth, your sole heritage from me.

"You dear folk, apple of my eye! If you witness the violence of tyranny in your time and wander through the gloomy hollows of darkness, if you see people in oppressed territories being transferred from one prison to another and the poor and rebellious being murdered, do not despair. You are the promise, so you cannot give up! Never will you trammel yourselves on the paths of despair and surrender, nor amid the legions of mayhem and tyranny.

"Go forth into the world and flourish among the weak and hungry. It is among such folk that sorrow grows in heart and body, and anger along with them. They are family and support, your primary cause in this world and the next.

"Dear children of mine, I am not the last martyr. Take my place, and make my life a part of your own. Turn your lives into a weapon with which to confront the enemies of love and knowledge. Never submit or throw down your arms. Keep yourselves forever alert and ready for action. Resist, and victory will be yours; resist and resist again with all your might. Should you lose the battle and should chance betray you, you are still the source of inspiration and wonder. You will be the leaders for campaigns yet to come. For your offspring and those of the poor, certain victory is guaranteed. Peace be upon them and you!"

chapter four
signs of refutation and merciful rain

1. Between Humor and Revenge: Cairo Burns

[Al-Hakim] summoned commanders and sergeants. He ordered them to proceed to old Cairo [Fustat] and set it on fire. Anyone they captured was to be killed. . . . The fighting between slaves and populace lasted for three whole days. Each day al-Hakim used to ride out to the Muqattam Hills, climb the mountain, and look down. From there he could watch the fire and listen to the noise. When he asked about it, he would be told that the slaves were burning and sacking old Cairo. A pained expression would show on his face. "God curse them!" he would say. "Who told them to do that?"

IbnTaghribirdi,
Bright Stars Concerning the Rulers of Egypt and Cairo

In the final months of al-Hakim's life, his mental breakdowns kept recurring. That forced him to stay within the confines of his own private domain of solitude and depression. "It's not a throne I'm sitting on," he kept saying to himself, "but rather a volcano, one that keeps spewing hatred, resentment, and anger."

During this same period the people's own volcano was itself spewing out manifestos and pamphlets of wide variety, all of which ridiculed al-Hakim and cast aspersions on his origins, lineage, and deeds. He used to spend long nights either in the Muqattam Hills or perched in the minaret of his mosque, perusing them over and over again. The ones with the biggest impact on his frayed nerves were those that had been widely copied and distributed, petitions that had already been forwarded either to him or to his father, al-'Aziz, before him. He focused on two of them in particular, confronting their scandalous contents with feverish eyes and stricken heart. The first was a placard that had once been placed right in front of al-'Aziz when he mounted the pulpit in a mosque:

> To tyranny and oppression we are inured,
> but not to heresy and stupidity.
> If you are so gifted with knowledge of the unseen,
> pray tell us who wrote this placard.

The second was the famous decree that the 'Abbasid caliph, al-Qadir, had issued, signed by a number of judges and religious leaders, including some well-known Shi'ites. It cast aspersions on the lineage and doctrine of the Fatimid caliphs. Its key section has this to say:

> They trace their descent back to Daysan ibn Sa'id al-Khuram. They are all colleagues of heretics and sperm of devils. Their doctrine is one whereby they seek access to God, believing themselves to be following God's injunction to the *ulama'*, namely to serve as a conduit to people at large. They all believe the current ruler in Egypt, Mansur ibn Nizar (known by the name al-Hakim—may God subject him to perdition, disgrace, and exemplary punishment!), to be the son of Mu'add ibn Isma'il ibn 'Abd al-Rahman ibn Sa'id—may God grant him no aid!—who, when he came to Tunis was called 'Ubaydallah and took the title al-Mahdi. He and his vile forebears—God's curse on him and them!— are pseudo-Kharijis; they have no claims to descent from the line of 'Ali ibn Abi Talib. The claim is totally false. They do not even realize that the true descendants of 'Ali

have always maintained that those Kharijis are all imposters. While the Fatimid pretenders were still in Tunis, this information was already so widely acknowledged in Mecca and Medina that no one could have been taken in by their lies. The current ruler of Egypt and his forebears are infidels, fornicators, liars, and heretics. They believe in the dualist doctrine of the Zoroastrians; they have abrogated legal penalties and legitimized prostitution; they have shed blood and cursed prophets; they have insulted forebears and claimed divine attributes. Written in Rabi' al-Akhir 402. This text is signed by a number of people.[20]

These texts, with their widely variant length and level of vitriol, had a dire effect on al-Hakim's entire mental state; they triggered a sordid retrospective beset by the foulest of memories and a sense of sheer panic. A savage whirlwind took control and dragged him inexorably down to self-destruction. While he was in such a frame of mind, his memory would take him back to a period a quarter of a century earlier when Egyptian humor at his expense had reached some sort of zenith. During a tour of Fustat, people had rigged up a female mummy in his path and covered it with a shawl and veil; in her outstretched hand they put a sealed letter which looked just like a petition requesting redress for some wrongdoing done to her. When al-Hakim took the letter and read it, he almost fell off his donkey, so foul was the abuse directed at him—disgusting language of a kind he had never heard in his life before. He was furious and ordered the woman to be tortured, then burned alive. They told him that she was actually a statue made out of strips of paper. That made him even angrier, but he decided to bide his time before taking revenge on the people of old Cairo for the way they had insulted and poked fun at him.

Had that long awaited opportunity finally come today, I wonder? By now, Egyptians were using houses and rooftops to send each other thousands of letters every day. They filled walls and gateways with slogans and placards, all of them trying to outdo each other in vituperative eloquence as they reviled al-Hakim's name.

The people in old Cairo dubbed their campaign against al-Hakim's tyranny "resistance by sarcasm"; their revolt was called the "papers revolt." These two tags were widely used; young and old adopted them as a means of expressing their desire for freedom and confrontation.

Al-Hakim found himself at a total loss in confronting this ever widening uprising and the efficiency of its publicity machine. He started blaming his own assistants and started describing his cohorts of young officials as transvestites and tarts' offspring. He got the idea of wreaking dire punishment on some of them as a kind of object lesson to others. The first of them to get this kind of treatment was Lu'lu', the police commander. One notable morning, al-Hakim summoned him to his presence and proceeded to lambast him in the foulest terms.

"Lu'lu', you pearl of disaster and foul stench," he said, "there you were a slave in irons, and I set you free. You were clanking around in chains, but I freed you and gave you high position. Now you repay me by being utterly incapable of curbing the populace's rowdiness or quashing the sources of these verbal assaults on holy and sacred institutions. So, just before I kill you, tell me: what are your last words—God shame you?"

In spite of his enormous frame Lu'lu' looked like a naughty child, quivering with fear. "My lord," he stuttered, "I ask your protection. Give me a day or two, and I'll bring you the rebellion's leaders and those responsible for distributing the leaflets."

"You've already brought me many severed heads," replied al-Hakim, "but the majority of them were obviously women and children. They have no role in such things."

"But, my Lord, it is precisely women and children who are the source of the entire problem!"

"But you've selected half of them from families that have sworn allegiance to me and are secretly committed to my cause."

"When rebellion is rife, my lord, it is hard to make distinctions. It's almost impossible to avoid implicating innocent people."

"No, no, you piece of black mush, you're more stupid than a blind woodcutter, more impotent than a barren palm tree. Get out of here. You've got just two days to come back with something better than a donkey's horns!"

A day went by, then another two. Finally Lu'lu' appeared again before al-Hakim and was forced to kiss the ground. Then he stood up and started laughing.

"By God, my lord," he said, "it's a losing battle! No sooner do you grab one leader than he's replaced by others. You can destroy tons of leaflets and placards, but they're replaced by double that and more. This kind of struggle is unprecedented. You strike with the sword, and it's as though you're hitting water; you raise the level of violence, and all you get back is scoffs and sarcasm. So here's my neck for the executioners to trim. Now with complete conviction I can simply repeat exactly what it is that placards and mouths keep saying: Death is so common that it's laughable; so let some of us die so that tyranny can be brought to an end."

"Cut out his tongue first," yelled al-Hakim, "then tear him limb from limb. Watch and take note!"

With that he rushed off to the Muqattam Hills, followed by two guards and a young chamber-boy. He had hardly reached his favorite spot before telling the guards to convey orders to his slaves that they were to wash Lu'lu''s body and bury him with full honors in the cemetery. "Now," he told the boy, "show me your moon." With that the boy stripped and bowed down before his master who spat in his anus and then left him there, sitting on a rock.

Al-Hakim started pacing up and down inside his residence. He was tormented by grim thoughts that crowded his vision with vivid tableaux filled with unending disaster and concentrated misery. Time itself seemed to have slowed down, as though enmired in an enormous slimy bog. Al-Hakim passed the time by making authoritative gestures or begging for evening to come in anticipation of nightfall. Such was his impatience that he used to go to a nearby outcrop of rock that was covered with fig trees and wild plants.

"You people of Egypt," he yelled, "so renowned for your tambourines and oily beans, I tell you all, by Him who entrusted me with dominion: I will never deal with you as weakly as that eunuch Lu'lu'. Today you can insult my dignity and high standing, but you'll eventually come to appreciate my lineage at the point of a sword and my nobility in the expanse of my treasures. Your only means of escape will come when you remind yourselves that my great ancestor, heir of the Prophet, lives among the clouds where his voice is thunder and his whip lightning."

Al-Hakim now yelled to the young boy to go and bring his historian, Mukhtar al-Misbahi. Within the hour the historian was standing on the outcrop waiting for al-Hakim to recover his consciousness. To avoid the tedium of waiting he recorded a document that included as much as he could understand of al-Hakim's ruminations as he sat there on the ground:

By my right to incandescence and whirlwind
I who am repressed have need of fires.
By the right of the dragon that sheds its skin and crawls
I shall leave to oblivion and rubbish heaps
My soul's mournful state
And kindle fire against humor and rebellion.

When the historian could no long follow what al-Hakim was saying, he cleared his throat, then stood in front of al-Hakim and kissed the ground.

"Your august majesty summoned me," he said, "so here I am answering the call. My paper is open and ready for whatever subtle, glorious words and clear, solid proofs you wish to have faithfully recorded.

"So recite to me, my lord, whatever you wish, and I will use it to ennoble the wheel of time and polish the memory of future generations."

Al-Hakim now got to his feet and moved toward the historian. He made him stand where he was while he snatched the papers and tore them up, then spoke to him, "Fear God, Mukhtar," he said in a melancholy tone. "Bow down to Him alone, not to the one you mention. Desist from elaborate rhetoric; it neither helps nor cures anything. The crisis has now become so great that both history and strategy are useless."

"May God protect you from all evil, my lord, and save you from every adversity."

"Very well, Mukhtar! Pray for me as best you can. In these recalcitrant times I only meet people who want to curse and scoff at me. Look at me, my friend! See how I have aged and how the procession has passed me by. Or do you think I've been in power too long? Tell me, great sage and officer of endowments, how old am I today?"

The historian looked astonished at what he was hearing. He started counting, using his fingers. "My lord," he replied hurriedly, "today you're two months short of thirty-six, no less and no more. At such an age men are at the peak of their capacities."

"Shrewdest of documenters," al-Hakim said, "that's the way it looks on the surface. But my inner age is three times that or more. I'm the only one to feel the impact and suffer its scars. For the most part your papers will never be able to truly capture living realities or the severing of links and hearts. You will only fill your pages with froth and peels."

"You seem somewhat depressed and caustic tonight, my lord. Shall I send for your doctor and have you sit in violet oil?"

"Neither medicine nor drugs can help me today. The only thing that can alleviate my illness and lighten my mood is fire. My sorrow is too immense to be understood, too enormous to be excused!"

Al-Hakim kept repeating these last words over and over again. At nightfall he suddenly emerged from his trance. With a deep sigh he hurried to his observatory and looked through the glass. "My unlucky star hasn't risen yet," he muttered. "How crafty it is!" With that he went into his retreat-house followed by his historian. The two men sat facing each other; between them were two candles that gave off a flickering light. For a long time silence reigned as al-Hakim let thoughts and ideas rage inside him; his mind was totally preoccupied by flashes of vision. He started muttering some of these thoughts, although he seemed somewhat reluctant to reveal them to his historian. "Were I to say what possesses me and shakes my mind and being, to reveal my private conversations with my Lord and my strange passion for my sister, the sultana, to apply brilliant rhetoric and the ultimate in clarity in order to simplify my message and revelation, I would still never manage to penetrate the circles of my historian's consciousness and understanding. This historian is a phony esoteric, an opportunist who goes to enormous lengths in his servile flattery!"

Al-Misbahi sat there, humble and withdrawn. He had to make every possible effort to keep an all-enveloping panic under control while he looked for a means of escape. With a superhuman effort he managed to unlock his tongue.

"My lord," he said as he mopped his master's brow, "if my presence disturbs you or disrupts your solitude and contemplation, then should I ask your permission to leave?"

"Leave when I have the greatest possible need of history? You want to escape? It's as if you are not convinced by my guarantee of safety. Apart from you, who else is there who can inform time and future generations about me?"

"There are still a few pages I need to write with your assistance, my lord. I've already completed the fortieth volume of my history which is entitled 'Book of the History of Egypt, Its Qualities, Its Wonders, Its Rareties, Its Curiosities, and the Regions and Monuments Within It, Along With Biographies of Governors, Commanders, and Caliph Imams, Forebears of the Commander of the Faithful, Who Lived There and Elsewhere.'"

"What are these few pages, Mukhtar?"

"Something quite simple: grandees and notables whom you condemned to death. I've already had the privilege, my lord, of linking all these death sentences to the relevant legal arguments and sections of the Shari'a law. I have cited al-Hamadhani where he says, 'When water is stagnant for a long period, it turns fetid; if the surface looks calm, decay is on the move.' However, my lord, I must admit that I haven't been able to fully understand two, or rather three, instances. The first one concerns your tutor, Abu al-Tamim Sa'id ibn Sa'id al-Fariqi."

"Do you remember the way Ibn 'Ammar used to parade his bigotry in front of me? It was the same with that crafty devil, Burjuwan, with his sword and thousand pairs of silk trousers. Al-Fariqi was just like them and others too. They all conspired to dominate me and retain power for themselves. They kept annoying me, so I took revenge."

"But my lord," the historian noted, "al-Fariqi had no part of either sword or bigotry. Quite the contrary, he was simply a giver of wise counsel."

"The kind of counsel that shackled my hands and turned abstraction into drivel. In politics, advice about how things should be is utterly useless in the context of dismal daily realities. Even so, al-Fariqi wasn't executed because of the ideas that earned him his salary, but because he insisted on inflicting his overbearing presence on me. His too many words of advice and warning prevented me from doing my job, and he kept interfering in all kinds of affairs and markets that were none of his business."

"One day, my lord, I was fortunate enough to be present at one of those moments when you lost your temper with him. 'The only lessons I learn,' you roared at him, 'come from my own efforts. The past is what I create through my deeds, my seals, and my monuments; there is no other. I append it to the world's memory as a token of my survival after death.' I have recorded that dictum of yours in my history. But let me ask you, my lord, about the other al-Fariqi, Malik ibn Sa'id, the chief judge . . ."

"If that judge—God shame him!—were to rise from his grave now, I'd slay him all over again. When I put you in charge of the salary bureau, Mukhtar, you saw for yourself how he disclosed my secret correspondence and perused all the information forwarded to me."

"That's perfectly correct, my lord. However you pardoned him for that particular infraction. At your command I sent him a strongly worded letter of reprimand."

"And do you think he changed his ways? Oh no, he carried right on with his duplicity and deceit. He devised ruses of every kind and fondly imagined they would somehow escape the notice of my spies and informers. It is proven beyond any doubt that he had sex with women who came to him with complaints; in fact Satan tempted him to infiltrate my own harem. He even started flirting with my sister, Sitt al-Mulk. Before I had him executed, I asked him during his trial what was the difference between a man and woman. Mukhtar, have you an idea how that crafty rogue answered my question? "Men have a sexual organ," he replied, and then continued like someone touched by the Devil in person, "and women are one great sexual organ."

Al-Hakim leaned over and whispered these tidbits into the historian's ear, while the latter sat there begging God's forgiveness. The historian continued with his questions.

"My lord," he asked, "as long as we're on the topic of judges, can I ask you about your choice of fire as the means of getting rid of 'Abd al-'Aziz al-Nu'man, the chief judge? Wasn't executing him a sufficient form of revenge for the scandals he perpetrated?"

"Mukhtar," al-Hakim replied, "the only outrages he committed that you know about were bribery and his regular tendency to cause trouble and incite people against me. As you're well aware, he gave secret support to Abu Rakwa and all other rebels too. He was the worst of descendants of the best of forebears. My sentence of execution was totally justified, as it was for his partner and relative, 'Ali al-Husayn ibn Jawhar. I only gave orders for his body to be burnt because the wretch used to rob and harass orphans. I was merely executing God's promise, He being the best of promisers: *Those who unjustly consume the property of orphans will taste fire in their bellies and will roast in hellfire.*

"May God shed light on your deeds, my lord," said the historian. "Now there's just one more case that worries me; I can't understand the real causes. It involves the way your general, al-Fadl, was killed. Since he had succeeded in defeating Abu Rakwa's army and saving you from a potentially enormous danger, he certainly didn't fail you. . . ."

"Mukhtar," al-Hakim interrupted as he paced the room nervously, "you should not be like everyone else, content merely to scratch the surface of things. God protect you, look deeper. You will discover that al-Fadl had no real role in my defeat of Abu Rakwa. The real reason for my defeat of Abu Rakwa was the enormous amount of money that was spent from both state coffers and my own resources, money that made it possible for me to dragoon mercenaries from a variety of countries and races. Look still deeper and do some research. You'll discover that I only managed to capture the rebel by giving in exchange gifts and supplies to his protector, the king of Nubia. In total I spent more than a million gold dinars. If I hadn't resorted to such stratagems, they being the only ones I still had at my discretion, I could not have offered any opposition to Abu Rakwa's army. But for that, Mukhtar, my superficial historian, I would not be here now giving you this explanation."

"You are right, Commander of the Faithful! Please excuse my inadequate research and faulty understanding."

"My other reason for killing al-Fadl was that he murdered Abu Rakwa without my permission and thus deprived me of the opportunity to give him an affectionate welcome. All he left me was a head with nothing to say. Ah, Mukhtar! How much I'd looked forward to talking to Abu Rakwa and debating with him! I relished the possibility of exposing the confused ideas and visions inside his head. If only I'd been able to do what al-Fadl made impossible, if Abu Rakwa had debated with me about his reasons for rebelling against me! If he'd won me over, I'd have made him my heir apparent."

"Would that have been legal, my lord?"

"The law always sides with whatever is most correct and beneficial. Didn't I decide not to make my legitimate son, al-Hasan, heir and instead selected my cousin, 'Abd al-Rahim ibn Ilyas? That broke the chain of dynastic succession to the imamate and favored the upright over the twisted and the capable over the weak."

"Yes, indeed you did, my lord. That's another issue I can't understand!"

"If I'd met Abu Rakwa and found he was better than the others, I'd have shared the caliphate with him and made him my heir after my disappearance."

Mukhtar was astonished, not knowing what to do or say. "Shall I write down what you've been saying about Abu Rakwa?" he asked.

"Do whatever you like. Actually leave out what I've just said. Even if you pass it on, you may not find anyone who'll believe you. But do write this down in your history: Only the most worthy and virtuous deserve the imamate."

"What about the chapter in my history on Abu Rakwa, my lord? Shall I include the verses attributed to him that I actually asked your poet, Muhammad ibn 'Asim, to write, the ones in which he asks you for forgiveness and pardon?"

"Recite me a few lines so I can decide."

"It's a long poem, but I'll select a short extract."

> I fled, but to no avail. No fugitive on earthcan withstand
>   the one with God on his side.
> By God, flight's only cause was fear of that death I now
>   savor.
> My entire body led me to you as a dead person shakes in
>   death's millstone.
> All are agreed that you are my killer but that is indeed a
>   false notion about you.
> It is a matter of revenge and is over; now are you bound
>   to use it as you must.

"Fear God, Mukhtar!" was al-Hakim's reaction. "Spare these poor dead folk the fancies and lies of poets!"

"But, my lord," the historian replied, "this poetic text will gradually be turned into a genuine document to be repeated by historians for all time. I think it's important and precious. It needs to be reproduced like all documents that may have started as poetry but later became history."

"If you like," said al-Hakim, "leave it for the course of history to determine. It's a mere drop in the ocean. But then who is to tell us we're not all living a bad dream or a total lie?"

With that al-Hakim rushed out of his residence, headed to his observatory, and pointed his telescope into the heavens. He came back inside, sat down again in the dark, and started repeating a phrase, as though to himself, "The heavens are loaded with stars, each one clasping the neck of another. My unlucky star has shown me its tail." Once he had tired of repeating this phrase, he fell into a troubling silence that al-Misbahi dared not interrupt. The historian was on the point of grabbing the opportunity afforded by al-Hakim's ever increasing somnolence to escape to his own house. At the sound of the first snore he stood up and started to sneak away like a thief in the night. However the roar that al-Hakim let out, along with expressions of disapproval, made him return to his place in short order.

"So, Mukhtar, are trying to leave without my permission? Aren't you capable of sharing my insomnia and gloom with me? God disgrace you for running away like that!"

"Forgive me, my lord. I'd noticed how melancholy you looked and how much the misery seemed to be weighing down on you."

"Then write that down. You know my penchant for innovation and putting a cover on the past."

"You were lost in a profound silence . . ."

"So record my silence then! You will see how my deeds ferment and my innovations fare in their labor pains."

"But, my lord, so gifted and splendid, I myself cannot take on such a complex, indeed impossible task."

"If you can't do it well now, then learn how to do so. It will be the same as learning astronomy and the interpretation of esoteric words and stars. Are we created for any other purpose than learning and searching for light? Mukhtar, how long shall I see you only at my banquets and receptions, as part of the procession to open the Canal in Cairo, or at the dedication of my buildings and other ceremonial occasions? Till when will your loyal pens only follow me during my nocturnal councils and affairs of state? Do you define history as simply weddings, ceremonies, ribbons to be cut, records and decrees to be recorded and sealed? That type of history has already covered all caliphs and sultans; they dominate the entire scene. Don't you think your opus could be expanded to include one of the weakest Buwayhi sultans like Bakhtiyari who turned his meetings with ministers and generals into a chain of weeping and wailing, and all because he had fallen in love with a young boy and lost him? Isn't what I'm asking you the truth?"

"Certainly, my lord."

"So then, where have you left my unique and splendid qualities? How can you manage to encrust the memory of time and future generations with the jewels of my era?"

"My lord, my own share of knowledge is very small. *Over every knowledgeable person is One who knows.*"

"This knowledge you have is less than it should be; it lacks profundity and interpretive power. It could prove very harmful, indeed useless."

"So how can I raise it to a higher level in order to satisfy my lord?"

"Mukhtar, you have to work hard and never flag. Interpret till you're sweating out of sheer exhaustion. Open up your senses so you can penetrate beyond the outer shell and reach the very essence of things. There you'll encounter useful ideas and wonderful proofs. But, if you don't go through those doors, you'll be like all other normal people who live in the visible world, and never move beyond the passage of time or cultivate anything beyond rust and dross."

"Just supposing, my lord, that I were to make the necessary effort till my veins stick out and my face turns pale, but still fail to uncover anything more than what I've already mentioned. In such a case I'd have no choice but revert to the things I've always relished writing about, the coterie of government and panoply of kingly power. Those are the things I've asked people about, and they in turn have directed me to the capital of your rule. I have questioned the inhabitants of your capital, and they have directed me to your court, my lord. It is in this prosperous court of yours that I have found my desired goal, the focus of those interests in matters of administration, warfare, and finance, all combined in the decision-making process and in creating events. Every person can find ease in the particular situation for which he was created. My lord, I have found my own ease in your service, just as I found it with your illustrious forebears. I recount your doings and relate everything to you. That's why you'll never find me consorting with the plebs nor bothering about their livelihood, plants, and paltry minerals. No, I have concentrated instead on precious stones, costly horses and livestock, and rare plants that are good for your health, my lord."

"Mukhtar, my court has attracted you and given you enthusiasms. But at the same time it's made your head spin so much that you've ignored everything else."

"But, dear patron, the attraction that I feel for the court and all the benefits connected with its firmament don't prevent me from alluding to other people as well. I can do that in marginal comments about revolts and major calamities like earthquakes, fires, droughts, and plagues."

"What you want is for the people's memory to vaunt my name; wherever they turn, my face is the only one they'll see."

"How could I wish for anything else, when you've afforded your humble servants throughout your widespread dominions a positive flood of your personal radiance and enveloped them in your cogent proofs?"

"But, Mukhtar, today people are in a very different mood from the one I'm used to or desire. Their lese majesty has reached the level of outright slander and censure. They're busy erasing me from their memory. Haven't you noticed the increase in pamphlets and the petitions plastered all over the city walls and gates? I've come to expect all kinds of unpleasantness from my people, but not lampoons and sarcasm."

"Pamphlets and petitions are never used, my lord, to write history. It is not bothered with people's fairytales. History is whatever I write, the things you tell me to record under the inspiration of Him who has made you His caliph to mankind on earth."

"Those very pamphlets scoff at your history, Mukhtar. They will take revenge on both you and me. They write another kind of history, one that will only recall my name with guffaws and curses. Had you read any of them, you'd realize what I'm afraid of: one traces my ancestry back to a donkey; another claims that I regularly seduce my own sister; a third announces that I stare at the private parts of young boys and palace pages, then accuses me of pederasty."

Every time al-Hakim talked about the content of a pamphlet, he leaned over and whispered things in al-Misbahi's ear. The historian squirmed in his place and asked God for mercy.

"And those pamphlets," al-Hakim went on, "don't even include others that invoke a malevolent eloquence to portray the way I have shed blood and ruined reputations. If only you could take a look at the disgusting pamphlets that Muzaffar brings to me under his parasol, you'd drown yourself in the Nile or else join me in thinking how to take revenge."

"But my lord," the historian replied, "such populist rubbish just goes back where it came from. Before long such obscenities are completely forgotten. That's what history has taught us, and it can serve as the most accurate teacher and guide."

"My current predicament has nothing to do with history, Mukhtar, but with my own depression. I feel slighted and demeaned. Inside I'm suppressing a scream, loud enough to shake palace and neighborhood. I am contemplating an idea that, if implemented, will put an end to old Cairo and everybody in it."

"My lord, I have already inserted the following passage in my history, referring to your actions in Rabi' al-Awwal of A.H. 395: 'You ordered a storehouse to be built at the foot of the mountain and to be filled with sanat wood, reeds, and alfa. Everyone—governors, generals, and secretaries in government service—was scared, not to mention the rest of the populace. Petitions increased, and there was much distress. All secretaries and administrators, Muslim and Christian alike, gathered on the fifth of the month and went out to the Rayahin in Cairo, kissing the ground all the way till their reached the palace. Once there, they stood by the gates, praying and begging forgiveness. They brought with them a document penned on behalf of all of them. When they entered the palace, they repeated their pleas for forgiveness, but no one bothered to pay any attention. They handed over the document to the senior general, and he sent it on to the caliph himself. With that, they were all pardoned and, by order of the senior general, told to leave and come back early the next morning in order to hear their pardon read out. So they all left in the afternoon. Next morning they heard read out separate decrees for Muslims, Christians, and Jews, in each one of which there was a pardon and guarantee of safety.'"[21]

Al-Hakim looked insanely happy. "How well you have memorialized me, Mukhtar!" he said acidly. "And you remind that I ordered the storehouse burned so that I could enjoy the fire. On those days the whole thing was a bit of fun, a kind of joke. But the fire I have in mind now is intended to wreak deadly vengeance on the people who make those pamphlets."

"Start your fires, my lord, and I'll be there beside you to write the proper description and justification."

"The people of old Cairo, whose attachment to life is their sickness, can try crawling to me on their bellies like lowly reptiles, but this time there will be no pardon and no safety for them. Night is almost over now, Mukhtar, so go home to your family. Tomorrow night look for me in the dome of the sky, in the desert by the Pyramids. Bring Hamid al-Din al-Kirmani with you. I will need him to explain certain ideas precisely."

No sooner had al-Hakim issued his command than al-Misbahi gave a bow and left as fast as he could. The caliph stretched out in a corner and snoozed for a little while guards outside kept watch in a desultory fashion.

Next evening, al-Misbahi and al-Kirmani went to their rendezvous in the desert by the Pyramids and sat inside a tent opposite al-Hakim. The caliph looked relaxed and serene; he seemed in a contemplative mood. These symptoms were the result of not only the clement weather and soft breezes, but also the awe inspired by al-Kirmani's large frame, radiant visage, and profound words.

Al-Hakim took a deep breath and rocked back and forth. "Greetings to the great authority of the Iraqis and eminent philosopher of our cause," he said. "How is it that you have been absent for so long? I have been in urgent need of someone knowledgeable in the highest and lowest degrees, thirstier than sand itself for the fresh water of truth."

Al-Kirmani placed his hand on his heart and gave his interrogator a sad, yet affectionate look. "My lord," he said, "I have only turned my attention from you in order to focus on your needs. My only concern and preoccupation has been the blessed calling and the reformation of whatever of it has been dissipated. Truth to tell, regions and islands still seem to me to be as I described them to Your Majesty more than two years ago:

"The heavens are shrouded in a blanket of clouds. People are suffering an enormous trial. The covenant recorded in former decrees has been broken; the works of the holy men of our religion have been cast aside; the ceremony of holding a council of wisdom in accordance with their past practice has been rejected. The lofty has been abased, and the lowly exalted. With my own eyes I have watched as holy and devout men of faith—may God extend their light!—men who have been fostered within the arms of the cause, have stood perplexed in the face of these circumstances that are enough to turn hair white. They have found themselves utterly bewildered by the kind of innovations that normally only send hypocrites and heretics to perdition. These days they are killing each other and charging their colleagues with fornication and criminality. They let evil notions and destructive rumors get the better of them, and seem totally unaware of the clear smoke that protects them and the fearsome trial they will face. Some have taken excess to its limits, others have renounced the bonds that tie them to their faith. A minority have totally shaken off the religion and devotions that were their choice and habit. They face a grim future of moral decline and dissipation beset by devils all too eager to snatch them away and rob them of their beliefs. Some people among them are content with their personal credo, in that their spirits are delivered through belief in God Almighty's own statement: *Those who go astray cannot hurt you if you are rightly guided.*" [22]

"Don't rub salt in the wound, Hamid al-Din," al-Hakim reacted, making no attempt to hide his exasperation. "You bring up such things about times past, when my remaining time is limited. How can I possibly embark on a campaign against my own adepts when I am totally involved in quelling my own conflicts and anxieties? Haven't you noticed how I've let notables and grandees strut about, using my titles and decorations? I no longer strip them of such things, just so that they can buy them back. Haven't you read my safety guarantee for non-Muslims where I allow them to rebuild the churches I've destroyed and celebrate their feasts and liturgies again? Eminent sage, I am tired and on edge. The things being said by the people of Fustat sicken me."

Al-Misbahi now broke his silence. "My lord," he said with a stutter, "exhaustion and disillusion are conditions suffered by all great leaders and overseers of peoples' destinies."

"Ah," al-Hakim went on, ignoring what al-Misbahi had just said, "how I long to live another life, not in order to be a ruler, but to write! Can you even imagine, Hamid al-Din, the things I want to write? Everything that historians do not see or appreciate, all the secret cries, rifts, and verities that are missing from their weighty tomes. For example, return with me to my youth and join me in watching this picture: In the Lu'lu'a Gardens there stands a lofty and eternal oak tree, one that allegedly goes back to Pharaonic times. When I was not yet ten, I used to climb it and spend hours daubing the leaves with glue mixed with seeds. Then I used to hide amid the leaves and wait. It was well before noon when my sticky leaves would be covered with the birds and insects I caught. I used to grab the nearest ones and either strangle them or slit their throats; the ones out of reach I used to get with a stick. The palace cats rushed to congregate under the tree to enjoy the feast I brought them. I'd often kill any cat that was too vicious or greedy. I kept on doing this till one day Burjuwan came along, made me come down, and told me that my father had died. With that, he placed the crown on my head, kissed the ground in front of me, and, along with everyone else, acknowledged me as caliph. As I submitted to the ceremonies of installation, I was also saying farewell to birds and insects. It was only with the greatest reluctance that I descended sadly from their realm, hoping to find the same consolation and serenity in the concerns and pleasures that would come with my new throne and control over people's lives. My historian has only included the barest skeleton of this particular story, and I wish to write about it myself since it is the origin of all the nightmares and horrible visions that have beset me, things I've had to carry inside me during dealings with my subjects—warding them off in good times and applying them in bad ones."

Al-Kirmani was upset by what he heard, but managed to recover his poise and equanimity. "My lord," he commented, "from my perspective the only conclusion to be drawn from this recollection is that you are indeed the imam indicated in God's noble words: *So wait for a day when the heavens will bring a manifest smoke to cover people. This is a dire punishment.* Like prophets and imams before you, you have been sent to baffle human minds with your deeds and to use them thereafter to test the secret intentions of mankind."

"Like all philosophers, Hamid al-Din," al-Hakim responded, "your words arrive when the sun is already setting and it is too late. Where are we now with our highest and lowest degrees? What of our creatures, our minds, our firmaments; our symbolic words, our integers, our alphabetic computations? The entire edifice is cracked, great sage, and our corporeal world is crumbling on our heads like so many specters and bubbles that vanish into thin air."

"In the name of Him who has no like or contrary and who cannot be sensed or comprehended," al-Kirmani replied, "it's only advocates of excess, ambition, and greed who keep sapping the strength of the mission. Such people seek shelter in the light of your divine presence, yet they still manage to distort things. As they tour countries and provinces, they deliberately and maliciously misuse the words of our imam, Ja'far al-Sadiq: 'Whoever spends a year without providing us with a portion of his goods, small or great, will not see God—praised be He and exalted!—on the Day of Resurrection.' They omit to mention these other words of his: 'Anyone who discloses our secret and then comes to us with a mountain of gold will find himself only further distanced from us.' So who are these people, other than purveyors of impossible idiocies, who have revealed our secrets and displayed them on walks and streets? Who else has exposed our divine calling to all kinds of calumny, something to be trampled underfoot by men and beasts? Up hill and down dale you'll find them yelling about how our lord's very hair is a manifest sign of divine revelation, his woolen garment is possessed of exegetical authority, and his donkey is living proof of the fact that he is empowered to speak. These are just some of the varieties of nonsense that Egyptians treat with such sarcasm."

Al-Hakim looked distracted and was clearly annoyed by what he was hearing. "Don't tell me," he interrupted, "about things that cannot be corrected. Al-Akhram has been murdered. Hamzah and al-Druzi have fled together, carrying word of our beliefs to the Syrian mountains. So there's no crisis. All that concerns me now is my own total self, and yet it keeps torturing me with questions: 'You who are close to relinquishing power, during your reign have you really exercised authority in accordance with stars and heavenly bodies? Or rather was it the case that one day your eyes overflowed with tears and a joy to make you smile? Have you experienced moments when you started trembling and fluttering enough to attract doves to you, or were you rather like someone who experiences orgasm during sex and then proceeds to spread the word of peace?' Great sage, how can I respond to such questions other than with absolute sincerity? So, the total unvarnished truth is that, throughout my troubled life, I've found myself transporting the onus of the heavenly coffin inside my head and suffering exhaustion and bleeding as I shouldered the seasons' dizzying succession. Anyone who aspires to delve deep into such mysteries should neither rule nor have authority. Indeed such a person should never be involved in ephemeralities or even in tangential dealings with people. The truth is that I have involved myself in contradictions, so I now see myself brought so low that I am a mere part of things rather than being master. I have plastered my people with signs, and they have hurled double them back at me. I have celebrated my feasts and celebrations, and they have always done precisely the opposite. I buried al-Akhram with all due ceremony, and they proceeded to bury his murderer with even more. We both watch each other. They greet all my serious initiatives with guffaws and my decrees with leaflets."

Al-Hakim's mood worried al-Kirmani; he was afraid of what fresh outrages the caliph might unleash. Mustering all his powers of persuasion, he decided to try to soothe the caliph's anxieties and cheer him up somewhat.

"My lord," he said, "so far nothing is lost. Just close the book on the past and send out new missionaries to your people. They can pass on the counsel of our imam, Ja'far al-Sadiq: 'Make it so people love us, not hate us.' Don't forget always to live by the hadith of our beloved Prophet (on Him be peace!): 'If there is to be just a single day left for this world, God will prolong that day, so that from my offspring may come one who will fill the world with justice just as it has been filled with injustice.' The message of that hadith is a powerful and noble one, sufficient in itself to provide my Lord with a release from hardship and hope after despair."

Al-Hakim now stood up, walked toward the tent-door, and started nervously pacing up and down.

"August sage," he said, "the people are no longer of a mind to wait till a final day for justice. They don't want any more tests or trials. Today what they want is equity and pride, and soon; they want instant gratification. In such a situation I have neither discretion nor authority. Should I go out and tell them, like Jesus, 'I am the Son of God on High'? Or should I threaten them with *I am the Mount, the inscribed Book, the inhabited House*, I am the Lord of Resurrection, imam of the faithful, the manifest knowledge, tongue of believers, buttress of monotheists?' By God, if I were to do such a thing, people would start banging drums, making fun of my words, and doing the belly dance and other salacious things. No, we've had enough arguing and chatter. The only possible solution is for me to become the raging fire that reaches their very hearts. Join me tomorrow night, Mukhtar, in the hills overlooking Fustat, that accursed and obstreperous den. Then you'll be able to write the most incredible part of your history. As for you, Hamid al-Din, I regret that you haven't been able to cure me of my depression, but you should realize—God take care of you!—that you need to bring your ideas at the right time, not at a moment which is beyond the scope of actions and rules of time."

With these final words, al-Hakim mounted his horse and rode off toward his palace, followed by retainers and guards. He left his two companions to convey their farewells in a state of total despair.

On the evening of the promised day, al-Hakim was to be found in the hills, picking up clumps of earth like a lunatic and hurling threats in the direction of Fustat. After a while he became exhausted and collapsed to the ground, muttering,

"On this night, in the folds of this mountain
I shall get drunk on a strange beverage,
One through which I shall come to love and adore my
    beloved fires.
With bubbles and wondrous herbs I shall get drunk.
In its heavenly sign my spirit will be crystallized by the
    aroma of plants and the light of the moon,
With insects, birds, and the silence of stone as companions.
I shall get drunk till my passion rages.
To slaves I give part of what I have,
Then I shall test people in homes and interiors
With the flame of my fire and the heat of my smoke,
Guided as I pass among them by the stench of slander
    and leaflets."

By nightfall al-Hakim was indeed intoxicated. Standing alongside him were his senior slaves, waiting for him to issue orders. "Cause dissension, and you can govern," he kept telling himself. "Set one group against another, and they will beg you to adjudicate. After all you are the one who governs by command of God [Al-Hakim bi-Amr Illah]. That is what should happen now!" With that he yelled at the top of his voice, "My slaves, flatten Fustat! Straighten its curves. Today it's all yours, to burn and pillage. That is my revenge for the slander and sarcasm they have shown toward me. They will escape neither me nor you. Their insults against me have transcended all bounds. Had I the power, I would send down a flood on them locusts, lice, frogs, and blood; I would even try to give them a new skin every time fire consumed it."

Having summoned generals and unit commanders he ordered them to proceed to old Cairo. Setting it on fire, they started to pillage and put to death any of the inhabitants they captured. Slaves, Turks, Maghribis, and all other categories of soldier, they all headed for Fustat. When the inhabitants heard the news, they all clustered together and defended themselves; they managed to stop the fire at the edge of town. The fighting between slaves and people went on for three whole days. Each day al-Hakim went outside the city and watched the scene from the hills, listening to all the shouting and demanding detailed information. Slaves are burning and pillaging old Cairo, he was told. Al-Hakim looked upset. "God curse those slaves," he said. "Who ordered them to do that?" On the fourth day, nobles and shaykhs all gathered in mosques, raised copies of the Qur'an in the air, and started crying and beseeching God Almighty. With that the Turks relented, took pity on them, and started fighting on the side of the people of old Cairo. Actually, most of them were already related by bonds of parenthood or marriage. The slaves were now left to fight on their own. Things turned yet more grave, and fighting intensified. The Kutama and Turkish soldiers gained the upper hand. They sent al-Hakim a message. "We are slaves and mamluks," it said. "This is part of your country, and we ourselves have family, property, children, and estates here. We have never known its people to commit the kind of crime that would require such appalling treatment. If there are other factors of which we are unaware, then tell us and wait for us to leave with our families and property. If the actions of your slaves contravenes your instructions, then allow us to deal with them like rene- gades and criminals." To which al-Hakim sent a reply, saying that he had never desired any such thing and called down curses on whoever it was had given such orders. "You are right to defend the people of old Cairo," his message went on. "I hereby authorize you to help them and attack the people who have mounted this assault." Simultaneously al-Hakim sent a secret message to the slaves, telling them to stick to their orders; he also replenished their supply of weapons. In so doing, his intention was to set them against each other and thus make use of the one as an instrument of vengeance on the other. People soon realized what he was doing. The Kutama and Turks sent him another message. "We understand what your intentions are," it said. "This will lead to the destruction of this country and its people and of you too. It is not right for us to surrender ourselves and other Muslims and to watch as women are murdered and property destroyed. If you do not call them off, we will burn Cairo itself, and we will ask the Bedouin and others to support us!" While al-Hakim was listening to this last message, they had already gained the upper hand against the slaves. He got on his donkey, rode into the space between the two groups, and ordered the slaves to leave. Once they had gone, he summoned the Kutama, Turks, and senior citizens of old Cairo and apologized to them all. He swore he was innocent of responsibility for what the slaves had done and thus broke his own solemn oath. They in turn kissed the ground at his feet and thanked him. They demanded a guarantee of safety for the people of Fustat, and he duly wrote one for them; it was read out from the pulpits of mosques. So the fighting came to an end. People reopened their markets and resumed their lives. A third of the quarter had been burned, and half of it pillaged. People started seeking out the soldiers who had made off with their wives, daughters, and sisters and bought them back from slaves, even though they had already been deflowered. Some of the women had actually committed suicide for fear of being dishonored. A group of Alawite notables now petitioned al-Hakim. They pointed out that some of their daughters were still living in misery with slaves, and asked him to get them released. "Find out how much the slaves are asking for them," he said, "and I'll give it to you." One of them said, "May God show you with regard to your own family and children the kind of things we have had to witness with ours. By allowing your own kind to be defiled in this way, you have abandoned all devotion and chivalry, whereas they have never showed you any anger or resentment." Al-Hakim decided to deal with him kindly. "Noble sir," he said, "your words are extremely provocative, but we are willing to be tolerant. Otherwise we would become very angry, in which case people would find themselves confronting more and more surprises because of the multifarious ways in which customs can be flouted and loyalties corrupted."[23]

Al-Hakim now spent several days in his palace, apparently content. His mood kept swinging from one of sheer delight to a fretful calm. He frequently took violet oil baths, reciting to himself:

> "Thus narrows the wound and memories of degradation,
> With images filled with flame that burn unchecked,
> With the advent of a terror that overwhelmed face and heart,
> Punishment with smoke, chaff, and whirling ash."

2. Sultana, Mistress of All

For four years following al-Hakim's murder Sitt al-Mulk controlled state affairs. She restored prosperity to the royal house, filled the treasury with funds, and gave a number of men assignments. Then she fell ill; a disease of the digestion caused her to become dehydrated, and she died. She was knowledgeable, well organized, and highly intelligent.

Ibn al-Sabi,
Book of History—Completion of Thabit Ibn Sinan's Book of History

Sitt al-Mulk arranged for someone to assassinate him [al-Hakim] during one of his nocturnal excursions. The caliph was killed, but the whole thing was kept secret until the Feast of the Sacrifice in A.H. 411. Shi'i apologists believe that he is in occultation and will inevitably return; concealed for the time being in his absence, he will surely be restored to his former position.

Ibn al-Qalanisi,
Afterword to the History of Damascus

Sitt al-Mulk was the daughter of the Fatimid caliph, al-'Aziz bi-Allah. She was much beloved by her father, the apple of his eye, and object of his greatest affection after God Himself. Whenever he felt beset by worries and problems, she would be his stalwart support. When al-'Aziz died, the succession passed to his son, Abu 'Ali Mansur al-Hakim bi-Amr Illah. During the dark years of her brother's reign (by the same father), Sitt al-Mulk was still able to radiate an aura of beauty, intelligence, and grace. Her star shone with the many hopes not only of the oppressed and cloistered women of Egypt but also of all classes of folk who adored her and referred to her as Mistress of the Kingdom, Sultana, and Lady of All.

Her beauty!

Poets composed odes that extolled her far and wide, to be repeated by bards and buffoons alike at their soirees and clubs. However none of these people (nor her many other admirers) dared mention her by name for fear of coming to a quick and gruesome end at the hands of her vengeful brother, lord and master of all. So they took to using various kinds of allusive phrase, such as: Treasuretrove of Glamor, Maid of Sunrise, Visage to Die For. They would vie with each other to describe her, pointing to her magnificent hair, her wonderful poise, exquisite waist, beautifully apportioned shoulders, and straight back. Her eyes were compared to those of gazelles and fawns, her neck to that of a silver ewer, her legs to palm branches, and her hair either to thick, unplaited silk or to clusters of ripe grapes. In addition to poets there were others who wrote belles-lettres and rhyming prose about her, penning such passages as, "She is slim, svelte and lovely, taut as a whip and lively, tall as a reed and comely." They would make use of prophetic imagery to describe her: "Her leg is visible from beyond the flesh of beauty." Adherents to the faith noted that certain unbelievers only needed to set eyes on Sitt al-Mulk's lovely face in order to regard its exquisite form as sure evidence of God's existence; they immediately expressed a belief in God and became Muslims of the Fatimid persuasion. Those people who had neither access to descriptive eloquence nor a portion of the pearls uttered by renowned poets could only gaze on every limb of her blessed body and proclaim, "All praise be to God!"

Based on evidence from everyone who was fortunate enough to attend her councils or stand close to her whenever she appeared, passed by, or spoke, Sitt al-Mulk used to radiate scents of perfume and musk. People are unanimous in stating that these fragrances emanated from the holy plants of paradise itself; they were not the products of human craft but came solely from her unique body and the scents that wafted through the gardens of her small palace. Everyone who approached her was stunned. "Can such fragrance really be for me?" they would ask themselves, whereupon they would render her all obeisance and admiration. Among the most prominent of these admirers were Najd al-Husayn ibn Da'us, chief of the Kutamis; Abu al-Hasan 'Ammar Khatir al-Mulk, senior minister; Muzaffar, who had charge of her majesty's shade; Nasim, master of her majesty's closet; Ibn Miskin, lancer-in-chief, and others. As a rule Sitt al-Mulk paid no attention to poetry written about her, but some of the more brilliant odes did manage to reach her ear in extracts. Some of these she would cherish; those that were the most sincere and modest she committed to memory. Here is an example; the majority of the poem is lost, as is the identity of its author and transmitter. When she was on her own or feeling downhearted, isolated flashes of poetry would come to her:

> From the handsome knight who courts the rose,
> These words: I come to you after season of decline
>   and gloom
> To declare that the bitter cold will no longer hold sway,
> Nor the iron grip of drought.
> Dearly beloved, I beseech you
> To root out the absurdity that controls your steps, one
>   by one,
> By the sea and the Lord of the Ka'ba I beseech you,
> From Dhu al-Nun al-Hamza, ascetic of tattered garments,
> The eater of barley on plates of exile,
> The lover who has lost kerchief and felicity,
> The ecstatic dwarf,
> The notebook of wounded hero

Where before his death he recorded:
From the handsome knight who died close to the rose
While the caravan encamped at twilight in difficult terrain,
These words: So where am I now regarding the burned book?
Has the stony night set me apart from the sweet lady of
    the rising sun?

And then there is her intelligence and composure! Sitt al-Mulk was
never especially conscious of her own beauty nor did she exploit it in her
relationships or general conduct. Instead she employed her own intellect
and composure to focus on things that were more important than her
own beauty; she was interested in more useful and enduring matters, in
particular those principles and fundamentals upon which the Fatimid
dynasty was grounded. She was especially happy to link this tendency on
her part to Fatima al-Zahra' (peace be upon her memory!) from whose
example she adopted principles of justice, enlightenment, and belief in
the one God. One of the clearest signs of her intelligence and composure
was that she quickly pledged allegiance to al-Hakim bi-Amr Illah even
though he was very young at the time. During the early part of his reign
she was the one who nurtured him lovingly, showed him affection, gave
him sound advice, and provided him with costly, wonderful presents.
That was the way she chose to celebrate his ascent to the throne and to
express her own pride in the dynasty of Fatima al-Zahra'. Historians
record that, when al-Hakim was acknowledged as caliph, she gave him
thirty caparisoned horses, one of them encrusted with jewels, another
with crystal, and the rest with gold. She also gave him twenty mules with
saddle and harness; fifty servants, of whom ten were Serbs; a jeweled
crown and skullcap; boxes of perfumes; and a garden in silver planted
with varieties of miniature trees.[24] Sitt al-Mulk never displayed aversion
or hatred toward her brother; any such bitter sentiments would have had
a negative impact on her intelligence and composure. Eventually, however,
she became all too aware of his tyrannical moods and bloodthirsty
instincts. She used to watch in horror and dismay as he proceeded to

slaughter God's own creatures with no just cause, thus making a complete mockery of the spiritual heritage of the Fatimid dynasty and demolishing its record through his intrigues and dark deeds. The very essence of the state was exposed to ruin.

How incredibly beautiful Sitt al-Mulk was! The series of troubling issues that she took on her shoulders only served to enhance its dignity and prestige. The few strands of white hair that sprouted from her head in no way diminished the number of her devoted admirers, nor did a few wrinkles in her complexion diminish the sparkle that radiated from her smile and her eyes. Then there was her intelligence! God be praised, it was only reinforced by her experiences and strengthened by the whole cluster of trials and crises that were the result of her brother, al-Hakim's, grim moods. She kept hoping for release from these misfortunes and spent many sleepless nights in prayer and supplication, cloistering herself with her own contemplations and anxieties. From time to time she would whisper secret prayers to God in a desperate quest for eventual triumph and release, saying,

> "Shi'i martyrs from across the history of travail,
> The face of the Lord of Sorrows is in a pit of mud,
> His people's women are locked up, complaining of violence
>   at home.
> This dire treatment brings them nothing but misery, languor,
>   and boredom.
> Lord of martyrdom and sorrow,
> If only you knew how gardens are on fire with grief,
> How faces crumble behind walls!"
> She would say:
> "On waking one morning I found myself in a country of
>   terror and massacres,
> In aggression's own empire.
> All that remained for me was your visage, 'Ali,
> A candle of paradise, a chart of justice;

Struggle and You, they were all I had left,
Along with words of salvation from the smoke that I recite
Directly from you, with no other authority,
Thou source of succor and support!"
She would also say:
"My dear brother, your entire reign is summed up as one
    vast graveyard,
Poverty, misery, murder, and terror, my Lord.
Have you heard the tales of panic and confiscation,
Stories of siege?
You, my Lord, who govern by outrage,
Woe to you, a thousand times, woe!
One day the peoples of Egypt, Tunisia, and Syria
Will inevitably occupy streets and roofs in God's land
And legislate in the name of justice and God's unity.
Then in God's name they will demolish your idols, my Lord."

This is how Sitt al-Mulk gradually came to a firm resolve that there
was indeed a desperate need for salvation and release. She was impelled
in that direction by a series of dreams in which Fatima al-Zahra' appeared
and enjoined her to take care of her beloved dynasty. She would stay with
Sitt al-Mulk until dawn's golden rays emerged; then she would vanish,
leaving behind her sacred sash across the ever brightening sky.

Sitt al-Mulk spent many sleepless nights like this. No sooner did she
fall asleep than Fatima al-Zahra' would appear and offer her advice.
Indeed Fatima al-Zahra' would even visit her in daydreams, always
enveloped in the same radiant halo of sanctity; at times she would be
accompanied by a bank of clouds, at others by various stars that augured
good fortune and happiness.

During her final apparition Fatima added a new injunction, urging Sitt
al-Mulk to go to her brother and persuade him to desist from his perverted and tyrannical behavior. After a good deal of thought during
which Sitt al-Mulk tested the validity of this proposition, she proceeded

to carry it out. One morning, a day to remember indeed, she went to al-Hakim's room in the palace. There they had a memorable conversation, one that augured the direst of consequences.

"How my heart boils when my sister defies me!" he roared in a fit of anger. "You've remained apart! May you never penetrate my subsoil, nor I uncover your secret. You dare to come into my presence without an invitation from me? Your spirit is suppressed to the point of exploding; you're poison just waiting for the right occasion. You are the foulest of stains on my state and kingly brow. Be gone from here, Christian's daughter. Reveal your secrets and explode before I vent my wrath on you!"

Sitt al-Mulk made valiant efforts to control her nerves and organize her thoughts. "Our lord, Imam Ja'far al-Sadiq," she replied, "had this to say: 'Remaining silent under tyrannical rule is a kind of religious servitude.' So how am I to remain silent when I too, my brother, am a part of this dynasty? How am I supposed to think positively and put worries aside when I spend all my time suffering through your moods and waiting for the inconceivable to occur? That I may die, my brother, or that you will inevitably do away with me, neither of those things scare me. No, what really frightens me is that you'll destroy this entire house and help our foes wipe out not merely us but our religion of Islam in some way yet unknown."

"And how do you dare to claim responsibility for this house?" al-Hakim interrupted, shards of loathing and anger spewing from his mouth. "We ourselves were the ones who raised it up on sturdy pillars of stone and iron. Don't talk about things you know nothing about. Talk to me instead about your own home. You've turned it into a brothel. You allow men and lovers to come there one after another and enjoy your favors and your accursed body. I've heard that a lewd poet with whom you've been consorting has even written a poem that begins, 'How oft I have sighed at a bosom that brought a wayfarer such luscious food!' not to mention similar outrages. As your brother, I should have kept you cloistered once you had attained puberty; that was when your lustful bosom started to bloom, and the obedient and innocent maid in you died for ever!"

In spite of strenuous efforts, Sitt al-Mulk's eyes filled with tears. "Shame on you, brother!" she said. "If you want to kill me, there are plenty of excuses. But for you to besmirch my honor, no and a thousand times no!"

"There no point in shedding tears in front of me," retorted al-Hakim, his expression and voice still a tissue of fury. I no longer have a heart for you to break or win over. By noble Fatima al-Zahra', I'm going to send some midwives to see you tomorrow, have them check on your virginity and examine that womb of yours for seeds of fornication. If I find out that what spies and old women are telling me is true, then I shall kill you myself without hesitation or mercy. Now get out of my sight before my anger gets to my sword and my sword to your neck."

Sitt al-Mulk left al-Hakim's palace and returned to her own. Now she was certain that her brother was a hopeless case; there was no room for either doubt or protest. It was hopeless to try to stop him committing acts of terror or to reform his tyrannical behavior. Once again Fatima al-Zahra's voice came to her at night to confirm her conclusions and urge her to act speedily so as to extirpate this sickness by the roots before it was too late and all was lost.

By dawn next morning Sitt al-Mulk had in place a carefully crafted plan to get rid of her brother. As spearhead she selected Sayf al-Dawla al-Husayn ibn Dawass, chief of the Kutama tribe that had suffered many hardships during al-Hakim bi-Amr Illah's reign. She went to his house alone and in disguise. Once she had entered and removed her veil, the chief bowed low and kissed the ground at her feet many times. However she grabbed him by the shoulder and told him to stand. Once he had done so, he addressed her, "How can I possibly deserve all this?" he asked, his heart palpitating in a blend of pleasure and amazement. "By God, after this hallowed visit I shall sleep sound and content, untroubled by thoughts of al-Hakim's swords or poisons. The nightmare is over. Now I'll be able to breathe fresh air, the sweet air of peace and liberty, things I have missed for so long! You, Madam, are the instigator of such joy."

"May all boons be yours, Sayf al-Dawla!" Sitt al-Mulk replied. "You are the lord of that tribe without whose courage and steadfastness the Fatimid dynasty would never have been established in Tunisia, Egypt, or Syria. You are the very embodiment of your people's glory and prestige; in your towering figure, one that has traversed seas and capped waves, I envision a wind-filled sail propelling our boat forward against our foes. Dear Husayn, you have wasted your oars in al-Hakim's evil swamp when what you really desired was to escape! How bitter the truth is! How long can you stand to watch in horror as blood flows like water and heads continue to roll with neither cause nor justification? How much longer can your sword remain buried in its scabbard collecting rust?"

"My lady," Ibn Dawwas responded, "your words are like the sweetest perfume, the purest amber. They weave a garment of resolve and warmth for me personally and the state as well. I feel as though the sweet rain of deliverance is about to fall. Droplets of mercy and healing are flowing through my mouth!"

"You are right, Husayn," said Sitt al-Mulk, "and so is your vision. The rain will indeed fall very soon. It will water the furrows of our parched land, sweep away the anxieties that have beset us, and let the water of our beloved Nile flow freely once more. That blessed era will only come when you put an end to the evil tyrant who has claimed divinity for himself and spread perdition and shame among us all."

Ibn Dawwas fell to the ground again, kissing Sitt al-Mulk's leg, clinging to her garment and begging to be relieved of such a risky task.

"This is a daunting charge, my lady!" he stammered. "I am even more afraid of failure. These days al-Hakim has managed to tyrannize and cow everyone to such a degree that you won't find anyone who'd dare strike a blow against him, even from a distance with a bow and arrow or catapult."

"Come now, Sayf al-Dawla!" Sitt al-Mulk retorted as she leaned over and wrapped his head in her garment, "do you imagine I haven't taken your fears into account? I don't want your hands to be besmirched by al-Hakim's blood; you don't even have to be there when he's killed. All I'm asking you to do is select two of your slaves who have never set eyes on al-Hakim, men whose strength and courage you trust implicitly. Just convince them that a traitor is bent on harming their master the caliph. Tell them that tomorrow night this nefarious criminal will be lurking in the Muqattam Hills; he'll be riding a gray donkey and imitating the caliph's own dress and habits. Promise them money, estates, and high positions if they bring you the head and guts of this traitor in a bag. They should bury the rest of his corpse along with that of the donkey and any companions he may have with him. If they succeed, you must do away with them, so this secret stays between just the two of us. Keep it firmly locked away inside your heart, and you'll enjoy every possible blessing. You'll be given charge of government affairs for al-Hakim's successor whom I shall appoint. For my part, I shall remain what I am, a woman behind a veil."

Sitt al-Mulk had allowed no leeway for expressions of fear or objections. In fact Ibn Dawwas started extolling her wondrous intelligence; as he saw it, the plan she had devised was flawless. When she was sure he understood it in every detail, she planted a kiss on his ear. She then took two sharp knives out of her sleeve and handed them to him.

"These are Tunisian-made," she told him. "I have complete faith in their efficacy."

With that she stood up and left. Ibn Dawwas followed her to the door, uttering expressions of obedience to her wishes. He promised to bring her the bag the next night, just before daybreak.

That very night, while Sitt al-Mulk was hatching her plan and giving Sayf al-Dawla ibn Dawwas the task of carrying it out, al-Hakim himself rode out to the water reservoir in the northeast of Cairo. There he inquired after the latest pilgrim caravan that he had sent on its way months earlier but had not yet returned. He was told that they had sought refuge at the Ka'ba in Mecca and were still there. When he asked about the presents and pilgrim dues he had sent with them, he was informed that Qarmatian robbers had waylaid them and stolen the holy Kiswa, as well as wheat, flour, oil, and even candles and perfume.

"There was a time," he said slapping his thigh, "when I used to prevent Egyptians from performing the pilgrimage. But then I cancelled the order. Today however I'm going to reimpose it, and there'll be no appeals."

Just at that moment al-Hakim felt a sudden stab of pain. He dismissed his servants and guards, then turned his mount toward the Lu'lu' Palace gardens where he planned to lie down for a while. However no sooner had he arrived than he started feeling even worse. Trees loomed in front of his eyes like soldiers; the branches were drawn swords, each one ready and eager to tear him limb from limb. He headed back to the palace by way of the Tarma stables where he insisted on moving all the horses and other animals out so he could spend the night in the company of his faithful donkey, al-Qamar. It was here in the pitch darkness that al-Hakim started uttering strange phrases, the audible parts of which sounded weird and obscure; his only accompaniment was the neighing of his donkey spreadeagled on the ground, coupled with the stench of straw and animal droppings.

The following morning found al-Hakim still ensconced at al-Tarma. His guards came in and asked if he wished to be taken back to his own bed. He agreed, but once installed there, he continued talking in riddles. He kept shivering uncontrollably, but eventually fell into a deep, yet fitful slumber. When he woke up, his final night on earth had already begun. He got up and summoned his astrologers. He was reminded that he had banished most of them and murdered the ones who were most skilled. There was only one left, and he was blind and crazy; no one knew his whereabouts. Al-Hakim looked up at the heavens.

"So there you are, O ill-omened star!" he said.

After contemplating the sky for a while, al-Hakim went to see his mother, Lady 'Aziza. He kissed her head and hands and told her about the unlucky star. His mother wept bitterly. She begged her son to break his normal routine just for this one night and not go out to the desert by the Muqattam Hills.

Al-Hakim responded to her pleadings, shivering as he did so. "This very night and early tomorrow," he said meekly, "I have much to do. My dear mother, I have led you to perdition, and now my own sister is out to destroy me. But you're the one I'm worried about, far more than whatever she may decide to do. Take this key, it's the one to the safe; in it you'll find boxes containing three hundred thousand dinars. Take the money back to your palace to keep as a reserve."[25] Now I see you kissing the ground and begging me to dispense with my nighttime ride, yet my restless soul tells me otherwise. Either I'll go out and come back unscathed, or else I'll die. If it's the latter, then farewell. We all belong to God, and to Him do we return."

Only the last third of the night still remained when al-Hakim left his palace, as though drawn by some invisible force. He got on his donkey and rode off toward the Muqattam Hills, instructing his guards not to come with him; all except for a single boy who brought inkwell, pen, and paper with him. Sitt al-Mulk was following his every move from her own palace. No sooner did he reach the hilltop and go down into the hollow than he started shouting over and over again, "Now you'll be rid of me! Now you'll be rid of me!" Coming to himself again, he kept on talking, loudly at times and then muttering,"This is a night like no other. It is the infinite abyss whose overwhelming beauty draws me onward. As I follow the stars and planets of this night sky, I see myself longing for my own demise and the totality that is indivisible. This night is the never-sleeping eye that lures me, pulling me toward the treasure-trove of eternity and the blessings of the world to come.

"On this night that remains unsullied in spite of your vigilance and efforts, my body disintegrates and my cells evanesce, and yet I no longer value them.

"I now belittle this earth of mine where I was welcomed before this dark firmament studded with lustrous pearls!

"Were my soul to fly away and quit the havens of corruption in order to blend with the elements, then my death would be so easy and pleasant!

"Yet what distresses me and kindles my ire is that I am to meet my fate after being betrayed, cut down, and torn apart by the weapons of scum.

"My unlucky star reveals to me how my own end has come about as a result of the scheming of a woman who is closest to my heart, and using a Tunisian knife. This woman will order me killed, then will kill my murderer, and all those who know about it.

"Woe then to the chief of the Kutama! And woe to all those who plot against me!"

The murder of al-Hakim bi-Amr Illah took place on the 27th of Shawwal 411. At the time he was thirty-six years old, and he had reigned for twenty-five years and one month. If the killers had not forgotten to bury the crippled carcass of the donkey, Sitt al-Mulk's plan would have worked perfectly. As it was, rumors were rife in every town and leaders started asking questions. But Sitt al-Mulk managed to brush aside this conspicuous error by responding to the rising tide of questions with a serene demeanor, "Al-Hakim informed me," she said, "that he would be absent for a while. Everything is fine. Al-Qamar, his donkey, either died of exhaustion from carrying too heavy a load or else al-Hakim killed it himself, something he's threatened to do many times."

Throughout the week following al-Hakim's disappearance Sitt al-Mulk was in a race against time. The long wait and al-Hakim's empty throne seemed to her like a sword; either she had to use it herself, or else it would strike her down. In order for her gamble to succeed, she would have to get the Tunisian and Turkish soldiers on her side, distribute cash and rewards among them, and make land-grants to their commanders and officers. In order to broaden her sphere of discretion, she found it necessary to let the Prime Minister, Khatir al-Mulk, in on the secret of al-Hakim's murder, in exchange for which she extracted from him a solemn oath of loyalty and total secrecy. She ordered him to bring the heir-apparent, 'Abd al-Rahim ibn Ilyas, back from Syria. Since she was adamantly opposed to seeing the caliphate transferred to al-Hakim's cousins, she also gave the minister the task of forcing the young man to commit suicide. A short while later Khatir al-Mulk did exactly that. His own retainers provided the following account: "We took the heir-apparent some poisoned fruit, dates, almonds, and pomegranates. 'The Lady Sitt al-Mulk has sent these fruits to you as a present,' we told him. 'They're fresh from this season's pickings. Enjoy them!' With that the young man grabbed a knife and plunged it into his stomach. As he began to lose consciousness, he swallowed the fruit all at once. 'A pox on al-Hakim and his throne,' he gasped as he lay dying. 'As I go to see my God, I have a never ending stream of disturbing questions.'"

At this point a whole series of strange tales and loaded rumors about Sitt al-Mulk began to circulate among the populace and even judges and justices. So she summoned a group of them to meet her.

"Woe to all of you!" she said in a harsh tone. "Are you supposed to be trustworthy servants of this state or merely scum of the earth? Are you all renouncing your faith in the esoteric, the occult, and the hidden, in the very bases of the Fatimid cause? Am I supposed to regard you all from now on as Sunni Muslims, a group of incompetents whose legal scholars and imams have had this to say: 'There is to be no hereafter for such people. When they die, their souls will not leave their bodies; instead they will be punished for evermore in torture's lingering grip.' Recant your folly and spare me your arguments. Purge yourselves in the pure water of virtue and the preservation of honor. Otherwise look forward to God's own curse upon you and the punishment of a woman behind the veil."

When Sitt al-Mulk put on such an obvious display of anger and sanctity, the justices and judges started whispering to each other that she was obviously guiltless. With that they all bowed down before her and begged her for forgiveness and a pledge of safety. That said, she duly pardoned them all and calmed their worries.

Once this first and last storm had died down, Sitt al-Mulk began to feel the road to power now fully open to her. She used the occasion of the Feast of the Sacrifice to install her own candidate on the throne and crown him. He was Abu al-Hasan 'Ali ibn al-Hakim, a young man to whom she assigned the title al-Zahir li-I'zaz Din Allah. She immediately summoned Ibn Dawwas.

"I am now exactly as you have always known me," she said, addressing him face to face, "and as I have pledged myself to you. Now you do likewise. The hearts of all free men are havens for secrets. Never forget that. I am placing this child in your charge; on your own head be it! You must hold his hand and teach him how to govern and manipulate the reins of power. Long live our glorious dynasty!"

As Ibn Dawwas listened to these words, he bowed low and kissed the ground in a show of obeisance. She would not let him go until she had also summoned Khatir al-Mulk and told him exactly what she had told Ibn Dawwas.

"You are to outfit a splendid carriage for the new caliph," she added imperiously, "then give him a slave escort and parade him before the people. You should inform them that she who is all-powerful hereby issues the following proclamation: 'Here is your new lord and guardian. Give him a pledge of your loyalty and obedience.'"

She had things her way. Khatir al-Mulk executed her orders with consummate skill. With the exception of a single servant whom she had killed because he refused to pledge allegiance and instead proclaimed the imminent return of al-Hakim, all the palace staff spent the day kissing the ground and rubbing their cheeks on the floor, outdoing each other in displays of fawning obedience. People from all walks of life arrived in droves to proclaim their pledges of loyalty and express their delight.

Soon after the coronation ceremonies for al-Zahir li-I'zaz Din Allah and all the accompanying celebrations and festivities, Sitt al-Mulk proclaimed three days of mourning for al-Hakim's disappearance. Once this period was past, everything gave the appearance of being in good order and on an even keel once again: waters flowing in their proper courses, swords back in their scabbards, and wayward tongues remaining silent. However it was not long before the general atmosphere inside the enormous palace began to echo with nasty rumors. A provocative whispering campaign started casting doubts on Sitt al-Mulk's innocence in the matter of al-Hakim's death. What fanned such doubts was a report issued by a group of investigative experts to the effect that, just three days following al-Hakim's disappearance, they had combed the Muqattam Hills from top to bottom. They had found his clothing close to a small pond east of Hulwan and Dayr al-Baghl—seven buttoned garments, all of them blood-stained. However the group was scared of Sitt al-Mulk's likely reaction to this news and also anxious to appease the new caliph, so they did not release their findings. Eventually however the news leaked out, and everyone heard the story.

For an entire day Sitt al-Mulk stayed secluded in her bedroom, while she tried to figure out how to fix things and find a solution. Right at sunset she began to feel flashes of a strong conviction, one she was powerless to quell, namely that such important secrets could only be safely stored inside a single heart. To reduce them to a single entity and keep them out of harm's way inevitably required that all the other versions would have to be eliminated. Simply stated, Sitt al-Mulk reached the conclusion that, if the secret of al-Hakim's murder was to be fully suppressed inside her own heart and prevented from spreading, then it too would have to be eliminated by killing everyone else who knew about it. As she saw it, such a course of action would not merely give her more leeway and cleanse her hands of his blood, but also accomplish other goals that were much needed in order to stabilize the government. Firstly, she would be rid of the rivalry for power and influence between Ibn Dawwas and Khatir al-Mulk which was all part of their bargain for keeping things secret. Secondly, it would squelch all talk about al-Hakim's temporary disappearance that his devotees were putting about among simple country folk and conspirators against the current government. Thirdly, it would stop all the stories being put about by lunatics, some of whom, before killing themselves, would claim to be al-Hakim's murderer, while others dressed themselves up to look like al-Hakim and then gathered a crowd around them with a view to bringing back his power and authority.

Sitt al-Mulk immediately summoned Nasim the Sicilian, the chief of security. She told him to stop kissing the ground in front of her and to get up. "Talk to me about secrets, Nasim," she said.

"My lady," he responded humbly, "secrets are part of my daily routine, my profession, a buried link, a veiled knot, something my eyes can envision but my tongue cannot speak. The secret is something I can neither understand nor seek to understand. The secret, my lady, is a priceless fundamental, a special core. Once spread abroad, it is lost. While the soul of the one who bears it may be troubled, that of one of who does not bear it is yet more so. In the political realm secrets constitute the key to authority; in war they provides the means to take the enemy by surprise and secure crushing victory. Secrets, my lady, are the most exalted and cogent things a man may carry in his soul to his very grave. This is just a small portion of what our shaykhs and elders have told us about secrets and the secret of secrets."

"Now, Nasim," Sitt al-Mulk continued, well pleased by what she had heard, "you're aware of the high esteem I have for you, just as my late brother did. In fact, mine is yet higher. I've no doubt you've heard all kinds of stories about al-Hakim's death. Today I want to put an end to all that by revealing what my own investigations have brought to light regarding certain senior officials who always dreamed of doing away with my brother. Go outside now and in full hearing of Ibn Dawwas instruct the slaves as follows: 'Our Lady has discovered and confirmed that it was Sayf al-Dawla who murdered al-Hakim. So kill him.' Then go and say exactly the same thing about Khatir al-Mulk. Insist that he be killed too, along with the entire coterie of both men. Once you have carried out these orders, come back and tell me what you have managed to do."

Nasim and his squad made their way to Ibn Dawwas's home, but he wasn't there. Next they headed to the Kutami quarter, and there they found him checking on his kinsmen and exhorting them to stick together. The Security Chief informed him that his lady required his presence immediately on an urgent matter. Once Ibn Dawwas had been escorted far away from the quarter, Nasim carried out Sitt al-Mulk's orders. When the guards drew their swords, Ibn Dawwas began to defend himself and called on his tribesmen to help him. He managed to kill two slaves, but within minutes he was dead, his corpse riddled with sword-thrusts.

"I managed to escape the hell of al-Hakim," he muttered as he lay there dying, "only to fall into the clutches of that viper of a sister of his. A pox on this state, with all its secrets and catastrophes!"

At that very moment Khatir al-Mulk was at home. He was describing to his wife a nightmare he kept having: al-Hakim would appear to him, sometimes in the guise of a terrifying ghost, and tell him to choose between revealing the real secret behind his own murder or else facing a gruesome act of vengeance; at other times, his guise would be a huge woman who would grab his neck in her numerous hands and amuse herself by throttling him. The only way his wife could find to calm his anxieties was to ply him with cup after cup of wine. Once they were both thoroughly drunk, she used to get up and take all his clothes off. Then, swaying slowly from side to side, she started to strip in front of him, her eyes and gestures serving as icons of seduction and grace. With that she fell on top of him, and his massive body welcomed her in a passionate embrace and an orgy of kisses. They both became as a single body, undivided and totally blended. It was at the very moment when they were in the midst of their passion and at the point of climax that Nasim and his guards burst in on them like a lethal lightning-strike. In stabbing them both to death, the slaves managed to tear their bodies to pieces.

Early in the evening of that bloody day Nasim returned breathless to Sitt al-Mulk's residence, accompanied by a group of sturdy slaves who were carrying bulging sacks dripping with blood.

"Here is what you ordered, my lady," said Nasim with a bow. "These seven sacks contain the corpses of those two accursed wretches, Khatir al-Mulk and Ibn Dawwas, and five of their equally treacherous henchmen. The rest will follow. Should we separate the heads and toss the rest to the lions?

"No!" shrieked Sitt al-Mulk, tears streaming down her face. "Nothing must be left. Bury the sacks in a single ditch outside the city. Keep your hands away from their necks. Let the blood course through their veins, not on the tips of your swords."

"And what about the young governor of Aleppo, Abu Shuja' Fatik al-Wahidi?" inquired Nasim in a affectionate tone that made no attempt to conceal its hard edge of determination. "Are we supposed to keep our swords away from him too, my lady? Throughout the late al-Hakim's reign he was constantly creating problems. He gave himself fancy titles like 'Aziz al-Dawla, Prince of Princes, and Crown of the People, struck coins in his name, and had his own name included in the Friday prayers. I've no idea what further mischief he'll get up to if my lady keeps on placating him and trying to win him over with compliments and gifts."

Sitt al-Mulk realized that Nasim was criticizing her decisions, but still managed to keep her temper under control. "What would you have me do?" she replied. "Send an army to obliterate Aleppo? Don't you realize that when you find a snake in your garden it's better to cut its head off, not set fire to the entire garden? I've promised myself not to kill anyone until my complete repertoire of tricks and machinations is exhausted. As far as the governor of Aleppo is concerned, I'm still looking for his particular weaknesses so I can use them to get rid of him."

Nasim lowered his head and cowtowed like someone in desperate need of forgiveness and approbation. "My lady clearly has things well planned," he mumbled. "God will grant her success and provide the surest counsel. If you would like information on the secret weakness of that rebellious wretch in Aleppo, just ask your servant, the Chief of Security. I can give you guaranteed information, things that will expose the way he really is and bring about his downfall. Discretion being out of place where matters of religion and politics are concerned, I can tell you, my lady, that the young governor of Aleppo is a prostitute's child. He's renowned among informers and spies alike for his innate aversion to women and his perverted social preferences. He has neither wife nor lover. His only true passion is an Indian boy whom he calls "the eternal youth." This boy is the only person he sleeps with; all he asks from his Creator—may He be exalted!—is to be in this boy's company on that fateful day when all bodies are to be gathered together. My lady, this very boy can be God's gift to us. He'll provide the precious means we can use in order to act. Let's make him a pliant tool in our hands, something we can use to destroy this enemy of our state. Once we've employed certain techniques to turn him against his master, we'll be able to make him the vengeful sword to remove this traitor's head. Once that is done, we can kill the boy. Everything else is for my lady to arrange, she being the one who inspires my thoughts and actions."

Sitt al-Mulk said not a word, but simply gestured her approval and agreement. She rushed away to her chamber, pursued by Nasim's expressions of loyalty and obedience. She lay down on her bed and wept bitterly, agonizing over the fact that she was compelled to order so many people killed—and all of it, by God, in spite of herself!

For a few precious days Sitt al-Mulk felt she could breathe easier. She allowed the palace maids to pamper her body with baths, massages, and beauty treatments; throughout this period she came to relish this level of attention and asked for even more. Meanwhile the maids were outdoing each other in their efforts to stimulate every limb, every single inch of her blessed body.

During this period Sitt al-Mulk actually felt reborn; it was as if she were finally rid of times steeped in blood and disaster and could at last take some comfort from harbingers of good times ahead. She started to supervise state affairs for herself, while in her shadow the new caliph, al-Zahir, learned how to achieve the necessary level of decision-making authority and how to annul the oppressive and contradictory policies of his own father. Before long she had fully restored the Fatimid dynasty and its administration to full order and provided it with both security and permanence. She started with a broad purge of the financial sector which in al-Hakim's time had fallen on bad times because of his profligate spending on gifts and land as well as on a wide variety of phony and illegitimate salaries. Along with such measures she also re-imposed taxes and duties at reasonable and fairly distributed rates. As a result of these urgently needed reforms, signs of a healthy economy began to appear, along with indications of a balanced budget. Sitt al-Mulk also pushed al-Zahir to rescind or annul all the edicts that al-Hakim had issued in the form of bans and prohibitions, along with the withdrawal of protection from Christians, Jews, and adherents of other faiths. No sooner had these new edicts reached the ears of the Egyptian populace than a general sense of tranquility was restored, and with it a new tolerance and co-existence among the people of every race, creed, and color.

At first, people found it hard to believe that life in their quarters was really returning to normal. Then gradually they started spreading their

wings and exercising their rights once more. Men and women from different classes and age groups, everyone started going out into the alleys and
streets again. They expressed their joy in praises to God and prayers for the
continuing success and victory of the new caliph and his aunt and for
crushing defeat and perdition on their foes. They formed processions and
threw roses and other fragrant cuttings at each other as they exchanged
politesses; all this as a way of giving expression to the overpowering sense
of joy and well-being they all felt, second only to heavenly bliss itself.

Everyone in Egypt now began to realize that al-Hakim's fabled
"smoke" had finally dissipated. When women started going out in the
evening to stroll along the banks of the Nile, it was clear that the dark
night of his reign was truly over. Nightclubs reopened, and once again it
was legal to purchase and drink liquor. Egyptians were allowed to hold
their festival celebrations again, and they resumed with even greater
splendor than before. Banquets resumed too, with all kinds of food and
drink; tables would stretch for a mile or more, loaded with roast lamb,
chicken, pullets, pigeons, trays of cheeses and sweets, and so on. People
from all classes of society turned up, ate as much as they could, and took
home whatever was left. These types of celebration were no longer
confined to the two big feasts, Greater and Lesser Bayram. Traditional
Fatimid celebrations were included, such as the commemorations of the
opening of the Canal, of the Nile flood, of the four candles, and other
recognized Fatimid holidays. The celebrations also included Coptic
ones, Nawruz, Pentecost, and other Christian feast days. Everyone in
Egypt now turned these occasions into a celebration of life itself and a
means of putting the era of al-Hakim far behind them.

During the dark days of al-Hakim's reign candles and lamps had only
been permitted to burn at night with the tyrant's permission. Now they
were to be seen everywhere on land and water, giving expression to the
outburst of sheer joy that everyone felt, and especially people who had suffered badly under the old regime. Nothing better reflected this reinvigoration of the national spirit than the lifting of the compulsory confinement of
women inside the house. Public baths once again rang with their voices,

and shoe-sellers, couturiers, and beauty parlors thrived. What a feast for the eye! Feluccas and river banks teeming with bevies of beautiful girls whose finery and perfume pervaded every space they chose to grace with their presence. Happy indeed were the young bachelors long deprived of such delights. They could now enjoy the spectacle every evening, and especially on major feast days! A group of pretty girls would parade past, svelte and lively, chewing gum and exchanging small talk. Another would gather round a brazier or an illuminated lake, singing and chanting poems. Yet another would be rowing a boat to the rhythm of a flute player, their long hair flowing like spread sails, their breasts open to the waves' embrace.

Faced with such overpowering beauty, young men, in fact everyone who set eyes on the girls—whatever their age, even those who considered themselves experienced arbiters of fashion, could only sigh and utter expressions of admiration, at the same time feeling a bitter pang of regret that so much beauty had been buried inside houses during al-Hakim's gruesome reign.

Now everyone had a sense of being released from bonds of oppression and prohibition, from murder and persecution. Such times were now far, far away. Instead life had a wonderful savor to it and a particular scent that revived and relaxed the soul. This existence could respond to love's call, to the expression of sweet words, to the aspiration for the beautiful. Sitt al-Mulk herself might also have been able to enjoy her share of this new life and accept the peace and well-being it offered, but instead a vestige of al-Hakim's "smoke" wafted in, taking the form of the last of his senior missionaries, al-Druzi. Unlike Hamza and al-Akhram, he had not yet died or been murdered, but was still to be found in the mountains of Syria. He kept proclaiming al-Hakim's divinity and suggested that the Holy Spirit had entered al-Hakim from Adam through the mediation of 'Ali ibn Abi Talib. He used his eloquence and oratorical skill to convince people that al-Hakim would soon be returning from his occultation; he would then restore justice to a world filled with oppression. Every time Sitt al-Mulk heard about al-Druzi's pronouncements, she requested God's mercy and help. Quaking in disbelief she would listen to reports of the *fatwa*s al-Druzi kept issuing. They began, "In the name of al-Hakim, the Merciful, the Compassionate," and went on to legalize things that were forbidden and to annul prayer rituals and Muslim laws.

Faced with this danger Sitt al-Mulk hurriedly created a planning group led by the caliph al-Zahir Li-I'zaz Din Allah. Every member of the group favored sending an army to crush al-Druzi and his followers and disciples, but Sitt al-Mulk thought it a better idea to stamp out the disease by cutting off the snake's head and thus eradicate sedition.

"How can that be done, lady of wise counsel?" they all asked.

"We don't want to spill the blood of innocent people and those followers who've been duped," she replied. "What we need to do is to infiltrate into the ranks of devotees someone skilled in the crafts of disguise and deceit, someone who can make a big show of loyalty and devotion to the cause. Then, once he's gained everyone's confidence, he can choose the appropriate moment to kill al-Druzi and bring us his head."

It was only a single month after the members of the group had listened to Sitt al-Mulk's idea and unanimously supported it that the Kutami cavalier who had been selected for the task returned to Egypt with the heads of al-Druzi and three of his major supporters and confidants. Those in the know about the scheme were overjoyed and wished Sitt al-Mulk still further successes of this kind.

When the severed heads were displayed in public, the Caliph al-Zahir started prodding them with his bamboo cane, and members of the group spat on them. Sitt al-Mulk on the other hand refused to have them anywhere near her or even look at them. Instead she had them quickly stored away in the repository for heretics' heads, then spent many hours locked away in her room, weeping bitter tears for the action she had been forced to take against al-Druzi—all of it, by God, in spite of herself! She spent many, many hours weeping over her own inability to solve a paradox, one that revealed itself to her in all its horrifying complexity: in order to stem the hemorrhage, yet more blood had to be spilled. The only thing that managed to dispel this vision was her joyous conviction that all factors pointing to yet another bloody episode had actually ceased to exist in view of the impossibility of al-Hakim rising from the ashes. Any such fears would result in the erasure of any idea of an honorable peace with the Byzantine emperor Basil II, who had announced himself willing to renounce all aid to enemies of the Fatimid state in return for a restoration to Egyptian Christians of those rights and freedoms that they were entitled to enjoy under the code of Islamic law.

On that notable day when al-Hakim's "smoke" finally dissipated and no trace of it remained, spring announced its arrival in the Fatimid domains in a spectacular and beautiful form that Egyptians had never witnessed before. The Nile was in full flood, bursting with life and reflecting the light of the clear blue sky. At its zenith the sun bathed land and people in a compassionate warmth. The moon lit up streets and roofs, providing lovers with a plentiful glow. The desert donated to these nuptials of nature a gentle breeze whose scented wafts were welcomed by everyone.

During this season Sitt al-Mulk came to have a powerful sense of well-being that she had never experienced before. She used to spend a lot of time walking alone in her palace gardens, where bushes, roses, and trees were garlanded with beautiful scented flowers, and where birds and butterflies filled the air with song and color. In sum, Sitt al-Mulk, like everyone else who had become inured to terror and grief, could hardly believe her own eyes or tolerate the presence of so much beauty. In such circumstances what she needed most was a continuous series of private communions with nature, unsullied by talk of politics or blood.

One spring evening when the sun had almost set, Sitt al-Mulk was sitting in the most beautiful part of her gardens and communing with nature. Her eyes glowed and her complexion shone with sheer emotion; a gentle, scented breeze was toying with her hair and every part of her body. At that moment she closed her eyes and surrendered to a strange, God-inspired sleep. No sooner had she fallen into its embrace that a group of naked and barefoot poets appeared, each of them reading from his own poetry and demanding from her body a touch or a kiss in exchange. They all fell silent and receded when the master poet among them appeared and recited the following line: O love of my life, have pity; for love of you I burn on fire.

Then the master of masters burst on the scene to recite his line of love: For love of you letters within my heart have been titled with tears and sleeplessness.

Lastly there arrived a thin poet. With great merriment he sang a poem fragment to the accompaniment of a chorus of transvestites who repeated the chorus while pinching anyone who objected:

> My fault in loving you I cannot, cannot see!
> That my goal is to please you That seems good, so good to me!
> If you choose to torture me, I care not, care not!

The poets kept topping each other's efforts in both poetry and drinking till they were all equally drunk and rowdy. They then started hugging and kissing each other, exchanging victory medals, and prancing around singing over and over again, "That seems good, so good to me!"

The way the poets were making a huge row around Sitt al-Mulk and fighting each other to get hold of her only came to an end with the rapid arrival of the senior officials and generals of the state: Ibn Dawwas, Khatir al-Mulk, and al-Druzi. They rudely drove the poets away and started to strip Sitt al-Mulk of her clothes, touching, grabbing, fondling, and kissing her body as they did so. Having decided to have sex with her, they all wanted to go first, whereupon they all started cursing and swearing at each other. They tried casting lots, but nobody won. Then they took up their swords and started fighting. The winner was al-Husayn ibn Dawwas, the Kutami chief. No sooner had he recovered his breath and savored the moment of victory than he started taking his clothes off and preparing to leap on top of Sitt al-Mulk's naked body and rape her as an act of revenge. He mounted her and started pressing down, but she kept resisting and calling out for help. Almost at once Nasim, the Security Chief, arrived on the scene along with Ibn Miskin, the Chief Lancer, and a contingent of slaves. They pulled Ibn Dawwas off their mistress and dealt him a series of deadly blows. The slaves then did obeisance to her and approached her on their knees. They too leapt on top of her in a crushing mass: one of them was kissing her limbs, another was squeezing her breasts, and still another was rubbing himself against her—all with devout blessings. All Ibn Miskin could do was to take spears to them and leave them either dead or wounded. When Nasim noticed signs of lechery in Ibn Miskin's expression as well, he grabbed his spear and killed him. . . .

Now only Nasim and Sitt al-Mulk remained in this place now crammed with the dead and dying. Night was bidding adieu to its last shadows, and only the groans of the dying disturbed the quiet of an elemental silence. Within this final circle of Sitt al-Mulk's dream Nasim stood in front of her and stripped.

"The keeper of all secrets, my lady, the victor in every battle, and yet a eunuch! As you can see, I am unable to serve you. Being myself at the point of death, I can no longer conceal from you the degree of my love and passion for you. You are the one I adore, my cause and my guide in this life and on the Day of Resurrection. It is this secret burning inside my heart that has impelled me to do away with all your lovers, one after the other, and to rescue you from all those who shared knowledge of the way you arranged al-Hakim's murder. Now you must kill my secret by killing me. Otherwise I shall reveal your secret and then kill myself."

Sitt al-Mulk did not utter a word. Her stomach was upset, her heart was palpitating, and she had difficulty breathing, as though she too were suffering death agonies. Faced with such a determined silence Nasim approached her and emptied a vial of poison into her mouth and another one into his own. He lay down beside her, suckling from her breasts and awaiting the advent of the angel of death.

Next morning, the seventh day of spring in A.H. 414, Sitt al-Mulk's dead body was discovered, locked in its eternal slumber and looking like one of the houris of paradise. Her hair had turned white, and lines had begun to appear on her face, lending her visage an even greater nobility and radiance.

In accordance with Sitt al-Mulk's own wishes, her funeral in the caliphal cemetery was a modest affair. A huge crowd walked behind the coffin, and the feelings of grief and loss surpassed even those normally

felt by the Shi'a community on the Day of Ashura. After burying the
sultana in her final resting-place, Egyptians spent an entire week walking
around barefoot, wearing only dark clothes, and only eating barley
bread, black lentils, cheese, and salted foods. They closed their shops
and thronged to the Azhar mosque and other places of worship where
they all prayed to God for mercy on the dead woman.

During that very same week a disturbed young man could be seen
walking around the cemeteries and quarters of Cairo. He was of olive
complexion and had a mole on his cheek and brilliantly white teeth. He
kept wandering about chanting:

> Where can I find the burned book?
> Whither has the stony night banished the maiden of sunrise?"

Just one year after Sitt al-Mulk's death, the Egyptians, now ruled by
al-Zahir Li-I'zaz Din Allah, set about ridding themselves of all their
suppressed anxieties and erasing for ever their fears and constraints. In so
doing they exceeded all limits. The young caliph was extremely fond of
food, drink, promenades, and songs, and so it was easy for the people to
draw him into their activities. For example, on the third day of the Christian
feast of Easter, Muslims and Christians gathered at the Miqass Bridge.
Tents had been set up, and a huge crowd spent the entire day playing and
indulging in all kinds of debauchery. Men and women commingled as they
got progressively more and more drunk, so much so that women had to be
carried home in baskets. This was a day of wholesale debauchery.[26]

In the year A.H. 418 al-Zahir started drinking wine and allowed the
people to do likewise, to listen to singing, to drink beer, eat mulukhiyya
and various types of fish. People spent a lot of time on amusements.[27]

Al-Zahir died in the second half of Sha'ban in A.H. 427, a few days
short of his thirty-second birthday. His caliphate had lasted for fifteen
years, eight months, and a few days. He loved entertainments and was very
fond of singing. In his time people in Egypt were very chic and hired
singers and dancers. The whole thing reached unprecedented proportions.[28]

Notes

1. Ibn Taghribirdi, *Bright Stars*, Vol. 4, p. 186.
2. Ibid., p. 196.
3. Al-Maqrizi, , *Homily for the Devout*, Vol. 2, p. 35.
4. Ibn Taghribirdi, *Bright Stars*, p. 202. Ibn Taghribirdi mentions that in this same year, "Al-Husayn ibn Ahmad ibn al-Hajjaj Abu 'Abdallah, the poet, died. He grew up among the workers and writers in Baghdad and served as morals supervisor for 'Izz al-Dawlah Bakhtiyar the Buyid. However he ignored his position in order to devote himself more to poetry, folly, and debauchery. I said: This very same Ibn al-Hajjaj was proverbial for his frivolities, jests, and lampoons. The majority of his poetry is comic and sarcastic verse, often obscene. Here is an example: "Heaven help me/with her cunt and my cock/they've both demanded sex/but it's enough to chop off my erection." [p. 205]
5. Ibn Kathir, *The Beginning and the Ending*, Vol. 12, p. 10.
6. As reported by 'Abdallah 'Inan, *Al-Hakim bi-Amr Illah and the Secrets of the Fatimid Cause*, p. 128 (based on the church manuscript, *Siyar al-bi'ah al-muqaddasa* (Biographies of the Sacred Space), n.p.
7. Al-Maqrizi, *Homily for the Devout*, p. 55.
8. Mentioned (with an incorrect date) in Ibn Khaldun, *Book of Exemplary Lessons*, Vol. 4, p. 76.
9. Al-Maqrizi, *Homily for the Devout*, p. 97.
10. Ibid., p. 77.
11. Ibn Taghribirdi, *Bright Stars*, pp. 222–23.
12. Ibid., p. 232.
13. Al-Qalqashandi, *Morning for the Night-Blind*, Vol. 10, pp. 444–45.
14. Ibid., p. 443.
15. Ibn al-Athir, *The Complete Work on History*, Vol. 7, p. 236.
16. Al-Maqrizi, *Homily for the Devout*, p. 64.
17. Ibid., p. 66.
18. Ibn Taghribirdi, *Bright Stars*, p. 216.
19. Ibid., p. 217.
20. Ibid., pp. 229–30.
21. Al-Maqrizi, *Homily for the Devout*, pp. 54–55. It seems likely that al-Maqrizi is copying the information from al-Misbahi whose history has not come down to us.
22. Al-Kirmani, "Cheerful News," p. 55.
23. Ibn Taghribirdi, *Bright Stars*, pp. 181–82
24. Al-Maqrizi, *Homily for the Devout*, p. 15.
25. Ibn Taghribirdi, *Bright Stars,* p. 187.
26. Al-Maqrizi, *Homily for the Devout*, p. 137.
27. Ibid., p. 29; al-Maqrizi, *Lessons and Reports*, Vol. 1, p. 354.
28. Al-Maqrizi, *Khitat, Lessons and Reports*, Vol. 1, p. 355.

Bibliography

Al-Antaki, Yahya ibn Said. *Silat tarikh Utika* (Appendix to the History of Eutychius).

Al-Dhahabi, al-Hafiz. *Tarikh al-Islam* (History of Islam). Cairo: n.p. 1985.

Ibn al-'Amid, al-Makin. *Tarikh al-Muslimin* (History of the Muslims).

Ibn al-Athir. *al-Kamil fi al-tarikh* (The Complete Work on History), Vol. 7. Beirut: Dar al-Kitab al-'Arabi, n.d.

Ibn Iyas. *Bada'I' al-zuhur fi waqa'i' al-duhur* (Bright Flowers Concerning the Events of the Ages). Cairo: Dar Ihya' al-Kutub al-'Arabiyyah, 1984.

Ibn Kathir. *al-Bidaya wa-l-nihaya* (The Beginning and the Ending), Vol. 12. Beirut: Dar al-Kutub al-'Ilmiyyah, 1987.

Ibn Khaldun. *Kitab al-'Ibar* (Book of Exemplary Lessons), Vol. 4. Beirut: Dar al-Fikr, 1981.

Ibn Khallikan. *Kitab wafayat al-a'yan* (Book on the Deaths of Important People). Karachi: Pakistan Historical Society, 1961.

Ibn al-Qalanisi, *Dhayl tarikh Dimashq* (Afterword to the History of Damascus). Damascus: Dar Hassan, 1983.

Ibn al-Sabi. *Kitab tarikh—Takmilat kitab Thabit ibn Sinan* (Book of History—Completion of Thabit Ibn Sinan's Book of History).

Ibn Taghribirdi. *al-Nujum al-zahira fi muluk Misr wa-l-Qahira* (Bright Stars Concerning the Rulers of Egypt and Cairo), Vol.4. Cairo: Dar al-Kutub al-Misriyyah, 1933.

'Inan, 'Abdallah. *al-Hakim bi-Amr Illah wa-asrar al-da'wa al-fatimiya* (Al-Hakim bi-Amr Illah and the Secrets of the Fatimid Cause). Cairo: 1959.

Al-Kirmani. "Risala: Mabasim al-bisharat bi-l-Imam al-Hakim bi-Amr Illah," (Essay: Cheerful News Regarding the Imam, al-Hakim bi-Amr Illah) in Muhammad Kamil Husayn, *Ta'ifat al-Duruz*. Cairo: Dar al-Ma'arif, 1962.

Al-Maqrizi. *Itti'az al-hunafa' bi-akhbar al-a'imma al-fatimiyin al-khulafa'* (Homily for the Devout Concerning Reports on the Fatimid Imams and Caliphs), Vol. 2. Cairo, 1972.

———. *al-Mawa'iz wa-l-ikhtibar fi dhikr al-khitat wa-l-athar* (Lessons and Reports Concerning Cairo Quarters and Monuments). Cairo: French Institute for Archaeology, 1911.

Al-Qalqashandi. *Subh al-a'sha fi sina'at al-insha'* (Morning for the Night-Blind Concerning the Craft of Composition), Vol. 10. Beirut: Dar al-Kutub al-'Ilmiyyah, 1986.

Sibt ibn al-Jawzi. *Mir'at al-zaman fi tarikh al-a'yan* (Mirror of the Times Concerning the History of Notables). Beirut: Dar al-Shuruq, 1985.

Al-Wazir Jamal al-din. *Akhbar al-dawla al-munqati'ah* (Reports on the Interrupted Regime).

Glossary

Dates in the glossary are given in their Islamic (Hijra) form followed by their Gregorian equivalent

'Alawite: a Shi'ite sect whose name is based initially on that of 'Ali, the Prophet Muhammad's cousin and son-in-law, who is the foundational figure in the 'Shi'at 'Ali' or Shi'a; more specifically the group is named after 'Ali al-Hadi (d. 254/868), the tenth of the Shi'ite Imams. The group, also known as 'Nusayris,' supported the notion of the divine nature of the Shi'ite Imam.

Canal: the *khalij*, a canal that extended North-East from the River Nile and was a prominent landmark of the city of Cairo until it was filled in during the nineteenth century. It is now Port Said Street.

Coptic festivals: Nawruz is the Coptic New Year's Day festival, celebrated in September; Pentecost is the traditional Christian celebration of the fifty days following the festival of Easter, culminating with Pentecost Sunday which celebrates the descent of the Holy Spirit.

Dar al-Hikmah: the most famous 'Dar al-Hikmah' (House of Wisdom) was a library founded by the 'Abbasid Caliph, al-Ma'mun (d. 217/833). From historical accounts, it would appear that al-Hakim bi-Amr Illah established a similar institution in Cairo.

Fatimid festivals: the ceremonies involving the opening of the *khalij* (see *Canal)* and the Nile flood were connected with the River Nile and the importance of its annual flood to the economy of the region (that is, before the construction of the Aswan High Dam, which now controls the river's flow further south). Both are described in detail in Edward Lane's renowned account, *Manners and Customs of the Modern Egyptians* (1863).

Kiswa: a black, brocaded carpet used to cover the Ka'ba in Mecca. Traditionally made in Egypt, it was transported to Mecca as part of the pilgrimage caravan.

Maliki School: one of the four major 'schools' (Ar. *madhhab*) of Islamic law, named after its founder, Malik ibn Anas (d. 179/796).

Mulukhiya: a favorite Egyptian dish to this day; a thick soup made from a herb usually known in English as 'Jews' mallow.'

Smoke Verse: Qur'an (8:26); "So be on watch for a day on which the heavens will bring a clear smoke."

Umm 'Amr's donkey: an ancient Arab proverb dating from pre-Islamic times. Umm 'Amr was a woman with a curse on her, who was expelled from her tribe and rode off on her donkey. The proverb relates that "she never came back, nor did her donkey." The donkey is therefore a metaphor for any undesirable person or entity who suffers a similar fate.

Qur'anic References

A little enjoyment, and then they will face a dire punishment. (16:117)

Every soul tastes death. You will receive your rewards on the Day of Resurrection. (3:185)

I am the Mount, the inscribed Book, the inhabited House. (52:4)

O people, a simile is being invoked here, so pay attention. The people to whom you pray in place of God could never create so much as a fly even though they all combined their efforts. If that fly were to rob them of something, they could never retrieve it; seeker and sought are simply too weak. They have not given God his true value; indeed God is powerful and mighty. (22:73)

Over every knowledgeable person is One who knows. (12:76)

O you who believe, you are responsible for yourselves. Anyone who goes astray cannot hurt you if you offer him guidance. God is the point of reference for you all. It is He who will inform you of what you are doing. (5:105)

Remember, when you were few in number and oppressed on earth, fearing that others would overwhelm you. God gave you shelter, granted you victory, and provided you with good things, that you might be grateful. (8: 26)

So wait for a day when the heavens will bring a manifest smoke to cover people. This is a dire punishment. (44:10)

The imminent is imminent. Only God can disclose it. (53:57)

There is no compulsion in religion. (2:256)

They schemed and God schemed, and God is the best of schemers. (3:54)

Those who go astray cannot hurt you if you are rightly guided. (5:105)

Those who unjustly consume the property of orphans will taste fire in their bellies and will roast in hellfire. (4:10)

Verily humanity oversteps its reach by thinking itself sufficient. (96:6)

When they angered us, we took revenge on them. (43:55)

Whoever associates with God anything, it is as though he has fallen from Heaven and the birds snatch him away, or the wind sweeps him headlong into a place far away. (22:31)

Modern Arabic Literature
from the American University in Cairo Press

Ibrahim Abdel Meguid *Birds of Amber* • *Distant Train*
No One Sleeps in Alexandria • *The Other Place*
Yahya Taher Abdullah *The Collar and the Bracelet* • *The Mountain of Green Tea*
Leila Abouzeid *The Last Chapter*
Hamdi Abu Golayyel *A Dog with No Tail* • *Thieves in Retirement*
Yusuf Abu Rayya *Wedding Night*
Ahmed Alaidy *Being Abbas el Abd*
Idris Ali *Dongola* • *Poor*
Radwa Ashour *Granada*
Ibrahim Aslan *The Heron* • *Nile Sparrows*
Alaa Al Aswany *Chicago* • *Friendly Fire* • *The Yacoubian Building*
Fadhil al-Azzawi *Cell Block Five* • *The Last of the Angels*
Ali Bader *Papa Sartre*
Liana Badr *The Eye of the Mirror*
Hala El Badry *A Certain Woman* • *Muntaha*
Salwa Bakr *The Golden Chariot* • *The Man from Bashmour*
The Wiles of Men
Halim Barakat *The Crane*
Hoda Barakat *Disciples of Passion* • *The Tiller of Waters*
Mourid Barghouti *I Saw Ramallah*
Mohamed Berrada *Like a Summer Never to Be Repeated*
Mohamed El-Bisatie *Clamor of the Lake*
Houses Behind the Trees • *Hunger*
A Last Glass of Tea • *Over the Bridge*
Mahmoud Darwish *The Butterfly's Burden*
Tarek Eltayeb *Cities without Palms*
Mansoura Ez Eldin *Maryam's Maze*
Ibrahim Farghali *The Smiles of the Saints*
Hamdy el-Gazzar *Black Magic*
Fathy Ghanem *The Man Who Lost His Shadow*
Randa Ghazy *Dreaming of Palestine*
Gamal al-Ghitani *Pyramid Texts* • *The Zafarani Files* • *Zayni Barakat*
Tawfiq al-Hakim *The Essential Tawfiq al-Hakim*
Yahya Hakki *The Lamp of Umm Hashim*
Abdelilah Hamdouchi *The Final Bet*
Bensalem Himmich *The Polymath* • *The Theocrat*
Taha Hussein *The Days* • *A Man of Letters* • *The Sufferers*
Sonallah Ibrahim *Cairo: From Edge to Edge* • *The Committee* • *Zaat*
Yusuf Idris *City of Love and Ashes* • *The Essential Yusuf Idris*
Denys Johnson-Davies *The AUC Press Book of Modern Arabic Literature*
In a Fertile Desert: Modern Writing from the United Arab Emirates
Under the Naked Sky: Short Stories from the Arab World
Said al-Kafrawi *The Hill of Gypsies*

Sahar Khalifeh *The End of Spring*
The Image, the Icon, and the Covenant • *The Inheritance*
Edwar al-Kharrat *Rama and the Dragon* • *Stones of Bobello*
Betool Khedairi *Absent*
Mohammed Khudayyir *Basrayatha*
Ibrahim al-Koni *Anubis* • *Gold Dust* • *The Seven Veils of Seth*
Naguib Mahfouz *Adrift on the Nile* • *Akhenaten: Dweller in Truth*
Arabian Nights and Days • *Autumn Quail* • *Before the Throne* • *The Beggar*
The Beginning and the End • *Cairo Modern*
The Cairo Trilogy: Palace Walk, Palace of Desire, Sugar Street
Children of the Alley • *The Day the Leader Was Killed*
The Dreams • *Dreams of Departure* • *Echoes of an Autobiography*
The Harafish • *The Journey of Ibn Fattouma* • *Karnak Café*
Khan al-Khalili • *Khufu's Wisdom* • *Life's Wisdom* • *Midaq Alley*
The Mirage • *Miramar* • *Mirrors* • *Morning and Evening Talk*
Naguib Mahfouz at Sidi Gaber • *Respected Sir* • *Rhadopis of Nubia*
The Search • *The Seventh Heaven* • *Thebes at War*
The Thief and the Dogs • *The Time and the Place*
Voices from the Other World • *Wedding Song*
Mohamed Makhzangi *Memories of a Meltdown*
Alia Mamdouh *The Loved Ones* • *Naphtalene*
Selim Matar *The Woman of the Flask*
Ibrahim al-Mazini *Ten Again*
Yousef Al-Mohaimeed *Wolves of the Crescent Moon*
Ahlam Mosteghanemi *Chaos of the Senses* • *Memory in the Flesh*
Shakir Mustafa *Contemporary Iraqi Fiction: An Anthology*
Mohamed Mustagab *Tales from Dayrut*
Buthaina Al Nasiri *Final Night*
Ibrahim Nasrallah *Inside the Night*
Haggag Hassan Oddoul *Nights of Musk*
Mohamed Mansi Qandil *Moon over Samarqand*
Abd al-Hakim Qasim *Rites of Assent*
Somaya Ramadan *Leaves of Narcissus*
Lenin El-Ramly *In Plain Arabic*
Mekkawi Said *Cairo Swan Song*
Ghada Samman *The Night of the First Billion*
Mahdi Issa al-Saqr *East Winds, West Winds*
Rafik Schami *Damascus Nights* • *The Dark Side of Love*
Khairy Shalaby *The Hashish Waiter* • *The Lodging House*
Miral al-Tahawy *Blue Aubergine* • *Gazelle Tracks* • *The Tent*
Bahaa Taher *As Doha Said* • *Love in Exile*
Fuad al-Takarli *The Long Way Back*
Zakaria Tamer *The Hedgehog*
M.M. Tawfik *Murder in the Tower of Happiness*
Mahmoud Al-Wardani *Heads Ripe for Plucking*
Latifa al-Zayyat *The Open Door*